Horseman

Book 2 in the

Norman Genesis Series

By

Griff Hosker

Published by Sword Books Ltd 2016

A CIP catalogue record for this title is available from the British Library.

Cover by Design for Writers

Thanks to Simon Walpole for the Artwork.

Prologue

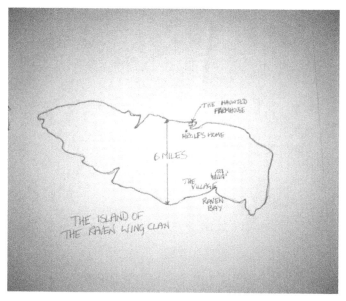

I am Hrolf Son of Gerloc although now they call me Hrolf the Horseman. It had been a year since we defeated Hermund the Bent and Black Teeth. They had tried to destroy us on our small island off the Frankish coast. It was a revenge raid; they hated me and Jarl Gunnar Thorfinnson. We had thought we were safe so far from their home but we were not. We had come close to being destroyed. They had besieged us and it took courage from all of our warriors to defeat them, drive them into the bay and destroy their drekar. Our Jarl, Gunnar Thorfinnson, had been generous both in his praise and his gifts. He had said to the whole clan that we would not have won but for me and my horse, Dream Strider. That was not true. Others like Rurik One Ear, Alf the Silent and Ulf Big Nose had done as much. Alf the Silent had paid the ultimate price; he had died. I did not like the elevation to hero. Jarl Dragonheart of Cyninges-tūn in the land of the Wolf was a true hero, I just did the best that I could. However I still believed that I was destined for greater things. I had met a witch on a lonely island off the coast of On Walum while serving the Dragonheart and she had said, *'His family will be remembered long after you are dead, Jarl Dragonheart, but they will not know that they would have been nothing without the Viking slave who changed the world.'* I had no family as yet and so I knew that I still had much to do.

The year since the battle had been a quiet one. We recovered from the deaths we had endured. We repaired our palisades and our ship and we prepared to do that which was in our nature. We prepared to raid. We were warriors and we had left the land of the Wolf to make our own land. It would be the land of the Raven. The island was but a start. Since the battle we had learned that the Dragonheart's son, Wolf Killer, had fallen in battle defending the Land of the Wolf. It made me more apprehensive about my future. Wolf Killer had been a great warrior. He would have been a Jarl like his father and now he was gone. The Dragonheart was, from what we heard, distraught. It was as though his heart had been taken from him. Many other fine warriors had also fallen and I wondered what would have happened had I stayed there. I had left and joined this clan because of a prophesy but also because I did not see my future in the Land of the Wolf but in Frankia, the land of the horse.

What set me apart from the rest of the clan on our little island was my love of horses. All Vikings could ride but I seemed to have a skill with them which others did not. My horse, Dream Strider, had been hurt in the attack. It had taken me six months to heal him. It had set me to thinking and I decided that I needed

5

more horses. I wanted to breed them. I kept that thought to myself. I was just one of the clan. The decisions and where we would raid would be the Jarl's or his brother, Gunnstein Thorfinnson. He and his crew now lived on the island with us. We had two drekar now and our clan was growing. I would just seize my opportunity when it came along. In the meantime I practised riding my horse wearing the mail that our smith, Bagsecg Beornsson, had made for me. I had used much of the gold I had saved to buy it. Already it had proved its worth. Had I not worn it then I would have lost my leg during the battle for our island. Now, a year after I had first worn it, Dream Strider was comfortable carrying both me and my mail. Along with my dog, Nipper, we regularly rode around our island. I knew every rock and blade of grass. This was my land and I would defend it with my life.

The other difference between the rest of the clan and me was that I lived alone. The rest lived close to the palisade and the hall of the Jarl. In order to help my horse to heal after his hurts in the battle with Hermund the Bent I had built a hut close by the haunted farmhouse overlooking the bay where the skeletons of the dead ships and their crews lay. The farmhouse was not haunted by the spirits of our enemies but the by those of the fishermen who had lived on the island before we came murdered by outlaws. I did not mind their spirits for I had not hurt them. I was not far from the others but it meant I could ride whenever I chose. Each night the gates of the clan's walls were closed. I sometimes like to ride at night or early in the dawn. I had built a hut, with the help of my comrades and I had built a stable and a store. With a pen for my horse to graze I felt I was in control of my own life. I enjoyed the freedom my lonely home brought. I had been a slave for many years and now I had my own home. I had my horse and my dog. I was content.

Chapter 1

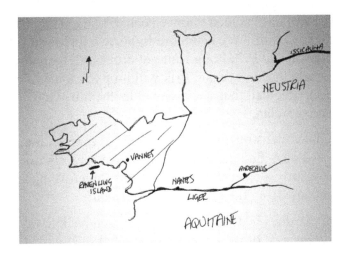

I had just given Dream Strider his first ride of the morning. I put him in the pen I had made. He had enough room to run and yet it was too high for him to leap. I put water in his trough and left him. He would be happy enough. I walked, with Nipper in close attendance, south to the home of the clan. It was not a large island and it did not take me long. I stood at the gate and watched the activity inside the walls. After the silence of my home it always seemed to be a noisy, bustling place. Bagsecg, the smith, would be hammering away at his forge. Children would be running around making noises and the dogs would be barking at each other.

Nipper, my dog, who walked next to me did not bark. He was a lonely dog. If any of the clan's dogs came near then he bared his teeth. He was very protective and they had all learned to keep their distance. He was an extremely good ratter. No vermin nested in Dream Strider's stable. He was my dog and Dream Strider and I were his priorities. I was lucky.

"Hrolf! You must have something of the galdramenn in you." Siggi White Hair strode over to me from his turf covered house.

"Why? I was here three days since. What has happened?"

"The Jarl has decided that we need to raid again." I cocked a quizzical eye at him. "We had more fights two nights since. Eystein Arneson and Erik Long Hair got drunk and fought over a woman. Eystein lost an eye and Erik will limp for some time to come. The Jarl decided that a raid would let them be violent to those outside our clan."

Fights such as this were normal but never welcome. Had one of the two men died then there might have been a blood feud. That could destroy a clan. One, Eystein, was Raven Wing and the other, Erik, came from the crew of *'Sea Serpent'*.

"Where does he think to raid?" I pointed back to my home. "The land to the east of us? The river there has many treasures."

"He has not decided. We hold a Thing, at noon. That is why I said you must have the second sight. I was about to fetch you."

"I am not important. Why does the Jarl need me?"

He laughed, "You were a slave too long. All the men of the clan take part in a Thing. We have to have the views of all. It saves arguments. Come, Brigid the ale wife has a fresh brew." He added, confidentially, "Erik One Hand also asked the Jarl if we could raid for his wife needs more barley and grain for the ale. It would not do to run out. This island is a good home but we cannot keep up with Brigid's needs."

Erik, along with Rurik One Ear, had helped me to defend the island from the band of murderers and outlaws. It made us close. As soon as he spied me Rurik One Ear came over. "You are like a hermit these days, Hrolf the Horseman!"

"You both have your women for company what do you need of someone who smells of horse sweat and shit!"

They laughed and Rurik said, "We put up with that for your wit, Hrolf. Are you here for the Thing?"

"I was not but now that I know it is here I will stay."

Erik put his good arm around me. "Then come to my home. Brigid will be pleased to speak with you. You should know you are the favoured one of all the women. I swear that if you asked her she would move in with you!"

I shook my head, "I doubt that." Erik had been, like me, a slave. He gave Brigid, also a slave, so much attention that she would never take another.

I enjoyed the rest of my morning as I sat drinking ale and catching up on the latest gossip and news. The two wounded warriors were being kept apart by the Jarl's hearth-weru. I guessed that would be part of the debate at the Thing. We would have to decide what to do about them. The Jarl could not afford to tolerate such dissension in his clan. Although only men could speak the women had an interest and they all gathered to watch. Few of them were Norse and this would be their first experience of our unique gathering. I had only seen one before and that was in the Land of the Wolf. Each clan did this slightly differently.

The only hierarchy was that the hearth-weru gathered around Jarl Gunnar Thorfinnson. The rest of us sat with friends and blood brothers. Siggi White Hair had told me of some clans where the debate became overheated and swords were drawn. That was expressly forbidden but the presence of the six hearth-weru ensured that all knew the rules. Anyone was allowed to speak. I decided to remain silent. Better to listen and let others give their views than make a statement which would fuel conflict.

The Jarl stood and began to speak, "We have not raided for some time. We had no need to do so for we had a good store of all that we needed. The fight that we had with Black Teeth and Hermund the Bent cost us men. But now I think we need to raid. We need grain and we need iron." He sat on the large log we had fashioned into a chair.

Ketil Eriksson, one of the Eriksson brothers, stood, "I care only that we find enemies to kill. My sword grows dull."

Gunnstein Thorfinnson, the Jarl's brother stood. He had his own crew. "My men and I are ready to raid now, too. We joined this clan because they were victorious. Since last year we have been farmers and fishermen."

I saw the Jarl flash his brother an angry look. Erik Long Hair was one of his men. This would just fuel the feud. Siggi White Hair saw the look and he stood. One of the oldest warriors he still had a fierce temper. I had seen him almost go berserk once. However, he was known as the voice of reason. His words, whilst quiet and considered were not conciliatory. "I think it is good that you wish to raid, Gunnstein Thorfinnson. I wonder why you have not done so before now. You have your own crew. What stops you sailing off and gaining great treasure, slaves and weapons? Go and find them and then boast to us, the men of *'Raven's Wing'*, that you are better warriors than we." He smiled, "I look forward to that."

I could see that Gunnstein Thorfinnson was annoyed. He was young and he was not yet a jarl. He flushed and as he stood his hand went to his sword. Jarl Gunnar Thorfinnson shouted, "Touch your weapon and brother of mine or not my men will cut you down! This is a Thing and men speak their minds however bluntly they phrase their words." The latter statement was a criticism of Siggi White Hair who nodded and sat.

10

This was not going well. I could see angry glances being thrown like weapons between the two drekar crews. Ulf Big Nose was our scout. I had been with him on many of his scouting expeditions. If we raided then it would be he who would be responsible for finding our target and ensuring we got there safely. He stood. He commanded respect from all, not least because he was a powerful warrior. He often fought without mail and yet had few scars. That took skill.

"It seems to me that we all want the same thing to happen. No one has said we should not raid." He scowled at everyone as he spun his head around. It seemed to make his nose even bigger! "Does anyone not wish us to raid?" No one said a word. "Then, Jarl, I think the decision is made and all we need is to decide where we raid." He smiled at Siggi White Hair, who was his friend. "And if one crew wishes to raid one place and the other does not then we can have two raids. It would be interesting to see how successful we both were."

The Jarl rolled his eyes. Having brought the peace Ulf now fanned the flames of animosity. The Jarl quickly stood. "Thank you, Ulf Big Nose, we will raid. I choose the Issicauna. I know we have raided there before but we have not been there for almost two years. They may have forgotten us. They have many churches and many settlements. It is close by and we know the land." He pointed to me, "And Hrolf the Horseman came from there and speaks their language." There was a great deal of nodding.

I turned to Rurik, "That is good. I had thought it might come to blows."

Before Rurik could answer Gunnstein Thorfinnson stood, "Then I will take my drekar to the Liger. I have yet to raid there. I know that the crew of *'Raven's Wing'* suffered losses there. I will avenge them!" It was a challenge to our crew as well as a veiled insult that we had, somehow, failed there. His men all cheered and brought angry growls from our crew.

The Jarl stood again, "Brother come with me to my hall. There we will speak in private!" As his brother stood the Jarl said to his hearth-weru. "Keep the peace!"

The six of them drew their weapons and stood between the two crews. Men had begun to stand. The Thing was over. Siggi White Hair was totally unrepentant, "That young fool nearly got all his crew killed on the second raid we had with him. Doesn't he know that his brother is the one who will bring us success. The Liger! Only a fool would go back there."

"But isn't it better to raid with two ships?"

Ulf Big Nose shook his head, "Only for the bigger places, Hrolf. We need grain. There are many smaller villages we can raid. The trouble is young Gunnstein is trying to prove that he is a great warrior. He wishes to be his brother. The Jarl served with the Dragonheart and learned much there. The younger Thorfinnson is barely finished sucking on his mammy's titties!"

"There is nothing wrong with that Ulf but you need to know how to fight first and he doesn't. Why, Hrolf here is younger but a better warrior already because he listens and he watches."

Just then we heard voices raised. We could not make out what they were saying but everyone in the settlement stopped talking and tried to listen. We did not have to wait long for the outcome. Gunnstein stormed out. He stood in the doorway of Gunnar Thorfinnson's hall and shouted, "Warriors of the *'Sea Serpent'*! To our drekar. Oleg, prepare for sea! We will show these old men how to raid. We will come back with so much treasure that we will have to capture three knarr just to carry it!"

His words did nothing to endear him to Siggi White Hair and the other original members of the crew. Gunnstein's men all followed him. Some made obscene gestures to our men. It was not a good leaving.

Ulf nodded, "Well that solves one problem. We do not need to keep Erik and Eystein apart!"

The Jarl was red faced and obviously not himself when he came out. He called over Sven the Helmsman, "Have the drekar prepared. We will sail on the morning tide."

Sven nodded and then said, "Is your brother sailing now?" The Jarl nodded. "Then I am sorry, Jarl, but he is a fool. It will take me the rest of the day to make sure that my sheets and shrouds are in perfect condition. I am not even sure he has cleaned the weed form his hull."

"It is not our problem now, Sven."

During the winter we had hauled **'Raven's Wing'** out of the waters and we had all scraped the weeds and barnacles from the hull before Sven had painted on the foul smelling liquid which slowed down their growth. It was not a pleasant task but we did it because we had to. The only task which was worse was ridding the hold of vermin. It was why I had trained Nipper to catch rats.

I turned to Siggi White Hair, "Will the brothers be reconciled?"

He shrugged, "Perhaps but it is in the hands of the Weird Sisters now, Hrolf. We cannot worry about that. We have our own journey to plan." He smiled, "Will you take your new horse mail?"

I shook my head, "It is too heavy to use on foot. I will just use the mail shirt I used to use and try to be quick on my feet. When I have grown and built up my strength then I will wear it on foot."

He laughed, "That is the spirit."

I went to Erik One Hand, "I will leave Dream Strider to run about the island. There is nothing to harm him and the grass is rich at this time of year. Nipper may come to steal titbits."

Erik nodded, "Brigid likes your dog. He keeps the rats from the grain. He is welcome here and he regards us as friend. I will look after your home while you are away. Take care, my young friend. Do not use all of your luck up at once."

"I am still learning, Erik. I watch more than I do and I listen more than I say."

I went back to my home and took out the old mail shirt I had. It only covered my chest and back but it would be enough for this raid. I had no doubt that I would be used as a scout again. As scout I had to move swiftly and silently. A full byrnie would encumber me too much. I found my leather jerkin. I would wear that beneath my mail shirt. Then I sharpened my sword and seax before finding as many arrows as I could. During the winter I had made my own arrows. I had a Saami bow. It had proved to be most useful as it had a longer range than ordinary bows. Then I went to Dream Strider. I did not bother to saddle him. I just jumped on his back and let him run. We would be away for up to five days and I wanted to enjoy the moment. He and I enjoyed a special bond. We were not horse and rider; we were one. Nipper raced along next to us. He loved the challenge. I did not return to my home until after dark. I rode Dream Strider down to the bay and we rode straight into the chilly sea. I enjoyed the salty water washing over me and Dream Strider seemed to enjoy it too. I did not ride him up to my home, I led him. These moments were special to me.

I took him to his stable and began to brush him. As always I spoke to him as though he were a man, "I will be away, Dream Strider, but you know that I will return. You and Nipper can enjoy the freedom of my home and the island." Others mocked me but I swear he knew every word I said. "I promise that I will return. Perhaps I will find a mare for you, eh?" He raised and lowered his head and then nuzzled my ear. It was late by the time I went into my simple one roomed hut. It was hardly a hall but I had made it big enough for my needs. It was longer on two walls than the others and had a turf roof and turf supports for the stones I had laid beneath wattle and daub. The central fire kept it warm. I had built

Dream Strider's stable close to my walls but I had room to expand my house should the need arise.

I had a rabbit I had hunted cooking in a pot and it was so tender that it fell from the bones. I ate it, with some bread I had been given by Brigid. The pain was scoured out by Nipper who crunched his way through the bones I had left. I would just need to rinse it in sand and the sea. I banked up the fire and went to bed happy but wondering what the Weird Sisters had in store for me.

Our two drekar were on the seaward side of the island. It meant that those on the mainland would not see us when we left. The Count of Vannes, Nominoe, was our nearest neighbour. They were not Franks but a people that were called Breton or Briton. The Jarl had made it clear that he did not wish to antagonise our neighbours and we never went near their lands. So far it had worked and they had not bothered us. I hoped that the Jarl's brother would have the good sense to stay well away from the Count's lands.

I had been elevated to one of the stern oars on our drekar. I shared an oar with Arne Four Toes and we sat behind Siggi White Hair and Beorn Beornsson. We had all day to sail around the coast and we were able to leave in full daylight. We headed out to sea until the land was a thin smudge on the horizon. Sven was a good navigator. We only had to row until he ordered the sail to be set and we caught the breeze from the south west. However, the first hour allowed us to become as one again and we sang as we rowed.

Through the waves the oathsworn come

Riding through white tipped foam

Feared by all raven's wing

Like a lark it does sing

A song of death to all its foes

The power of the raven grows and grows.

Through the waves the oathsworn come

Riding through white tipped foam

Feared by all raven's wing

Like a lark it does sing

A song of death to all its foes

The power of the raven grows and grows.

The power of the raven grows and grows.

The power of the raven grows and grows.

"In oars!"

As we stored our oars I felt my muscles ache. We had only rowed for a few miles but our rustiness showed. Siggi White Hair spat over the side and said, "Jarl, we will have to have the crew out more. We have forgotten what it is to sail the seas. Our island is too comfortable. Warriors should be tired each night!"

"You are right Siggi White Hair." I could tell the Jarl was distracted. He was not looking north but south. He was looking for his brother.

Knut One Eye, Ketil Eriksson's brother, said, "Do we have a target in mind Siggi White Hair?"

"I spoke with the Jarl and we agree that the old Roman town close to the mouth of the river would bring the greatest rewards."

"They have walls, Siggi White Hair."

"Aye, Erik Green Eye, but they are not well maintained. The Romans built them. These Franks are lazy bastards."

As I stared at the horizon I wondered about that. It had been two or three years since we had sailed this way. We should have scouted rather than going in blind. Ulf's nose would have sniffed out the danger. I said nothing. I was too young to venture an opinion.

Ulf Big Nose was not only a skilled scout he also stored places in his head. "And there is an abbey there. I remember it is close by the settlement on a hill. It has no walls! Who knows what trinkets we might pick up."

That seemed to satisfy the men. They liked to raid churches and abbeys. They were rarely defended and the priests had no weapons with which to fight back. Odin had decreed that they be slain. If a man did not fight for what was his then he was no man and did not deserve to live. It was brutal and it was cruel but we all understood the code.

Rurik joined me at the bow where I stood looking at the coast. "This village is on the north shore is it not?"

"As I recall, yes. I lived further upstream for some years."

"Good, for your knowledge of their words will come in useful." He tapped my short mail shirt. "You did not wear your new mail?"

"I am not yet fully grown. When I am then I can wear it on foot or on Dream Strider. I do not want to slow you down. Ulf Big Nose does not wear mail and he says that a scout must be fast or he will be dead! I doubt that we will encounter men wearing armour here."

"Do not tempt the Sisters, Hrolf. They listen. But you are right. Speed is worth more than mail when you are alone and surrounded by enemies."

"And I have yet to fulfil the prophecy. I have no family. When I have a family then I might worry."

"You have much faith in an old woman who lives alone on a rock."

"She was a witch, Rurik, and she knew things about me that no one else could possibly have known. Aiden, who is the

17

Dragonheart's galdramenn, also saw my future. I will live on the land one day and ride horses."

"You will leave the sea?"

I shrugged, "For most of my life I lived on the river we shall visit. The sea was something I was told about. I do not think it is in my blood as it is in yours." I pointed, "That land draws me. Our island is somewhere on my journey but I do not think my journey is done."

"That is why you live alone?"

"Partly and partly because it suits me to be with Dream Strider. I am learning, each day, to be a better horseman. I make small adjustments to my stiraps and my bridle. I am becoming more skilled at staying on his back even when he jumps and gallops over uneven terrain." I laughed, "It is better that others do not see my falls."

The wind was perfect for us. It took us gently around the coast towards Neustria. We prepared to go to war in an almost leisurely fashion. I did not do as many of the Dragonheart's warriors did. They put cochineal on their eyes or blackened them to make them more frightening. I just tried to be as ready as I could be. I had replaced the leather on my shield over the winter. I had had more metal studs. I hammered them in and they picked out the head of the horse I had painted upon it. My seax and Heart of Ice, my sword, were sharp enough to shave with. My hair was plaited and would add extra protection to my helmet which Bagsecg the smith had attached mail to. I had on my sealskin boots. They were more waterproof than the leather ones I used when I rode.

My helmet lay next to me. That would be the last thing I would don. As Sven turned to sail, with the sun behind us, towards the wide estuary I ate some of the bread and ham I had brought. The ship's boys came around with beer for us. In all probability we would only be ashore for hours but you could never tell. I smiled at

18

some of the rituals other warriors practised. The two Erikssons banged chests as they tried to become more fierce. Rurik just sharpened his already sharp sword. He would do it until we left the boat. We each had our own ways but, once ashore, we would be as one. The clan would fight for each other. Sven took in some sail as we were approaching the mouth of the river too quickly. He wanted to arrive after dark.

Jarl Gunnar Thorfinnson said, "We will take the settlement first. If we have little opposition then we will spend a day finding this abbey we have heard of. We will go back laden."

The men cheered. We were miles away from shore and any noise we made would not be heard above the sound of the river and the sea on the shore. I did wonder if he was trying to outdo his brother. I had no brothers. I did not understand this rivalry but I knew that it existed. The Eriksson brothers were always trying to prove that each was better than the other.

"Ulf Big Nose, I want you and Hrolf to find this abbey when we have subdued the village. See what else we can take back."

I nodded and Ulf Big Nose said, "Aye Jarl."

The sun finally started to slip below the horizon. We headed due west. Sven would take us to the southern bank and then we would row north. They had a watch tower to the north but they only looked for enemies coming from the land of the Saxons or the lands of the Danes. They did not expect to be attacked from the south. As soon as the sun set we took to our oars and waited for the order to row. Sven waited until he could feel the current from the river and then he nodded. We would not sing and the beat was given by Siggi White Hair. We watched the nodding of his silver hair. I knew that he sang in his head to keep the stoke steady. We pulled together with long powerful sweeps. We could only see the faint glow in the west; the setting sun. We relied on the ship's boys and Sven to ensure we hit the right place.

We were close to the shore and Sven used hand signals to slow us down. I could hear the surf. Our helmsman had managed to have us row upstream and now, as he turned, he could signal us to bring in our oars. The current would take us gently to the bank. We quickly stacked our oars and then each warrior grabbed his shield and helmet. I donned my helmet first. My vision narrowed as I had a half mask over my eyes. It could be a problem but I would be safer with the metal around my eyes. I did not draw my sword. I had seen too many warriors stumble as they tried to clamber over the strakes while holding a shield and a sword. It could either be merely embarrassing or result in a serious wound.

The ship's boys were ashore first and they ran to a pair of large rocks to wrap the ropes around them. The Jarl and his six hearth-weru were the first to leap in the water as was their right. They ran towards the wooden walls we could see just a hundred or so paces from us. I could smell the wood smoke and flashes of firelight showed us how Sven had managed to make such an accurate landfall. I followed Ulf Big Nose. If we were to be the scouts then I needed to be with him. We ran up the bank towards the wooden wall. We had been seen. I could hear, even through my helmet, the shouts of alarm. That was to be expected.

I found myself close behind the hearth-weru. All six wore good mail. There was a ditch around the wall but it was neither deep enough to deter us nor did it appear to have traps. Arne and Vermund, two of the hearth-weru, ran to the wall and placed their backs against it. They held Vermund's shield and with hardly a pause the Jarl leapt upon it and sprang up to grab the top of the wooden palisade. Olvir was a heartbeat behind him and then Einar followed too. The three of them helped up the rest of the hearth-weru.

"To the gate Hrolf!"

I followed Ulf and we ran to the gate. Inside I could hear the clash of swords and the screams of men who were dying or wounded. The rest of our men formed up behind us as we waited for the gate to open. I heard the bar as it was dropped and Ulf Big Nose pushed it open. I saw Vermund and Olvir, they were bloodied but unwounded.

Siggi White Hair, waving his war axe, burst through shouting, "The Jarl is alone! Raven Wing!" He ran forward and hewed down a Frank who was leading six villagers armed with swords and spears to stop us. Ulf and I hurried to his aid. He did not need it. He swung his axe at shoulder height. One man was slow to duck and lost his head while two others fled and left the warrior to fight Siggi White Hair almost alone. Ulf led me through the village to the northern wall. There would be a gate there and we needed to stop the Franks from fleeing. There was a lord in the village and we saw him as he tried to form a shield wall close to his hall. He had fine mail, a good helmet and four oathsworn around him. The Jarl would have his work cut out with him.

Jarl Gunnar Thorfinnson saw him and yelled to his oathsworn to follow him. Ulf put his hand on my shoulder. "We do not wear mail and they do. Come, Hrolf, we will stop their escape." He led me down a gap between two daub and wattle huts. A man stepped out from behind one of them. He held a spear. Ulf was so close to him that he was unable to use his sword properly and he just hit him with the side of the head with his hilt. Ulf turned left and ran behind the line of huts. I saw, fifty paces from us, people as they crowded towards the gate. They were trying to flee. It was still closed and guarded.

When the guards saw us they shouted an alarm. The four of them held their spears before them. The crowd before them dispersed. They did not wish to risk the wrath of a Northman. Ulf shouted, "Stay close Hrolf!" He did not pause but ran straight at the four of them. Both of us had our huge shields gripped tightly, close to our bodies. Heart of Ice was out already. The four men held spears and small shields. Their first mistake was in allowing a gap between themselves and their second was in waiting for us.

21

I ran at the two warriors to Ulf's right. The one in the extreme right was the danger. As he thrust his spear at me, I flicked the head aside with my sword. The second spear smashed into my shield. I did not stop but lowered my head and head butted the sentry. His helmet was open. His nose was crushed and blood spattered. He fell to the ground. I whirled around, swinging my sword as I did so. A spear is unwieldy at close quarters. My sword bit into the ash shaft of the spear and stuck. I punched with my shield. The metal boss hit the sentry on his shoulder. I jerked my sword back and it freed itself. Pulling my shield around to my front I brought my sword to stab over the top. The Frank was shorter than I was and I could just see the top of his helmet. I stabbed downwards. I hit something soft and I pushed harder until I met bone. Then I twisted and pulled it out.

"Well done Hrolf. He is dead." I lowered my shield and saw that my sword had pierced his skull. Ulf walked over to the unconscious Frank and plunged his sword into his throat. I did not know how he could do that yet I knew it was right. Enemy warriors were to be slain. There was no purpose in keeping them alive. They had to be watched and if they were warriors such as we they would try to escape. "You guard the gate. Let no one escape. I will find the Jarl."

I stood with my back to the gate. It was dark before me but I could hear the screams and the shouts as the rest of the clan fought the Franks. For a moment I was alone with the four dead sentries. I glanced at them. They had no mail and only two had worn helmets. The shields they had used were half the size of the one used by me. Only one had had a sword. I began to wonder; would we get anything worthwhile from such a poorly defended place?

There was a movement ahead, in the dark. I pulled my shield tightly to me again and held my sword above it. An old man, some women and three children emerged. I did not want to hurt them but I had my orders. I shouted, in Frank, "Halt! I will not let you leave!"

I saw the surprise as I spoke to them in their own language. I think the old man was going to risk attacking me for he pulled out a seax. I did not want to kill an old man. There was no honour in that. Then Siggi White Hair, Rurik One Ear and Arne Four Toes arrived. Siggi White Hair knocked the old man to the ground with his shield and picked up the seax. "The Jarl sent us but I see you have held the gate. The village is ours! Their lord is dead."

Chapter 2

By the time dawn had broken the wounded enemy warriors had been despatched. The villagers were all gathered close to the Frankish lord's hall. Ulf and I stood before the Jarl. "I can see no danger to us here. You two go and find this abbey. It should be somewhere close. See if there are any other targets close by. We will begin to load the drekar."

Ulf nodded, "Aye Jarl. Come Hrolf."

I had already used my nose and I pointed to a building close by the lord's hall. "There are horses close by. We can cover more ground that way."

Ulf nodded, "I should have known. But you are right."

I laid down my shield and hurried to the stables. There were four horses within. I saw that there was a stallion and three mares. It was a fine horse. I could see that it was a noble's horse. However it was the mares which interested me for one had a colour of red and gold. She was beautiful. Next to her was another even more beautiful. She had a lighter coat and her mane was almost blond. I left the two there as I saddled the stallion and the third mare for Ulf. I did not want the two mares risking. I had plans for them.

"I do not need a saddle!"

"Trust me we can ride faster and these horses are used to such things."

"You are the horseman. Where is your shield?"

"I thought we go to find a church. We should not need them and they are an encumbrance on a horse. But if you wish to take yours..."

"You may be right." He laid his down before we left the settlement.

We galloped through the open north gate. Ulf's skills and knowledge came into its own. He pointed to the higher ground to the north east of us. "They like to build their churches on higher ground. We will try there first."

As we rode I noticed that they had few animals in the fields. The ones we saw looked to be almost wild and there were so few of them that I think they must have been animals which had escaped. The animals we had found below were their only livestock. I wondered if others had raided them. We had captured grain and a few slaves but that was not enough. If we could not find the abbey then we would leave with just that which we found in the village and that looked to be poor return for the two warriors who had died.

Ulf did not take us along the sky line. He kept us below the top. He suddenly stopped. I could see nothing but it was obvious that he had sensed something. He slipped from his horse's back and handed me the reins. He bellied up the slope and, taking off his helmet, peered over the top. It seemed a quick glance was all that he needed for he slid back down, replaced his helmet and walked back to me. "We have found it. I will go back and tell the Jarl." He pointed up the valley. "Ride east but keep out of sight. See if there is any danger further upstream. Do not wander too far." He grinned, "I would hate to have to train another scout. Sometimes I think we might actually make of you someone I could rely upon!"

I took that as a compliment and as he headed back to the village I kicked my horse on and continued up the valley. I had a great responsibility. If I found Franks and they did not see me then I would have done the clan a great service. If they saw me, however, then all that we had gained could be lost. I regretted not bringing my bow. With that I could kill silently.

I decided to head down towards the river. Once I could find that I would have a better idea of where our drekar was in case I had to return quickly. It was the smell of smoke which told me where the people were. I stopped and dismounted. There was a stand of trees to my left and I walked my horse there and tied him to a sapling. I hung my helmet from the saddle and, drawing my sword, headed up the slope. Once I was just below the top I dropped to the ground as I had seen Ulf do and I crawled the last few paces. Peering over I saw, nestling in a dell with a small tributary of the Issicauna, a walled village. This one had a stone gate and towers at each corner. It looked to be bigger than the one we had raided. It reminded me of the one in which I had grown up. That had been further upstream. Even as I watched I saw three horsemen leave by the north gate and ride north. I had seen enough.

Once mounted I rode down to the river and followed the greenway which ran alongside it. I rode quickly for the danger was to the east. I galloped into the village and my arrival made the Jarl and the others turn. Pointing to the east I said, "There is a walled town with towers four or five miles to the east of us.

The Jarl said, "Did they see you?"

"No, Jarl. But I saw three horsemen leave the walls."

"Then we have time to raid the abbey and escape before they come. You and Rurik go and keep watch on them. Ulf will take us to the abbey."

I nodded, "Jarl I would like to take two of the horses we captured back to the island."

He smiled, "Horses! If you can coax them on board then you may take them!"

"Thank you Jarl. Come Rurik."

Rurik could ride; I had taught him but he was never happy about it. I returned the way I had come. Once we reached the stand of trees I led my friend to the vantage point I had found. I saw that they had fishing boats in the river. If they went to the sea then they would see the drekar. I hoped that the Jarl would not spend too much time at the abbey. I saw the riders I had spied before as they returned to the town. It looked as though they had been hunting for one had an animal across his horse's neck. That was good. It meant they would be less likely to leave again. The Jarl had not said how long we had to stay there but I made the decision to leave by noon. I watched the sun in the sky as it rose higher.

It was not long before noon when two more riders left not by the north gate but the west. To my dismay they began to ride along the road which ran west. I tapped Rurik on the shoulder and we returned to the horses. "We need to follow them. If they see the Jarl we shall have to stop them returning."

As we mounted he said, "I cannot fight from the back of a horse!"

I pointed to the stiraps. "That is why the Franks use those. They allow you to have control over your horse and your weapon. We just need to stop them." I led us further north. We rode above and behind them. I used the folds in the land to hide us but they did not turn as they headed along the ancient road. I could tell that they were heading for the abbey. I had hoped that they might also be going hunting but that seemed unlikely now. When we drew close where I knew they would see the abbey I led us down to the road. The Jarl would have sentries watching the road and I hoped they would take care of the two Franks with their bows.

The two of them were half a mile ahead and I could see the abbey rising to the right of the road. When they stopped I knew they had seen something amiss. "Draw your sword!"

I kicked my horse in the flanks and he leapt along the road. Two things happened at once. One of them heard our hooves as they clattered along the road and Ketil Eriksson and Karl Swift Foot spied them. They both released arrows. The two Franks drew their weapons and galloped towards us. Ketil and Karl sent more arrows after the two Franks. They managed to hit the horse of the one at the rear. It reared in the air and threw the rider to the ground. The wounded animal's cries made our horses skittish. I pulled back on the reins of mine but Rurik lost control and his horse charged down the road towards the oncoming Frank. I urged my horse on as I raced to catch Rurik. He was so busy trying to control his horse that he would be an easy target for the Frank. I saw that Ketil and Karl had reached the other Frank and killed him but at that moment the Frank swung his sword at Rurik. My friend bravely tried to block the blow with his own sword but he was still trying to control his horse. As the swords came together with a ring Rurik fell from his horse.

I held my sword slightly behind me as I raced towards the Frank. He had despatched one Viking and I saw his grin as he pulled back his sword to strike at me. As he pulled his horse to charge at me I rose in my stiraps and began to swing my sword above my head. He had not been expecting that and he brought his own sword around to block my strike. My sword was straight, true and finely balanced. It hit his sword and it bent. The tip continued down and struck first his helmet and then his face as it raked down. I continued with the blow and it bit into the neck of his horse. The rider and horse overbalanced and they tumbled into the ditch which ran along the side of the road.

28

I pulled my reins and turned. Leaping from my horse I ran to the ditch. The Frank was dead. His neck was broken and the horse had broken two of his legs. I took my sword and placing it next to his throat said, "Go to the Allfather; you were a brave mount." I slit its throat. The warm blood gushed over me.

I saw that the Frank was richly dressed. He was a noble yet his sword had been poorly made. I took his rings, his purse and a dagger which was in a richly decorated scabbard. I walked back to the sword. Its hilt was bound in silver but the blade itself had not been tempered as well as that which Bagsecg's father had made for me. I took the sword for Bagsecg could use the metal and I would take the silver.

Rurik had risen to his feet and was leading his horse. "I do not mind riding the beast but how you fight from its back is beyond me."

"It is a skill you can learn. Come let us return to the village."

Ketil and Karl approached. Ketil was grinning. They too had found that the Frank they had killed had coins and rings. "An easy victory!"

I nodded, "Perhaps we should call you Ketil the horse killer! What was wrong with hitting the warrior?"

Karl shook his head, "Not all of us have a Saami bow such as you, Hrolf the Horsemen. It turned out well enough."

When we reached the village Sven and those the Jarl had left to guard the villagers were already loading the drekar. Sven nodded at my approach. "Sven, the Jarl said I can bring aboard two horses if I can coax them."

He laughed, "If anyone can it is you. There is a gangplank. It is strong enough to take a horse. Put them at the bow and you can stay with them during the voyage." I nodded. "And you get to clean the horseshit!"

"Of course." I went to the stables. I would saddle the two mares I wanted. It would make them easier to control. "Rurik, come and give me a hand."

He came over. "You are taking two horses?"

"Mares for breeding." I handed him my helmet. "Put this and my shield aboard the drekar. I will saddle them and lead them." As I headed towards the stables I met Sven the Helmsman. He had a coil of rope he had found. Rope was always in short supply. "The Jarl says I can bring two horses back with me."

His face fell. "You get to clean up the drekar after them."

"Of course. It is good for the crops. It is like gold!"

Shaking his head he said, "And you stay with them on the voyage home. If they charge around the boat it could sink us."

"Of course." I entered the stable and fitted a halter over the head of the larger mare. "I take you and the little one to a new home. You will like it there. You shall run free." She whinnied and seemed unafraid.

By the time I had saddled them and Rurik had returned, the men were coming back from the abbey. I led the first mare. I spoke to her in the Frankish tongue. I did not know her name yet. She would tell me eventually. I stroked her as I spoke. When we reached the gangplank I thought she was going to baulk as a wave lifted the drekar a little. "Come, I have a fine stallion waiting for you! Dream Strider is handsome and he is brave. You will make a fine pair." She raised her head and whinnied but she put her hoof on the gangplank and let me walk her aboard. "Rurik, come and hold her while I fetch the other."

Rurik took the reins. He began to stroke her neck. As sheep and pigs were brought aboard so the noise rose. By the time I had brought the second one down to the drekar it was a cacophony of noise. She became quite skittish. I climbed on to her back and turned her around. I would not lead her aboard, I would ride her. I started to sing. I used the song they had made up about me. It was in Norse but it had a gentle rhythm.

The horseman came through darkest night

He rode towards the dawning light

With fiery steed and thrusting spear

Hrolf the Horseman brought great fear

Slaughtering all he breached their line

Of warriors slain there were nine

Hrolf the Horseman with gleaming blade

Hrolf the Horseman all enemies slayed

With mighty axe Black Teeth stood

Angry and filled with hot blood

Hrolf the Horseman with gleaming blade

Hrolf the Horseman all enemies slayed

Ice cold Hrolf with Heart of Ice

Swung his arm and made it slice

Hrolf the Horseman with gleaming blade

Hrolf the Horseman all enemies slayed

In two strokes the Jarl was felled

Hrolf's sword nobly held

Hrolf the Horseman with gleaming blade

Hrolf the Horseman all enemies slayed

31

Gradually she calmed and when I came to the chorus risked approaching the gangplank. I knew we did not have much time for the Jarl was already aboard. To my great relief she walked aboard calmly. I dismounted and stroked her head. "Well done! You are a brave one." I handed her reins to Rurik as I tied a piece of rope to the raven prow. I then tied the reins of the two mares to the rope.

Sven's voice carried down the drekar, "Ready oars!"

"You had better get to your oar, Rurik. Sven wants me to watch my prizes. He does not wish two horses careering about his ship."

"Better you than me!"

The first mare which I had led aboard had a proud look about her. She was not young but she held herself well. I stroked her and said, "You I shall name Freyja for you are like the goddess herself. You are fearless and proud."

I turned to the other. She had a golden colour and her mane seemed like a beautiful woman's hair. She also seemed younger, "And you are like the jǫtunn, Gerðr. Your foals will be the most beautiful while Freyja's will be the boldest and bravest!" They both seemed content but I spoke to them until we were well out to sea and the sail had been set. The crack of the sail almost made Gerðr start but Freyja turned her head and nuzzled the younger mare. It was then that I saw the similarity. Freyja was just a little darker than Gerðr. She was her dam! She had foaled already. This was *wyrd*.

Siggi White Hair came forward to bring me some ale and some ham when the oars were stored. "I see you have your treasure."

"Aye they are beauties. I can start my own herd."

"What for? We live on an island!"

"Someday we may not." I did not want to share my dream yet and so I changed the subject. "How was the raid on the abbey?"

"We have two holy books, much fine linen and two golden crosses. We also found much grain. It was a good raid. We lost no men and the wounds the men suffered were slight. It was the hearth-weru who needed healing. They and the Jarl fought the only warriors in the village. The women we took are all young."

I looked beyond him to the mast fish. There were ten captives there. They were mainly girls and young women. "Is the Jarl happy with the slaves we have taken?"

"He is. They all have broad hips. You will need to teach them our words."

"Brigid can do that too."

"Aye." He looked south. "I wonder how the Jarl's brother fared."

"This animosity between the brothers cannot be good, Siggi White Hair. This rivalry divides our people."

"Aye but it is *wyrd*. Brothers are always thus. When Gunnstein Thorfinnson realises that he has to walk before he can run, life will return to normal. A Jarl has to learn how to raid and how to lead. Jarl Gunnar learned that with the Dragonheart. He left when he was confident he could raid alone. Do not worry, when he returns with less than he thought he will swallow his pride and raid with us."

I nodded but I was not too certain. I was no galdramenn but sometimes I sensed things I did not understand. This was one such time. I put those dark thoughts from my head and I spent the rest of the afternoon and early evening singing to my two new horses.

As there was a wooden quay of sorts in the bay where I lived, Sven put in there. The fishermen who had lived there before us had built it so that they could tie up their boats and land their catch. It would make it easier to offload not only horses but also the other animals. When they were landed he would take drekar, with most of the crew, to the place we called Raven Bay. I waited for the captives and other animals to be taken ashore under the

33

supervision of Erik Green Eye and six warriors. Then I mounted Freyja and rode her down the centre of the drekar. When we reached the mast I turned her. It was a short jump to the jetty but, when we jumped, it felt further than it had looked. We landed and I took off her saddle. I went back for Gerðr. She would be a little more nervous but the fact that her mother was on the jetty would make it easier. She halted at the sheerstrake the first time I tried to jump. I smiled as the warriors on the drekar backed off nervously. They knew the effect of a wild hoof.

I spoke to her gently and backed her a little more. Her mother whinnied as I approached the second time and she jumped cleanly to land on the wooden walkway. The crew cheered and Sven hoisted the sail to take her to Raven Bay. I took off Gerðr's saddle too. I left the saddles on the jetty and led the two mares up the path to my home. Dream Strider had been running free but he must have smelled the mares for, as I approached the haunted farmhouse, he appeared along with Nipper who stood well back from the new horses. He, too, knew the danger of a nervous horse. I had to pull them to the pen I had made for Dream Strider. It was too high for them to jump out. I opened the gate and let them enter. Then I shut the gate to keep out Dream Strider. The two mares had had enough excitement for one day.

I slipped a halter on him and, as I stroked his neck said, "You will get to meet them by and by. I will ride you when I have fed and watered your new companions."

I took two wooden pails of grain and bran and put them next to each other in the pen. The water trough was still full. They were both thirsty and drank greedily. I saddled Dream Strider and rode to the village. The drekar had landed and the men were bringing up the sacks of grain and booty we had captured. The captives were huddled fearfully together.

Erik Green Eye said, "The Jarl asked if you would speak with them, Hrolf. He wants them calmed. They were keening all the way back." I nodded; I had heard them. It had been an eerie sound and it had unsettled the horses.

I dismounted and let Dream Strider's reins drop. He had been ridden and he was content. I had left my helmet on the drekar but I still had my sword. I took that off and slipped them over my saddle. I approached the women with a smile. When Brigid and the others had first been brought as slaves they had said that my smile made them feel slightly safer and that they liked my soft voice.

"You have been captured by our warriors but I am here to tell you that you will not be mistreated. None of our warriors will take you against your will. You will serve us on the island. You will work but you will be fed and well treated. There is no escape from this island but you will be safe here. We will not use a yoke and you can move freely but you are captives and, until a warrior chooses you as his woman, you will be used as slaves." I saw their predicament sinking in. I do not know what they had expected but now they knew the reality. "You will need to use our language. I will teach you." I pointed to Brigid and the other women. "All of those were slaves and could not speak our language. Now they can and they are happy. Ask them. They are now free. Their captivity did not last long. They can help you speak our words. Until such time as you can speak easily ask me and I will give you the words."

One of the young women, a little bolder and prettier than the rest put up her hand, "Lord, will you not sell us back to our people?" I noticed that she finer clothes than the others and sat a little apart.

"What is your name?"

"I am Mary daughter of Lothair of Reims. He was a noble. Your men killed him but my mother has money. She would buy me back."

"You should know, Mary, that we have all the gold we need but girls and women are in short supply. None will ask for ransom."

She pouted. I think she thought it was a defiant gesture. "Then I will throw myself from the rocks!"

I nodded, "You follow the White Christ. Does that not mean that if you do that you cannot go to heaven? Is it worth that?"

"I will not lie with an unwashed barbarian!"

"You do not need to but you will work." I looked at her hands which were soft and smooth. She had not had to do any hard work in her life. "I am afraid it will be hard work."

She sat down and her face showed resignation and despair. I thought she had been a little selfish. She would have been the only one who would have been ransomed. The rest would still be slaves. I saw resentment on some of their faces.

"Are there any other questions?"

Another, a little younger than Mary, put her hand up, "I am Hildegard, daughter of Otto the swineherd. Do we have to call her, my lady?" She jabbed a finger at Mary.

"You call the Jarl, 'lord', and the men in the village master but what you call each other is not our business."

She smiled, "Then I am content. Life cannot be any harder here than in our village and at least the men here look like they know how to fight. I would like to learn your words."

Some of the others nodded and said , 'Aye'. I noticed that they moved further away from the noble's daughter, Mary.

I spent the time it took the crew to unload the drekar teaching them the basic words and telling them the names of those who would be in charge of them. Night had fallen and the fires had been lit. Brigid had come over while I was speaking. I knew that she wished a word and I nodded. She spoke a little Frank and she said to the slaves, "Work hard and obey orders and life will be good. Do any of you know how to make ale?"

One girl of about twelve summers put up her hand.

"Who are you?"

"I am Emma and my mother makes ale. I have watched her."

"Then Emma, you can work with me." The slave jumped up and she had a huge smile on her face. For her life would be almost the same. She would be used to obeying orders. Instead of her mother it would now be Brigid.

Jarl Gunnar arrived and I said, "I have told them that they are slaves. Most are resigned to their fate."

"Good." He turned to me. "Ketil told me how you stopped those scouts. Thank you Hrolf. Your skills have aided us again."

"I am glad to be of some use, Jarl."

We ate a basic meal and the slaves were put into a hut we kept for them. I was about to return to my home when there was a commotion and two of the slaves came tumbling out. Hildegard and Mary had come to blows. They each had hunks of the other's hair in their hands and I saw bite marks on Mary's arm. Siggi White Hair strode over and bodily separated them. They were both sobbing but Mary, even though she was the elder, looked to be the most distressed. Siggi looked at me and I shrugged. "The one with the bite on her arm was the daughter of the lord. The other resented her. I fear they will take things out on her."

Jarl Gunnar had appeared along with some of the women and they had heard my words to Siggi. Brigid said, "Lord, I will house her in my home for a while but I am not certain if she has any skills which we can use. Perhaps it might be as well if we sold her back to her people."

I walked over to her and said, "What did you do in your father's hall?" She was still sobbing and I said, quietly, "Take your time. You will not have to share the hut with others, not for a while anyway. Brigid will care for you. What did you do?"

She seemed to breathe a little easier when I said that and she said, "I helped to teach others to read." That would not be a skill we would need.

"And was there anything else which you did well?"

"And I sewed with my mother. We made tapestries."

I smiled, "She can sew. That is a useful skill."

Brigid and the Jarl smiled, "It is indeed. In the morning take her to old Seara. She could do with some help." Seara was a slave we had brought on an earlier raid from the land of the Saxons. She was older than the ones we normally brought but we had discovered that she could sew and make clothes. Those unmarried warriors paid her to make them kyrtles and cloaks. She was however old and her eyes had been failing of late.

I turned back to Mary, "Tomorrow you will be taken to Seara who will watch over you. You will sew."

She took my hand and kissed it. "Thank you, master."

"I was a slave once amongst your people. I know how you feel but you will find that life goes on. This is your god's way of testing you."

I rode home in the dark but Dream Strider and I knew the path well. I heard my two mares whinny as we approached and Dream Strider responded. "Tonight you sleep in your stable tomorrow you and your mares can become acquainted."

For some reason I slept well for I felt contented. The population of our island was growing but, more importantly, my dream was coming to fruition. I was up before dawn. I went down to the quay and fetched the saddles. I placed them in the manger above the stalls. The mares would not need them for a while. I finished off the last of my ale and ate some stale bread and cheese. I did not even taste it for I was eager to see how my herd got on with each other. Dream Strider was equally keen and he stamped in his stall. I took him out and let him drink from the pail. I then went to the pen and opened it. This was all new to me but instinctively I knew I had to give them the freedom to get to know each other. As soon as I opened the gate the two mares bolted. We were on an island and they could go nowhere. Dream Strider reared and then took off after them. It was only then I realised how much bigger than the two mares he was. His hooves ate up the ground as he followed them. They would return.

I set off for the village. I needed more ale and some bread. I was also keen to see how the slaves had settled in. I knew that my language skills would be in great demand. The village was a hive of activity. We had a barn where we stored our grain. It was off the ground to prevent the rats from feasting upon it. The slaves were busy moving the sacks of grain we had captured. There were many jobs we could now do. With the increased number of slaves we were able to harvest more salt from the sea. The island had few beaches but there were areas we had used to turn sea water into salt. We had built dams so that the sea water did not flow back to the sea but dried, over time, in pans. The salt was placed in sacks. It was a time consuming task to cart the sacks of salt up from the shore to the village. The Jarl had his men organise that. At the same time there were more homes needed and there were many warriors helping to build the wooden houses with turf supported walls and roofs. Brigid and her new assistant were boiling up great vats of beer. We had the grain and our supplies needed increasing. Bagsecg was already sorting out the weapons and mail which could be repaired and would be reused.

As I passed he said, "I still need some boys to work my bellows. Girls tire too quickly."

I shrugged, "I will speak with the jarl but we take what we find. Many of the boys in the places we raid either run off or choose to fight and then they die. But I will watch out the next time we raid.

I went, first, to see the Jarl. I had my share of the raid to come. The coins I had taken and the weapons from the dead warrior were mine for I had killed him alone. That which we had taken from the village was to be shared. The Jarl took one third as was his right. He gave some of his share to the hearth-weru. The other two thirds were shared between the warriors who had raided. My two horses would be deducted from my share. Even so I was given two chickens and a small purse of silver. With that which I had got for myself it would do. I was becoming richer. I had my horde buried in my home.

I went to the baker and bought enough bread for the week. Then I went to see Erik and his wife, Brigid. "I have run out of beer, Brigid. I need a firkin."

She nodded, "If you can wait until this evening I have a new batch I am making. I roasted some barley while you were raiding. It will be a strong dark ale. Do you want it watered?"

"No, Brigid. I have a spring by my home. I can water that which I need."

"That will be five silver coins but I need the barrel back when you have finished. They do not grow on trees."

I saw a mischievous look on her husband's face. "Actually, my love, they do grow on trees but they need a cooper to make them!"

She threw a wet cloth at him as she laughed, "One armed fool! Do something useful, mark Hrolf's barrel."

As he went to do so I said, "How are the slaves?"

"You mean the high and mighty one?" I nodded. "She slept and she seems happy to be with Seara. I still think we would have been better to sell her back. This will cause bad feeling with the men of Neustria. The Count will want back this daughter of a noble."

"Perhaps but they do not have ships and they war with the men of Vannes and the people twixt us. I noticed that they had few animals. I think they have been raided from across the river."

Brigid wiped her hands on her apron and stood looking at me. "I came from Hibernia; I know not the people of Frankia." She smiled. "Is there one among the slaves whom Hrolf the Handsome would take to his bed?"

"I have enough to contend with just surviving. I now have three horses besides I am still young."

"There are many younger who are fathers yet! Many of the women here would happily take you to their beds Hrolf! You are well thought of!"

"I will know when the time is right." I was uncomfortable talking like this. "I had better see if there are any tasks for my horse."

Emma the slave, was stirring the mash and she smiled as I passed. She spoke to me in Norse, "Good morning Hrolf the Horseman!"

I smiled, "Well done! You have learned some of our words."

She reverted to Frankish as she added, "I could learn much from you, master. If you need a slave to work in your home and keep it organised for you I would be willing to be your thrall."

"That is not your choice, Emma, nor mine. You have a skill and you are using it. Be content."

She looked disappointed. "I am happy for you to take me, master. You said that we would be sought after by the men of the village. You are less hairy and smelly than most."

41

I shook my head, "I am not yet looking for a woman. I thank you for the offer. There are many young men looking for women to bear them children. Look for the ones with warrior bands on their wrists. They are rich and good warriors!"

She looked sad, "I think I would prefer someone gentle with a shaven face, like you."

"That cannot be. Choose another."

I left my bread and ale with Erik while I sought out my horses. I tramped back to my home and found all three of them on the headland contentedly chewing the grass. Dream Strider came to greet me and his mares followed. I had a herd. I saddled my stallion and headed back to the village. To my surprise the two mares followed. As we entered the gates the villagers stopped and stared. I dismounted at Brigid's hut. "This is good Hrolf the Horseman. We now have three horses to fetch and carry. Perhaps I will see if I can afford to buy one from you. If I had a cart it would make my life easier." She nodded towards Erik One Hand, "Especially with a one handed husband!"

"I hope that they will breed. When they do it will be easier to train a foal to pull a cart. These are used to being ridden."

Erik was intrigued, "How will you get the barrel, the grain and the bread home?"

"Balance." I handed Freyja's reins to him. "This one is strong. I will tie the barrel to one side of her and the grain to the other. The weight will balance out. It is not far. It would be better if she was trained to the cart but she is not. The younger one can carry the bread."

It took some time but eventually I rode home, very slowly. I had tied ropes to the two mares and they followed. When we reached our home I could see it had taken much out of Freyja. "I am sorry I worked you so hard." After I had unloaded them I went to my apple store and brought out four apples. I gave them to the mares. As it was a pleasant and cloudless night I put the three of them in the pen. I would have to build two more stalls in my stables but that could wait until the leaves began to fall.

After I had eaten I took a horn of the ale out to the headland and looked at the land of Vannes just across the short stretch of water. I wondered why the Jarl had not visited with the Count. It would be better to have our nearest neighbours as allies. I knew that they often fought with the Franks. It would be a mutually beneficial arrangement. I was not Jarl. I was one of the youngest of his warriors. He made those decisions and not me.

Chapter 3

Like the other warriors who had land or animals to tend I had task to perform when we were at home. The sheep and chickens needed little care but my horses did. I began to gather the wood I would need for the stalls. I made sure that I rode a different horse each time I sought the wood and I chose a different part of the island to hew the trees. Wood would soon become scarce. We would outgrow this small island soon enough. It took me some time to both gather the wood and then work it so that I could use it. I added two stalls to the stable. When Erik, Rurik and I had built the stables we had allowed for expansion. I had dreams. Thus it was six days before I returned to the village. I walked, for my herd seemed to want to be together. They were a family.

As I reached the gate Rurik accosted me, "The Jarl is worried about his brother. He says he should have returned before now." I agreed with the Jarl but I said nothing. "Siggi White Hair and Ulf had words with him. They say that it is Gunnstein's own fault that he went off alone."

"Does the Jarl wish to go and find him?"

He nodded, "It is a hard choice. If Gunnstein has found trouble then they will be watching for another drekar. Siggi White Hair said we could end up losing all because of a headstrong wastrel."

I shook my head. Siggi White Hair was always forthright. He was much older than the Jarl and sometimes he was impatient with our leader's decisions. I think Siggi thought of the Jarl as the son he never had. He wanted him to be the best he could be. I went with Rurik to the hall. It was a pleasant day and men were outside talking. Everyone had an opinion. I heard raised voices. Some remembered the arguments between the two crews and thought that this was *wyrd*. Others said that Gunnstein had come to join us and we had been grateful for his help when we had fought Hermund the Bent. I could see the arguments on both sides. I kept silent as I watched. This was not a Thing where there were rules. This was a clan arguing amongst themselves. We were oathsworn to the Jarl but we were warriors and men had opinions.

I could see that the Jarl was becoming angry. His hearth-weru were also becoming nervous and fingered their weapons. The Jarl stood, "*'Raven Wing'* is my drekar! If I decide we will seek my brother then we will do so!"

Silence fell. This was not like our Jarl. The jarl was rarely autocratic. He liked to hear opinions. If he had to judge a matter he did so fairly but he never imposed his will upon us. Something like this required a Thing. He was behaving like a king or a lord. We followed him by choice. For myself I was quite willing to seek out the errant brother but I knew that there were many like Siggi White Hair and Eystein One Eye who did not.

Siggi White Hair stood and weighed his words, "Can you sail *'Raven Wing'* with your hearth-weru, Sven and the ship's boys, Jarl?" It was said with respect and calmly but the threat was obvious.

"Do you stir up contention, Siggi White Hair?"

Such an act was against the rules by which we lived and Siggi White Hair shook his head. "No Jarl; I ask because I for one will not risk my life to sail after a foolish and arrogant youth who probably lies dead along the Liger." He spread his arms. "I do not doubt that there are many others who feel the same."

45

I watched as the hearth-weru gathered around the Jarl. This was almost a rebellion. One or two of the clan stood by him but the majority stood by Siggi White Hair. The clan was about to fall apart. If swords were drawn then it would be a bloodbath. The Jarl and his followers would die but then so would many other members of the clan.

I had decided to keep silent but now I saw that I could not. I stepped between the two groups. "We are in danger of falling out and destroying this family. That is not good." The two sides stared at me but I could see hands were still on swords. It was like a forest fire which has almost gone out but a small spark remains and just needs a breeze to fan it. "I am a new member of this clan but, since I left the Dragonheart, you have become my family." I saw hands relax at the mention of the Viking hero. I had fought with him and served him. That bought me some time to speak. "I agree with Siggi White Hair that it would be irresponsible to risk our ship searching for someone who may be already dead." I had appeased some but the Jarl's eyes narrowed as he glared at me. "On the other hand Gunnstein Thorfinnson and his men fought with us and helped to defeat Hermund the Bent. We cannot forget that. I suggest a compromise."

Every hand went from their swords as they considered my words. There were quizzical looks as they wondered what I had come up with and they had not. Every man woman and child in the clan was watching me. They had been drawn by the heated debate. I felt naked and exposed.

The Jarl said, "Speak. You have my interest."

I took a deep breath, "How well do you know your brother?"

"What?"

"If you wish us to find him and sail *'Raven Wing'* to seek him where do we look? The Liger is a long river. Do we look upstream or downstream? The north bank or the south bank? If we sail blindly then we are doomed Jarl. We will all die."

He had not considered that. I saw him chew his lip. "You are right, Hrolf, I should try to think like my brother. I cannot believe that he would risk attacking Nantes for the Count Of Vannes regards that as his city. " He rubbed his chin and then looked into my eyes. I willed him to speak that which was in his heart. "Our greatest treasure came when we raided Andecavis. He will try to outdo me and attack that city!"

Siggi White Hair said, "Then he is dead! We barely escaped with our lives! He grounded his ship in the river there. He would be a fool if he did so."

"Nonetheless, Siggi White Hair, if this was your brother would you not wish to find out?"

Siggi White Hair nodded but I could see that he was not convinced that we should all risk our lives on what would probably be a wasted chase.

"Then here is my compromise." Every eye was fixed on me. Every ear heard my words. "If we sail past Nantes then you can land me and my horse, Dream Strider. I will ride to Andecavis. I can speak the language of the Franks. If I go dressed as a Frank then I can go into the city and find out his fate. The clan can wait in safety. It will be me alone who takes the risk."

Siggi White Hair turned, "Why would you do this?"

"Because this is my clan and this threatens to tear us apart. I am but one warrior. My loss would not harm us but, if I succeeded then we would be as one again."

Ulf Big Nose came over and put his arm around me. "A fine gesture, Hrolf but one doomed to failure."

"How so? You taught me how to scout."

"You would have to get into an enemy city and if the Jarl's brother is there then they will be wary of strangers. If you did find them what could you do? Could Dream Strider carry them all back?"

I looked at the Jarl. "I could return to the Jarl and the clan. I could tell them of the fate of Gunnstein Thorfinnson."

Siggi White Hair asked, "And if you found no news?"

"Then that would eliminate one place we had to search. It is my own life and that of my horse which I risk. I ask no man to put his own life in danger."

Siggi White Hair nodded, "If Hrolf is willing to search for your brother, Jarl, then I am willing to sail down the Liger with you. But if he finds no trace of him then we forget this venture."

The Jarl stared at Siggi White Hair, "Let it be so."

There was a collective sigh of relief. Rurik One Ear put his arm around my shoulder, "Hrolf you are as mad as a cat in a sack! I admire you and wish I had half your courage but I fear that when you leave us we shall never see you again."

Erik and his wife came over. Erik put his good arm around me and Brigid kissed me full on the lips. "Do not throw your life away, horseman, you could have any of the women of the clan tonight. It is a noble quest. I have children I would do as you if one was lost."

The Jarl waved me over. I stood next to him. "This is a fine gesture. How long would you need?"

"It would take at least a week, lord. If I was lucky and found the drekar then I would need to find the crew and then report back."

"You do not think you will find the drekar." It was a statement and not a question.

I nodded, "I expect to find her burnt bones but I go not for a drekar, Lord. I go to find your brother and the crew, We both know that drekar can be destroyed but her crew can survive."

He looked surprised, "You think to find men alive if the ship is destroyed?"

"Answer me honestly, Jarl Thorfinnson. If *'Sea Serpent'* had successfully raided would not your brother return here and boast of his success?"

He winced as though I had struck him, "You cut to the quick, Hrolf, but you are right. Are you certain you wish to do this?"

"It is for the clan. I do."

The Jarl nodded, "We sail on the morning tide. We take a crew to row and no more. We go not to war. We go to find our brothers!"

I turned and sought Erik. "I need to ask a boon. You will need to feed my two mares each day and let them run in their pen. They will not be happy that I have left them and their stallion has gone."

Erik shook his head, "You risk your life and ask me to feed horses! Of course we will care for them and your home. Brigid is right, Hrolf. You are worth more to the clan than this. Do not throw your life away."

Erik, I have been told my fate and it is not to die on the Liger. I cannot fulfil my destiny if the clan falls apart. This is but a step on a longer journey. I cannot see the end yet for I am barely started. My path has been determined by the gods and the Norns."

That night as I prepared, I chose what I would take carefully. I would leave my sword, and my helmet as well as my shield. They marked me as a Viking warrior. I took the curved sword I had taken from a Moorish warrior years before and his small round shield. I did take my bow. It looked like one used in the east. I left my wolf cloak behind and took a faded, old red one. I knew that there were simple round helmets on the drekar. I would wear one of those. I had decided to play a Frank. My mail vest had been taken from a Frank. I would look and sound like a

49

warrior from the north. There were many such mercenaries who fought for a lord and then moved on. When I had lived in Neustria I had seen bands of them. They were poorly dressed and armed but they were their own masters. Of course it would not guarantee my safety. That was in the hands of the Weird Sisters and I just hoped that they had not finished with me yet. I reached the village before dawn having said goodbye to my mares and to Nipper. I dismounted by the Jarl's hall. He came out with his hearth-weru.

"This is an act worthy of a saga, Hrolf."

"If it binds us together then I will be satisfied."

As we left by the south gate, I was touched by the fact that people came out to wish us, and me in particular, well. I saw Hildegard, Emma and Mary and they were crying. I knew not why. Boarding the drekar with Dream Strider was not as easy from Raven Bay. In fact I was not even certain it was possible. It was Harold Fast Sailing who came up with the solution. Spare strakes were laid from a rock which rose from the sea to the deck of the drekar. I managed to coax Dream Strider up the slippery, weed covered rocks. He was glad to jump into the drekar and I rode him to the prow. We cast off and I dismounted. I gave him another of my previous store of apples as a reward.

'Raven's Wing' would not wait for us but return to the island. It would be too dangerous for her to lurk on the Liger. We had agreed that I would not be back any earlier than seven days from when I was dropped off. I would be on my own for that time. Ulf Big Nose came to speak with me. He was our best scout and he was there to give me sage advice. "The best place to hide is in plain sight. Where you can then pay for your bed." He handed me a purse with small Frankish coins. A mercenary would not have gold. "You are good with people Hrolf. Smile and talk to them."

"Will they not think that strange for a hired sword?"

He laughed, "They will think that your smiles are the reason you are so poorly dressed. You have chosen a good disguise. By using old and damaged mail, helmet and shield you look the part. You will be a young warrior fallen on hard times. The difficult part will come in Andecavis. If the drekar has been there they will be suspicious of any strangers especially those coming up the river."

"I was going to approach from the east. If I ride around the city I could appear to have come from the Empire."

He clapped me around the shoulders, "You learn quickly Hrolf. I do not think that you need to do this for in my heart I believe that Gunnstein Thorfinnson is dead but I admire your courage in volunteering for the clan."

"Do not make it sound so noble, Ulf. I will be riding Dream Strider and riding freely. Perhaps I will stay and become a soldier of fortune!" I said it lightly but I was beginning to worry. If someone like Ulf was concerned then did I have the skills to achieve what I had promised?

We sailed into the Liger estuary in daylight and boldly. We did not have shields along the sides. The Jarl hoped that the men of Vannes would know that we meant no harm. The ship's boys watched for signs of the drekar as we passed the harbours along the coast. There was none. Sven stopped us at one of the many islands on the river. This one was six miles upstream from Nantes. He would drop me and then they would turn around the island and head back to sea. Sven would bring the drekar back to the same island. I would wait on the island when I had completed my task. A gangplank was run out and I clambered ashore on Dream Strider's back. I had a skin with wine and one with water. That would mark me as a Frank and not a Viking. I had some ham and some cheese. My food would only last me a few days. I had sixty miles to travel and I planned on thirty miles a day. That would not exhaust my horse.

Siggi White Hair came to the side, "Be careful, my young friend." He flashed a look at the Jarl who was watching from the stern. "Young Gunnstein is not worth your loss! If they are dead then come back quickly!" His look left me in no doubt that he wanted me to say that Gunnstein was dead even if I did not know that for certain. I could not do that.

"I will return." I kicked Dream Strider in the flanks and we headed down the greenway which abutted the river. I did not look back. The sight of the drekar sailing downstream would have made me even more aware that I was alone.

My helmet hung from my saddle and I rode easily as though I had not a care in the world. I could not travel too far from the river as I was looking for signs of the *'Sea Serpent'*. I knew from our previous forays that there were few settlements along the river. Those that we had seen had good protection against floods. The greenway along which I rode showed signs of recent flooding. In places it was sticky and muddy showing where there had been an inundation. At one point the greenway was impassable. I turned north to skirt the boggy section and I found the Roman Road. Easier for travel it made it more likely that I would meet someone.

As I trotted along the cobbled road I ran over my story in my head. Ulf Big Nose had told me to believe what I said; the lie would be harder to spot. I was about to turn south and head back to the river when I spied a handful of huts close to the road. I had been seen and if I left the road would incur their suspicion. If I was who I said I was then I would welcome the chance to rest and water my mount.

As I approached I saw that they had neither gate nor wall. There were no visible arms but there was a reaction to my arrival. Children ran to their mothers and the men emerged from their huts and workshops, some holding weapons. I saw that they had a variety of activities. There was a forge; fish were being dried and women were weaving. It was a thriving little community. I smiled and halted in the centre. Dismounting I said, easily, "Am I glad to find people. This is a lonely road."

An older man with broad shoulders; I took him to be the smith asked, "Where have you come from stranger?"

"I have been travelling these many days. I was at Reims on the river and I have travelled down from there."

Another nodded to my sword and shield. "You are a warrior?"

"I am." I leaned forward. "I had a falling out with my Captain. I did not like the men he chose as our employers. I go to seek a permanent job. I hear Andecavis needs warriors."

My words and my smile seemed to put them at their ease. The smith said, "They always need warriors there but your sword has seen better days."

The curved Moorish sword had not been used for some time. There were flecks of rust on it and the scabbard was poor. "Aye. I have coin if you could put an edge on it smith and if there is any food..."

The chance of making money was not to be missed and they smiled. "Of course. Bring your horse to my forge. There is water there for him to drink. Anya, fetch food for this warrior. What is your name?"

"Bertrand of Bruges."

"You are far from home."

"When you are young and seek adventure the world is not big enough."

The smith had a cut log as a seat and he gestured for me to sit. He took my sword and placed it in his fire. "This may take some time. This sword has seen much wear. You might think of buying another."

"Have you any for sale?"

"There is little call for them here. It is peaceful."

"Then you and this village are lucky."

His wife had come out during our conversation with a small jug of wine, some fresh bread and the local cheese and butter. "Do not listen to my husband! Ten days since we feared for our lives for a dragon ship with fierce warriors sailed up the river. As it has not returned I fear for our lives. When they come back they will kill the men, rape the women and eat the babies!"

Her husband laughed, "I told my wife that if it had not returned it was because it had been destroyed by the men of Andecavis. What say you? You are a warrior and know such things."

"I think your husband may be right. Unless of course it slipped south during the night."

The smith shook his head, "We may not have a wall but we watch the river at night." He pointed south. "We have fishing boats there and some have been stolen before now. Each night two men watch the river. No one has come down since the Northmen went upstream. They are dead and I do not believe that they eat babies."

"Then your husband will be right, lady. You can sleep easy at night." I gave her my broadest smile and she smiled back.

"We could find work for you here, warrior. We have asked the lord to have men here to protect us from brigands and bandits but he is too concerned with fighting the Count of Vannes."

I nodded as I ate, "It is a pleasant place but it is too much like my home. I will try Andecavis and if I have no work there then I may return and take you up on your offer." I was planning my escape already.

It was late afternoon when I left. I paid for the work on the sword and my food. They pressed me to stay but I said I was anxious to get to the city. The smith told me that there was another village fifteen miles down the road. I stored that information and headed along the ancient road, east. I now believed that Gunnstein had come to a bad end. I had to discover what that end was. I owed that to the Jarl for he had given me the life I had. The drekar could not have survived upstream for ten days. When I was far enough from the village to move without being seen I left the road and headed back to the river path. I had eaten well and I was anxious to see the river for myself. Who knew what evidence there might be.

I rode until dusk and then found a clearing close to the river. There was a large willow which would afford shelter in case it rained. After giving Dream Strider water I allowed him to graze the rich and lush grass close to the river. I went to lay out a fish line. I had a fancy for fish for my supper. I left the line, baited with a juicy worm and went back to light a fire. The light had almost gone in the west but there was still a half light. I saw my line being tugged. I began to haul it in. It was a brown speckled fish, half as long as my forearm. Icaunis had smiled on me and sent me bounty.

I took the hook from its mouth and laid the fish on the bank. I carefully rolled the line and hook and placed them back in my leather pouch. Who knew when I would need it again. I quickly gutted the fish and threw the guts back into the river. They were for the river god. Soon the fish was crackling and spitting on my fire. Later, as I finished the last of the succulent fish I reflected that it had been a good day. It had gone better than I had hoped and, after hobbling Dream Strider, I lay down to sleep.

I awoke not long before dawn. I took Dream Strider's hobble from his legs and went to the river to make water. It was a different light this morning. It came from the east and what had been shadows were now bathed in light as the sun rose. I saw an arm. It was in the water and appeared to be waving. I drew my sword and approached it. I saw a tattoo and recognised it. The arm belonged to Sven Dragon Arm. He was one of Gunnstein's crew. When I reached him I saw that he was dead; he had no head. Had it not been for the distinctive tattoo I would not have recognised him. His body had been caught up in the bend of the river. I took his arm and pulled his body free. I let it catch the current and, bloated, it floated down the river. "Farewell Sven Dragon Arm. May you find your way to Valhalla."

I saddled Dream Strider. There was little point in travelling up the river. I decided I might as well head directly for Andecavis. I would sweep around the town further north than I had planned. As I rode along the road I felt sad for the crew. They had been a young crew. Sven Dragon Arm had been one of the warriors who had been with old Jarl Thorfinn Blue Scar on Ljoðhús. I hoped that some were still alive; it was possible but I suspected that if one of the more experienced warriors had perished then so had the rest. I could have turned around then with the news for the Jarl. No one would have blamed me but I had been given a task and I would stick to it.

The road followed the river and I passed through a few small villages. I smiled and I paid for a little food at each one. I was questioned for I was a stranger and I told my story each time. It became easier and more believable the more I repeated it. There were still some mile stones left from the times of the Romans. I saw one which told me there were five more miles to Andecavis. Just ahead I saw a crudely made road which headed north. I decided to take that one. Now that I knew the drekar had come to harm then I had to be even more circumspect.

After two miles I saw a forest to the east. The road north was not turning and when I spied a track I took a risk and headed east. It was a well worn track. There were fresh horse droppings along it. It was used by travellers with horses. That suggested nobles or merchants. It was a thick forest and it was dark and filled with shadows. The air was oppressively hot. I wondered if I had made a mistake. When I deemed it was noon I stopped. It was hard to tell but my stomach told me that I was hungry and Dream Strider's head drooped. When I spied the stream which obviously led to the larger river I stopped. While my horse drank I ate some of the cheese and the ham I had brought. I washed it down with the rough wine from my skin and then drank some water. There was little grass for Dream Strider and I gave him some grain. I used my helmet for a bowl.

We rode on and the forest seemed never ending. Ulf Big Nose had taught me to move silently and I had perfected the technique with Dream Strider. My horse picked his way along the path. He avoided any broken branches or twigs and did not step on stones which might clatter. Thus it was that I heard the shouts and cries from ahead. I stopped Dream Strider to listen and took out my bow. I strung it and took out an arrow. I let my horse move a little closer to the noise using my knees to guide him. I caught a flash of colour and metal ahead and heard more raised voices. I slipped from his back and tied his reins to the branch of a tree. I headed to my left.

I saw that there were some merchants and they were being robbed. There were four bodies lying on the ground and five bandits held swords to the throats of the four merchants who cowered on their knees. I knew there must be more bandits and I thought to leave the merchants to their fate. Then I realised that this was work of the Weird Sisters. I was being tested. I donned my helmet. I might need it. I readied an arrow and, as one of the bandits raised his sword to decapitate a merchant I let fly. Even while the arrow was speeding towards its target I was heading left. The arrow plunged into the bandit's back and he pitched forward. Two more bandits raised their heads. They had been behind the merchants' horses. They were looking to my right and I sent another arrow at the one bandit who was looking at me. My arrow smacked into his face before he could cry out.

I spun around and flattened myself behind a tree and prepared another arrow. I held a second in my teeth. I heard the last five bandits shouting to each other and seeking me. I turned around the other side of the tree and loosed an arrow at a bandit who was less than thirty paces from me. Even as he fell with an arrow sticking through his body I had loosed my second at another bandit fifty paces from me. It was hurriedly released and it just spun him around as it hit his shoulder. Now that they had seen me

57

the three ran at me. I had slain or wounded the two closest and I aimed carefully at the nearest bandit who raced towards me with an axe ready to slay me. My arrow hit him in the chest but he kept coming. I knocked another arrow and hit him when he was just twenty paces from me. The other two had grown wise and they had split up and gone to ground.

I saw that the merchants had taken advantage of my attack to free themselves. They were hurrying south towards Andecavis. I ran back to Dream Strider. I was closer to him than the last two bandits were to me. I slipped my bow over my back as I flung myself in the saddle. I drew my sword and turned. They would not be expecting a horseman and they would not expect me to have stiraps. I rode towards the bandit to my right. He had an axe and I saw him hold it behind him ready to hack into Dream Strider. The path between the trees was narrow and what I planned was risky. When I was four paces from him I jerked my reins to the left and leaned out. The axe scored a line along my right leg but my sword found his neck. The edge the smith had put on was a good one. The sword was torn from my hand.

I looked to the other bandit and saw that he and the wounded one were heading back into the forest. They had had enough. I passed the scene of the ambush. It looked to me like the merchants had had three guards. The bandits had killed them but lost one of their own. I was tempted to stop and pick up a sword, I knew I would need one, but the wound to my leg was more pressing. I soon caught up with the merchants. I saw that it was one merchant and three servants. They turned at my approach and then the merchant smiled, "Thank you for your timely intervention. I am indebted to you. My name is Phillip of Chinon."

"Thank you."

One of the servants said, "Master, he is wounded."

The merchant looked anxiously down the trail. I said, "There are two left and one is wounded. They have fled."

"Then see to him." He smiled up at me, "Those were fine hits with the bow." He then noticed my empty scabbard. "Where is your sword?"

"I lost it when I slew the last bandit."

He undid the baldric from his waist and handed the weapon to me. Take this as recompense and if you escort us to Andecavis then I will reward you with a purse of gold."

"And then I will be indebted to you."

The servant had put a crude bandage around my leg. "That will do until we reach a physician."

As we walked south the merchant explained that he had taken the path because it was reported that Vikings had attacked Andecavis. My ears pricked up at that. I feigned ignorance of the town. "Then why go through the forest?"

"The last time they came here they had more than one ship and they attacked those using the river road. The Count now has a night watch and it was they who spotted the ship. Had they not then heaven knows the outcome. The Count will have to increase his vigilance. I have lost three soldiers to bandits. Perhaps they were part of the same band?"

"Perhaps."

The servant who had tended me said wryly, "But you will not need to pay the dead men, master and you can ask the Count for an escort home."

That seemed to please the merchant. "You are right Abelard. There is always a silver lining behind every cloud and they did not damage our goods."

We chatted amiably for the last three miles. The forest ended and we found ourselves on a cobbled road. Ahead of me I saw the walls of the mighty city. To the right I saw the monastery we had burned the last time we had been here. There was a framework up. They were rebuilding it. There was a heavy presence of mailed men at the gate. Fortunately Phillip of Chinon was recognised. He must have been a man of some importance.

"Good day Master. I see not your usual guards. Who is this vagabond with you?"

"He is no vagabond. If it was not for him then we would lie dead in the forest. He came along and slew ten of them!"

I looked at Abelard who shrugged. We both knew he exaggerated. I daresay the merchant hoped to make capital out of this.

"The Count must do something about the bandits. It is not safe to travel and what with the Vikings too; it is too much"

The sergeant of the guard said, "Do not worry about the Vikings. We captured their ship and most of the men were executed. We have eight slaves left and when they become unfit to work then they will be executed." He pointed to the monastery. "We have them rebuilding that which they destroyed the last time they were here. It seemed right that they repair what they damaged. They have paid the price."

The merchant seemed a little mollified, "Perhaps. Come we have been delayed enough."

We entered the gate and I saw now the plan of the Norns. I would not have been admitted alone. Nor would I have known where the crew were. I could now plan to rescue them. I just hoped that Gunnstein was with them. As we descended to the river the merchant stopped. "Well Bertrand of Bruges, here is the physician." He handed me the small bag of gold. "If you are ever in Chinon then feel free to call and see me. I can always use someone as handy with weapons as you."

He then turned and left me. Abelard said, "Do not think unkindly of him. It is just his way. We thank you too. We know that without your intervention then we would be dead."

And then they were gone. I dismounted and felt the pain course through my body as I stepped to the ground. I knocked on the door and a servant looked at me somewhat disdainfully. "Yes?"

"I need the doctor."

He was about to slam the door in my face when I reached through and grabbed him. "I have money!"

"Master! I am being attacked!" He began screaming and shouting as though I was trying to give him the blood eagle!

"What the...?" A small, neatly dressed man with a totally bald head appeared.

"I am sorry sir but Phillip of Chinon brought me here. I was wounded in the forest rescuing him. I have money..."

The doctor smiled, "Out of the way Richard! You are a spineless excuse for a man! Come in...?"

"Bertrand of Bruges."

"There, do you see? He is not a Viking! You see them everywhere! Now go and bring his horse to the yard. Come sir. I know Phillip of Chinon. He is a good man. You have done this town a great service if you have saved him."

The doctor was a cheerful little man and he prattled on as he first washed and then sewed my leg. When he had finished he nodded. "Unlike Richard you have courage. You did not flinch once. That will be two silver pieces." I looked at him in surprise. It should have been much more. He shrugged, "You are a brave man and you do not have much. I will make it up the next time I have to lance one of Phillip of Chinon's boils!"

I handed over the money. "Thank you sir. I appreciate it."

"What brings you to Andecavis?"

"I am looking for work."

Shaking his head he said, "I fear that the Count is only employing those from within the city. He fears strangers. The Vikings..."

"I was told."

"I know not why they worry. The first raid, some years ago now, that was dangerous. There were many of these barbarians but this last one was almost harmless. They were seen as they rowed up the river and the Count had men waiting for them. They fought bravely enough but they had no chance. As a soldier you may be interested in seeing them. Their heads adorn the western gate as a warning to others."

"Perhaps but I need a bed and a stable for the night."

He led me to the door and pointed down the street. There was a sign with a bunch of rotting grapes hanging from it. "They have rooms and a stable. *'The Grapes'.* Tell Geoffrey that Doctor Manet sent you. He will not rob you." He turned and shouted, "Richard! The horse. Fetch it around!"

He was right. The mention of the doctor's name made the scowl become a smile. I found they had a room for me. The stable boy seemed happy to look after Dream Strider. The other animals in the stables were asses and donkeys.

Chapter 4

When I had washed and cleaned myself up I arranged my few belongings neatly for I knew not how quickly I might have to leave. I decided to walk around the streets. I needed a plan. I knew where the survivors of the crew were working but I did not think for one moment that they would allow them to sleep there. I went first to the river. I had taken off my mail shirt and my helmet. The new Frankish sword I had was the only sign that I was a warrior. My poor clothes did not afford me a second glance. I avoided looking into the faces of any I met. I wished to be invisible. I stooped slightly as I walked and I trudged rather than strode. I would not be remembered. Ulf Big Nose had taught me well.

I heard the hacking and chopping by the river. I headed there. When I saw *'Sea Serpent'* I became angry. They were tearing her apart. The fine prow was already being chopped into firewood. A drekar has a spirit. It should die in battle. If it is too old to be sailed then it is used as either a home or as a grave for a great warrior. It is not chopped for kindling. The spirits would not be happy. My hand went to my horse amulet hidden beneath my kyrtle. I had to go to the western gate. I had been told that was where the heads of the crew where. I needed to know who lived. I was not the only one interested in the macabre decoration. There were twenty heads adorning the gate. I dared not go out of the gates to see their faces for that would be seen as suspicious. I recognised Sven Dragon Arm's head. He had had bright red hair in three pigtails. As I looked down I recognised one or two others including the shaved head of Oleg the helmsman. But it was the one over the centre of the gate itself which made my heart sink. It was Gunnstein. His hair was as yellow as corn and he did not wear it tied but flowing over his neck. It did not shine and the bottom was covered in blood but I knew him. The Jarl's brother was dead. I turned and made my way back to the inn.

I was in no mood to eat but I knew I had to. I needed to find out where the captives were being held. To do that I needed to talk with the landlord and the other residents of the inn in which I stayed. I forced a smile as I ordered food and wine. My heart was not in it. As the plate of chicken stew and rough red wine was placed before me I said, "This looks good! I have a fine appetite for I saw the heads of the Vikings over the gate. That is the right end for such barbarians."

The landlord nodded and wiped his hands on his already greasy apron, "You are right Master Bertrand and if you are here at the end of the month you will see another eight heads; fresh ones! They are working on the monastery to pay for their sins. They will be executed when they cannot work."

I laughed. They would not know it was a false and hollow laugh. "Perhaps I will go and see where they are held. I have never seen a live Viking!"

"I am afraid that the only place you will see them is at the monastery where they are working. At night they are thrown into the Count's dungeon. They are fed the swill we normally give to pigs. Even that is too good for them."

I could not do as I had hoped and rescue them here in the town. It would have to be at the monastery. After I had eaten I went to the river and stared at the skeleton of the drekar. It took time but by watching the water and letting my mind empty, thoughts and ideas crept in like a fox into a coop filled with hens. Suddenly I saw the answer and I returned to my lodgings. I would need to spend the next day formulating my plans and making sure I could do it and the next day put it into action. It would mean a fast departure else I would miss *'Raven's Wing'* but it would be worth it if I could save those eight men.

I said to the landlord, as I ate the bread and cheese they had provided for their guests, "I will stay one more night. I will see if I can gain employment."

He pointed downstream. "I would try Nantes. The Count of Vannes is threatening that city again. They need fine swords and the men to wield them."

"Thank you."

I first went down the river and I sought what I needed on the stalls at the market. The plan was coming together, albeit slowly. Then I left by the north gate. The sergeant at arms recognised me, "Have you sold your horse?"

"No, I am just going to look at the Vikings. I have never seen one close up before. The landlord at the grapes said that they have tattoos and they file their teeth."

The sergeant nodded, "It is true and I have also heard that they drink the blood of babies and virgins."

I feigned fear, "Really?"

"Do not fear, Robert is the Captain of the Guard and he has them tethered, They will not be able to harm you. Besides they get weaker each day." He laughed, "The lime they crush to make the mortar is killing them!"

I left them and made my way up the track which wound around the hillside to the site where they were rebuilding the burned abbey. The problem would come if one of the *'Serpents'* crew recognised me.

As I approached I saw that there were six guards including the captain. Four of them had crossbows. I had heard of them but never seen them. What I did know was that they were accurate and anyone could use them but they were very slow to reload. An archer could release five arrows in the time it took to send one bolt on its way. The captain of the guard was armed with a fine looking sword and the sixth had a whip. His sword and shield lay by the logs the guards used to sit on. There were other slaves apart from the '**Serpents**' but the ones doing the backbreaking work, mixing the concrete under the supervision of an overseer, were my countrymen. I had brought a jug of wine with me from '*The Grapes*'. I shouted as I approached, "Captain Robert I am Bertrand of Bruges and I would like to see what these frightening barbarians look like. Do you mind if I approach?" He looked at me suspiciously. I held the jug before me, "I have brought wine to refresh us."

His face broke into a smile, "In that case come ahead. They are not dangerous. Raymond here has whipped all the spirit from them." He took the jug from me and picked up two beakers. He had huge hands. He poured some in the two and offered me one. He walked towards the men mixing the concrete.

Erik Long hair recognised me and his eyes flashed. I gave a shake of my head and said, "Pathetic really! And to think I was afraid of them!"

He nodded and went back to his work. "That one is lame. I have a bet with Raymond that he will be the first to die. They do not look so fierce now do they?"

"No. I would have thought that hauling the timbers and the stones would be harder work than mixing the concrete."

He shook his head. "The lime will kill them. They might last a month hauling timbers but it is ten days when working with lime. That is why they are fed so little. We give them just enough to keep them alive."

I nodded and finished my wine. "It will be a fine church when it is finished."

"It was a fine church before the barbarians destroyed it." He wiped his mouth with the back of his hand. "This is good wine.

If you want to see the heads of the others they are on the western gate. They are well worth the visit."

I handed him my beaker. "Thank you! I will. I shall go now." I pointed down the path to the river. "Is that the fastest way down?"

"It is. I apologise for the smell of these barbarians but they will not harm you!"

I laughed, "Now that I have seen them close up I know not what the fuss is all about. They look like ordinary men and nothing to fear!"

He nodded, "Do not be fooled. With a sword in their hand they can be dangerous."

I waved goodbye and headed past them. Raymond was at one end and his whip flicked out to slash across Erik Long Hair's back. He cried out and I forced a laugh. As I threw my head forward I hissed, in Norse. "Be ready tomorrow. This time!"

Olaf the Bear gave the slightest of nods. I now had a plan. I just needed to make some purchases. I took the opportunity of going through the western gate. My eye was drawn to the grotesque skulls. The birds had already pecked out Gunnstein's eyes but I recognised him. It confirmed that he was dead.

The sergeant at arms said, "Where have you come from?"

"I was talking to Captain Robert. He said I would enjoy the sight of these barbarians. He was right."

The guard nodded and waved me through. The first place I went to was the river. I needed a boat. It had to be large enough for the eight men who were left from Gunnstein's crew. Most were too small. I found three that looked to be the right size. I saw their owners. The three of them were sharing a jug of wine by the river. Fishermen went out early.

"Gentlemen, are any of your boats for sale? I was a warrior but there appears to be little opportunity here. I though, perhaps I would fish."

They laughed. "It takes more than a boat and good intentions."

"I have skill. I was brought up by the water."

One of them said, "My brother and I are happy enough with our boats but Theobald here is getting a little fed up with the work."

The man they pointed to was the oldest of the three and the least well dressed. "Would you consider it?"

"Perhaps, if the price is right."

"And which is your boat?" He pointed to the most dilapidated of the three. The other two laughed. I nodded, "I can see she floats but does she sail?"

"Good enough for me."

"And that is why you are willing to sell for she needs work and you wish to buy wine and not fish."

One of the others laughed and said, "He is here but a short time, Theobald, and already he knows you."

Theobald waved an irritated hand at them, "Twenty silver pieces and she is yours."

I laughed and stood, "Thank you gentleman but I think I will go back to soldiery and find another town."

Theobald stood and put his hand on my chest, "Stay. What would you say is a fair price?"

"I will give you two silver pieces and tomorrow I will try her out. If she does not sink then I will give you another ten. What say you?"

"And if you do not like her what of the two silver pennies?"

"You may keep them."

He held his hand out. "Then we can do business."

I shook his hand and handed him the two silver pennies. I kept hold of his hand. "First we sail the fishing boat down to the wall by the gate. I want to make sure she floats."

I saw him torn. He wanted to spend the coins but he also needed to make the sale. "Very well."

We clambered aboard. As my feet splashed in the water in the bottom I gave him a sharp look. He shook his head, "That is rain, sir, just rain."

"Is there a sail?"

"Aye, sir." He hoisted the sail. It had a couple of holes in it but it began to fill with the breeze. I cast off and we moved with the current. The steering board appeared to work.

"You can lower the sail." I took an oar and sculled us close to the stone quay which was very close to the town wall. There was a metal ring and I said, "We will tie up there."

"And walk back?"

"I wish to familiarize myself with the boat. You have your coins and I will return the boat tomorrow with the other ten if it sails."

He nodded and climbed out to tie up the boat. After he had gone I made sure that there were no holes in the hull. It looked just to be old and leaky. I would need to buy a rope which was twenty paces long. I headed back into the town. There were merchants at their stalls. Some were packing up but one had the rope I needed. I slung it over my shoulder. I saw that he had a pair of leather saddlebags and I haggled and as he was ready to go home I bought it at a bargain price. I found another stall where I bought a short sword and a seax. They were cheap because they were not well made. They would have to do. I hoped to get some of the guard's weapons the next day but I needed to have some extra ones with

69

me. Finally I bought a small axe. It was the kind the Franks liked to throw. That done the only thing I had to do was to buy some bread and some cheese. I told my landlord I would be leaving the next day, early, and I paid him. I think I had been a better customer than most of the ones he had and he was genuinely disappointed to be losing me. What he would do when he found out that he had been harbouring a Viking I did not know.

Before I retired I went to the stables. All depended upon Dream Strider. He appeared to be in good condition. The stable boy looked up as I went in. "He is a fine horse master. I groomed him."

"I can see. His mane shines. Here." I gave him four copper pennies and his eyes lit up.

"Thank you master. Will you be staying here longer?" I saw the anticipation of more coins fill his eyes with expectation.

"No. I shall leave tomorrow for Swabia. I hear there is a war there which needs warriors."

I went directly to my bed for I would be up early. We were close enough to the north gate for me to hear the watch as they did their rounds. I woke an hour before dawn. I slipped out of the house and went to the stables. The stable boy was asleep and I did not wake him. I had packed the saddlebags with the seax and axe. The sword I hung, along with my bow, from the saddle. I took the rope and food and returned to the streets which were just coming alive as the poorer people prepared to work. I spied the two fishermen. They and their crews were already preparing to set sail.

"Where is your crew?"

"I want to sail it first before I commit."

"We were teasing yesterday you know. Theobald is a fair man. His boat is sound but, like him, she is old."

"Then he will get his payment and we shall all be happy."

"Good."

I wandered down to the boat and tied the new rope to the bow. I put the food in the bottom and covered it with my cloak. I let the rope out to its full extent and then tied the end to the mooring ring. The current took it down so that it protruded beyond the wall. It was as close as I could get it to somewhere beyond the wall. That done I returned to my lodgings as dawn broke. I had my last meal there and then I went to saddle Dream Strider. I strung my bow and slung it over my shoulder. I put the short sword in my belt but I left the helmet and shield hanging from the saddle. By the time I reached the north gate it had just been opened. I did not recognise the sergeant at arms who was on duty but one of the sentries remembered me.

"Are you leaving us?"

"I shall head for Swabia. There is little work here or, at least, little work which pays well enough." I turned east and headed along the river road. As soon as I was out of sight of the towers I turned north and headed into the forest. I gradually worked my way back to the road I had first used to enter the city. I crossed over and sought the vantage point above the monastery. I had spied it when drinking with Captain Robert. I counted on the fact that they would do the same things the same way each day. Garrison soldiers are creatures of habit. When I reached the place I had identified I dismounted and led Dream Strider. I stopped just ten paces from the edge of the trees. Below me, forty paces away I saw the slaves and captives as they were led, hobbled at the ankles by the guards. I donned my helmet. Soon I would be going to war.

I saw them have their hobbles removed as the four crossbowmen sat on their log. Raymond seemed to do all the work. I wondered if he was paid more. I took out four arrows and jammed them in the ground and then with a fifth arrow ready I waited. I wanted the Captain and Raymond close together. They were the leaders. It took some time for them to oblige but after Raymond had applied the lash a few times the two of them closed with each other. I loosed one arrow and even while it was in the air a second. As they fell the four men with crossbows turned. At

71

the same time Erik Long Hair and the others grabbed the weapons from the two dead men.

The crossbowmen were on the horns of a dilemma. One turned to shout and sealed his own fate. My arrow struck him at a range of thirty paces. Only the goose feathers could be seen as it tore into him. Then the other three seemed to realise they had a weapon and they sought this archer. I loosed my next arrow as the three bolts hit the tree behind which I sheltered. That was my signal. It would take time to reload. Erik led the others to charge the three men with crossbows as I mounted Dream Strider and charged the crossbowmen. They were so busy with me that they failed to notice the eight vengeful Vikings running towards them. They butchered them. The overseer turned to shout. I sent an arrow towards him. It struck him in his arm and then the other slaves fell upon him.

"Grab the weapons and follow me down to the river!" I opened the saddlebag and gave the axe and seax to Erik. The sword I gave to Olaf. Then I headed down the path. At the bottom I slowed up. The sentries on the western gate were too far away from the construction site to have heard anything and I rode casually. The problem would come when they saw the eight men with me. I turned to them. We could not be seen from the gatehouse. As they halted, chests heaving with the exertion, I said "There is a boat tied just beyond the wall. One of you must swim to it and cut the rope. Sail down the river. The Jarl will be at the wooded island close to Nantes in two or three day's time."

"And what of you?"

"I will slow down the pursuit and lead them through the forests. I will catch up with you at the island."

They nodded, Erik Long Hair said, "We are in your debt."

"Wait until we are back in Raven Bay before you say that. The Weird Sisters are listening. Now walk until the alarm is given. I will put the horse between you and the gate." I held the bow and an arrow in my right hand as we walked out of the forest and across the road. I could see, thirty paces away the prow of the boat. Olaf the Bear nodded. He had seen it. There were four sentries lounging in the gateway. They had swords and shields. I stopped as though I had a problem with my reins. Then a sentry in the tower shouted.

As I lifted my bow I shouted, "Run!" I calmly sent one arrow at the leader of the sentries. He wore mail but I was so close that it hit him in the middle. My second arrow missed for the three dived for cover. I heard a splash and knew that Olaf the Bear had gone for the boat. Then there was a cry as Sigtrygg Red Hair was hit by a crossbow. I sent an arrow towards the second crossbowman who took evasive action and ducked beneath the battlements. I could hear the noise of the alarm being sounded. Ironically they closed the gate which helped us. They thought they were being attacked. The danger to us lay in the men on the gate tower and my bow had made them keep their heads down. It was a situation which would not last.

I heard Erik shout, "Ride Hrolf! We have the boat!"

I needed no urging and I kicked Dream Strider hard as a flurry of crossbow bolts splashed around the stern of the fishing boat. They were raising the sail even as they were moving west. I knew that they would send horsemen after me. The boat might be safe for they could not reach them once they reached the wider Liger but I was not. I would ride for as long as I could before I took to the woods. The road ran parallel to the river for a mile or so and I kept up with the rapidly moving boat. I felt guilty about robbing old Theobald but the clan came first. When the boat struck the Liger it began to move quickly and our courses diverged. I waved farewell and then kicked hard. Leaning forward I said, "Now we just worry about each other my friend. What a tale you will have to tell when you are back in my stables."

I knew my horse and what he was capable of. He liked a steady pace and I gave him that. When the road allowed I turned and looked behind for pursuit. I had seen the stables. They were close to the north gate. They would either have to ride up to the half built monastery or negotiate the streets. Either way I would have a lead. The question was when would they reach me? As I rode I slung my bow. I needed both hands to control Dream Strider. If I saw anyone coming the other way I would need to jerk his head around quickly. I used the remaining milestones to estimate my progress. I knew there was a town coming up in a few miles but I was loath to leave the road. As I began to turn a bend I saw a flash of colour ahead and I pulled Dream Strider to the north. There was no path but I plunged into the forest. I now had to use the skills, taught to me by Ulf Big Nose to outwit the Franks of Andecavis.

Chapter 5

Instead of riding parallel to the road I rode north and west to go deeper into the forest. I was looking for one of the many small streams which flowed into the Liger. The forest was silent and I walked Dream Strider to allow him to pick his way through the trees. I saw a lighter patch which indicated a clearing or water and turned his head. We found the stream and I head up it. Although it took me deeper into the forest I would be leaving no trail. I counted Dream Strider's steps and when I reached ten hundreds I let him clamber out of the water. I had given my name suggesting I came from the land of Bruges and Flanders. I wanted them to be confused. I allowed him to drink while I listened. There was nothing. I heard no sound of pursuit. I turned due west and rode in a line which would mirror the river. Ulf had told me that when you were being pursued often it was in your interests to let them get ahead of you. That was what I had done. I had no doubt that they might send men into the trees to seek me out but it was a large place and they would have little chance of finding me now that I had covered my trail. They were more likely to race ahead and set up ambushes along the road. If Ulf Big Nose had taught me well I would avoid them.

I walked Dream Strider until darkness began to fall. Night came much earlier in this tree filled world. I stopped by another of the streams which cut my path. The one I chose was in a larger clearing than I had seen before. I took off Dream Strider's saddle and used my helmet to pour water on him and clean the sweat which had accumulated. It would make him more comfortable and he was the only way I would escape this forest. I would not risk a fire and, as he drank, I prepared my bed. I cut some of the pine branches to lay on the ground. I put Dream Strider's blanket upon them and laid out my food. I filled my helmet with grain and allowed my horse to eat. There was little grass but he would graze while I ate. I tied a halter to his neck and to the branch of a tree and then I devoured the bread and cheese I had bought in Andecavis. I was ravenous. I washed it down with the last of the wine and then filled the wineskin with water from the stream.

With my weapons at my side I lay down in the inky black forest to sleep. I had done all that I could for Gunnstein's crew. They could all sail and, with luck, they would be lying up on one of the many islands along the Liger. When you sailed the Liger you saw them every few hundred paces. They were uninhabited for there were no bridges. If they landed then they would be safe. I had seen no boats which could have followed them and they would not be keen to be recaptured. They would hide. I had to put them from my mind and concentrate on evading the hunters who would be waiting for me. I had done what I had promised the Jarl.

I woke in darkness but something had disturbed me. I looked up and saw that Dream Strider had licked me and was now nodding his head above mine. My horse had sensed something. I quickly saddled him and as I gathered my weapons I listened. In the distance, to the east I could hear movement in the forest. It did not sound natural. However I did not hear dogs. I slipped on to Dream Strider's back and headed down the stream. After a count of a hundred I turned west. The stream's flow gave me the rough direction of the Liger. The slightly sloping land told me that the Liger was to my left. I glanced over my shoulder and saw that the sky was becoming lighter. Dawn was not too far away. Its first rays brought me bad news. The forest was ending. The tree began to thin. Through gaps ahead I saw terraces of vines and open fields. I had seen this part as I had travelled east. I knew exactly where I was. I was less than thirty miles from Nantes but there was little cover for me from now on. If men were waiting ahead then I would have nowhere to hide.

As I headed down through the trees I saw that they were thinner and more open here. There were terraces of grapes above the road. I could be spotted. Riding east I had been able to ride openly now I would have to fight. I rode Dream Strider with my knees as I strung my bow. I had but ten arrows left. After that I would be reliant upon my sword. The men who would be hunting me were experts at fighting from the back of a horse. I was not; not yet anyway.

I smelled smoke. There was a house nearby. I slowed. The edge of the trees was just thirty paces from me and I could see the river. It looked to be half a mile or so away from me. The land hid the road. They had terraced the fields to give maximum sun to the precious grapes. I dismounted and took off my helmet. The grapevines would not hide me but if I rode then I would be clearly seen. I dismounted and led Dream Strider through the fruit laden vines. I took a bunch as I passed. They would be sour but my store of food was lessening. I kept my head down. If anyone was watching they might just see a horse wandering through the trees; it would be interesting but not a cause for concern. I wanted no shouts until I was close to the river. I had a plan.

Each step down the terraces afforded me a better view of the road ahead. I could not make much out but the occasional glint of sunlight on metal told me that there were warriors waiting ahead. I had expected that but it still had an effect on me. The chances of my escape had now diminished. The noises I had heard in the forest were the Count's men driving me west into their trap. The route I took was my only possibility of escape and that was a slim one.

I spied the farm house to my left. I was hidden from it by Dream Strider's mane. I was now within sight of the road. I saw no one upon it. I listened. I could hear no one. I walked to the edge of the field. There was no fence. They needed none but there was a drainage ditch ahead. I put on my helmet and slipped on to Dream Strider's back. I lay along his neck to keep a lower profile and then I kicked him in the flanks. He easily jumped the ditch but his hooves clattered on the road. It was like the sounding of an alarm bell. As I headed towards the river which lay ahead beyond some bushes and willows I heard a shout from my right. Hidden there had been sentries. There were four of them and they had horses. I unslung my bow and, pulling an arrow loosed it at the four surprised sentries. They had no mail and were so close that even loosed from the back of a horse my arrow hit one in the chest. A hurriedly released second hit one in the thigh while a fourth struck a third man in the shoulder. I slung my bow from my saddle horn and raced at the fourth man. I drew my sword as I did so. The horses, frightened by my charge bolted, and the last warrior stood almost frozen to the spot. He belatedly tried to draw his sword. I leaned forward and hacked at his right arm. My new blade bit through to the bone and he screamed in pain.

I whirled Dream Strider around and headed back for the river. The four sentries could do nothing to stop my escape but their cries and the bolting horses would alert the larger number of men I had seen further down the road. I had no intention of pushing my luck any further. I would not be risking the road. As I reached the river I kicked Dream Strider and he jumped into the fast flowing river. It was wide and I could see no islands. I had done this before and I lay along Dream Strider's back and tried to steer him to the south bank. I kept hold of my precious bow. I was not safe yet and the Saami weapon might save my life yet. The flow inevitably took us diagonally. I kept kicking. It was little enough but it helped Dream Strider's powerful legs. The water stopped me hearing anything and I did not want to turn around. I focussed on the opposite bank. It seemed to take an age to reach it. When we were across Dream Strider struggled to clamber up the slippery bank but eventually his hooves found purchase. I kept hold of the reins and the bow and rolled on to the bank. Dream

Strider managed to clamber out. He shook himself. He had tired himself out in the swim.

I allowed him to catch his breath as I turned and looked at the opposite shore. There were ten horsemen there and they were pointing at me. I could not risk riding Dream Strider yet. The swim had taken much out of him. His eyes were wide and frightened. I took my bow and restrung it with my spare bow string. I had seven arrows left. I took out three and watched. I could see a debate on the opposite bank. They had seen a Viking cross the river. The Franks of Andecavis were renowned horsemen and were discussing if they could do it. Of course if they had never done so then it might be a daunting prospect. The fact that I had not moved spurred them on. Four of them headed into the water. I stood and watched. One tried to stay on his horse's back. As its head was pulled downstream the horseman lost his seat and fell into the water. The horse turned around and went back to the shore while I saw the man's hand flailing for a while in the river before it disappeared. He had never tried this before.

My bow was accurate up to a couple of hundred paces but I had too few arrows to waste. When they were a hundred paces from me I aimed at the leading rider. He was lying flat along his horse's back. My arrow score a line along the horse's neck and then smacked into his shoulder. I took my second arrow and aimed at the next man. He had seen his companion's fate. He put his head and body below the water. I sent my arrow into his horse's neck. The dying horse with the man clutching to the saddle were swept downstream. The last man had little choice. He could either risk my arrow or the river. Knowing I had only one enemy left in the river I waited. I kept my arrow aimed at him. He had little choice over where he landed. His horse determined that decision. I saw resignation on his face as he came closer to me. His horse managed to struggle up the bank and then stood, shaking close by Dream Strider. I gestured with my bow for the warrior to climb on to the bank.

"Drop your weapons!"

He was young; he was about the same age as me. He shouted at me, "They will catch you Viking! They know of you! The Count has put up a reward of ten gold pieces for your head!"

I nodded, "Then drop your weapons or I shall kill you where you stand."

He looked surprised, "You will let me live?" I did not answer but he eventually dropped his weapons.

"Now take off your boots and your breeks." He looked surprised but complied. I still had the bow pointing at him. "Now walk east and you shall live." I saw that he was undecided. "You saw what I did to your companions at a range of a hundred paces. Do you think I would miss this close to you? Walk!"

He turned around and began to walk east. The river bent around in a loop and when he was two hundred paces from me and about to disappear I picked up his weapons and put them on Dream Strider. I slung my bow on his saddle and then went to the young man's horse. I spoke quietly to it as I took its reins. "I will not harm you." I slipped onto his back and, taking Dream Strider's reins rode west. I knew that there were no bridges crossing the river. The men of Andecavis could however, cross at the many islands. They made fording slightly easier than where I had attempted it. As I headed west I saw them copying me. The would follow down the river and look for an island. I kicked hard and my new mount responded. I would tire this one out before remounting Dream Strider. Those pursuing me outnumbered me; there were six of them but their horses would be more tired than Dream Strider. In a long race I might win. I still had five arrows left. They would be wary of my bow.

There were no towns or villages on this side of the river but there were farms. However the sight of an armed warrior galloping along the greenway was enough to send them scurrying back into their homes as I passed. I knew that they would sound the alarm but I had seen few villages on the south bank. By the time help came I would be gone... or dead. I saw that I was keeping pace with the horsemen on the north bank. They had been joined by three more. The fact that they were keeping pace told me the effect the ride would be having on their horses. They were tiring for I was now going at a fast pace. They still had to cross the river. As we approached the first of the many islands I saw half of them plunge into the water to cross to the island. I took the opportunity to change horses and I tied the new horse's reins to the back of Dream Strider's saddle. The island hid them from view but also hid me from them. The river was just forty paces wide.

I waited, with an arrow aimed at the island. As the first warrior appeared I sent an arrow which hit him in the chest and threw him from the saddle. I had a second arrow ready as the next warrior appeared. He tried to hide behind his horse's head. At fifty paces I had a big target and my second arrow hit him in the thigh. I did not see the other three and I kicked Dream Strider on. I would put as much space between us as I could. I knew that they would struggle to rise from the water. They would also be cautious because of my arrows. They did not know how perilously short of them I was. They would ride together and hope to catch me unawares.

The greenway was firm underfoot and we made good time. When I spied the island where I had left the drekar my spirits soared and then plummeted as I realised that the drekar's mast could not be seen. I deluded myself into believing that they had stepped the mast. As I neared the western end of the island I saw that just the fishing boat was there. The drekar had not arrived. Perhaps they had struck trouble.

I dismounted and allowed a thirsty Dream Strider to drink from the river. I tied my captive horse's reins around the saddle and then broke a spiky branch from a riverside bush. "I am sorry for this." I lifted the saddle and placed the spiky thorns beneath. As I dropped the saddle I slapped his rump and he took off as though stung. The thorns dug into his flesh and he galloped down the greenway. I took Dream Strider's reins and slapped his rump. He jumped into the river, almost pulling the reins from my hand. I held on and kept pulling on the right rein to keep him heading for the island which was just twenty paces from me. Undisturbed by man it was covered in thick luxuriant foliage, Dream Strider scrambled up and I followed. We quickly vanished into the undergrowth. Leaving my horse I ran to the southern end of the island and in one slash of my sword severed the rope tethering the fishing boat. It began to drift with the current and headed downstream.

"What are you doing?" Olaf the Bear suddenly appeared from a bush in which he had been watching.

I pushed Olaf to the ground under a bush as the three horsemen's horses approached. They saw the boat speeding down the river and one shouted, "There he is! After him!"

I waited until they had disappeared around the bend in the river before I stood and allowed Olaf to stand. "That was our way off this island! The Jarl has not come! We are trapped."

I led him back to my horse. "Where are the others?"

"In the middle. They are hiding."

"Lead me to them. Are they all safe?"

"Sigtrygg Red Hair weakens."

"Did you take the bolt from him?"

He shook his head. "We had not the skill."

I had forgotten that this crew was young. "That is why he weakens." I followed him and discovered their improvised camp. They were lying in a clearing in the middle of the island. They rose when I entered. Olaf the Bear pointed accusingly at me, "He let the boat go!"

I shook my head, "If you wished to use it again you should have hidden it. I saw it. There are men searching for you. They would have found it." I went to Sigtrygg. He was sleeping but he was hot. The wound in his shoulder was red, inflamed and angry. "This needs cleansing. Find me maggots."

A bolt is not barbed like an arrow. A barbed arrow tears flesh when you pull it out. Often the only way to remove it is to break the flights and push it through. A bolt could be pulled clear. I got a good grip on it and jerked it out. His body arced and he opened his eyes in shock. Pus and blood poured out. The flesh was beginning to blacken and it did not smell good. If I did not act quickly then he could die. If it had been in his arm or his leg I would have amputated. I did not have that luxury.

Erik Long Hair said, "Are you not going to stem the flow of blood?"

"It needs cleansing. The blood will take some of the bad from the wound. If I could then I would have burned it but we cannot afford a fire. Men still seek us. Here take my helmet and fetch me water to wash it."

Sigtrygg said weakly, "If I am to die give me a sword, Hrolf."

"You are not going to die! At least not yet. If I think you will die then I will give you your sword. Close your eyes and rest."

Erik returned with the water and I poured it over the wound. The blood flowed clear. I lifted his body and saw that the bolt had not gone all the way through. That was good. There was some moss on a rock and I took it and packed it into the wound. I had seen Aiden, Dragonheart's galdramenn do this. It slowed down the bleeding and it seemed to have something in it which helped to heal wounds.

Olaf The Bear returned with a handful of squirming maggots. "There was a dead bird yonder."

"Good. I need a cloth to bind this." Lifting the moss I packed the maggots underneath. Erik handed me a piece of cloth. It was none too clean but the moss would help. I tied it around the wound.

83

I saw that all of them were looking at me. They were expecting me to perform another miracle and conjure the drekar.

"Why were there no guards watching? I could have been a Frank, slipped ashore and you would all be captured."

Erik Long Hair said, defensively, "We watched the boat."

I shook my head, "There are men searching for us on both sides of the river. Einar and Karl one watch the south bank and one the north."

Olaf The Bear said, belligerently, "Who are you to order us?"

Erik smacked him on the side of the head, "He is the warrior who risked his life to save ours and is the only one who seems to know what to do." He turned to the other two, "Go, we will relieve you before too long."

I stood and went to Dream Strider's saddlebags. There were two loaves left. They were a little stale. They were a couple of days old but these men needed food. A lack of food made it hard to think and I needed these to be able to think and do as I ordered when the time came. I broke one into four and handed a piece to each of the two sentries.

"Thank you Hrolf." Karl looked at Olaf. "Forgive Olaf, his brother was one of those executed. What of the others?"

"Others?"

"The ones who brought word that we were captured."

"No one came. This was Jarl Gunnar Thorfinnson's decision and the clan of the Raven Wing agreed to the rescue."

The two of them went to their sentry post. Olaf The Bear said, "So when you came you did not know where we were?"

"No. I spent two days travelling up the river in the hope of finding you but when I found the body of Sven Dragon Arm I feared the worst."

"Then I am sorry for my words. I thought we had been abandoned by Jarl Gunnar Thorfinnson."

"Then you do not know him. He was angry with his young brother but he would not leave him to die. He will be saddened by his death."

"Why is the Jarl not here yet?"

"I know not. He will come but we must be ready to fight. Do you all have a weapon?" They each held up one. Finni's was a dagger. I gave him the sword I had taken from the Frank I had captured. "Here." He balanced it in his hand. A Viking is always happier when he has a sword in his hand. "Now they will find us. Let us not be in any doubt about that. When they find the empty boat and the horse I freed they will know that we are between the hunters and Andecavis. They will search every piece of cover. This was the last place they saw me and where they spied the boat. We have to be ready to fight them until *'Raven's Wing'* comes sailing up the river."

Thrand the Bold said, "They will not take me prisoner again. If I have to fight them with tooth and claw I will do so. Had you not come for us...."

"Then the lime you used would have killed you."

They stared at me, "Truly?"

"Aye, Erik Long Hair. The guards were laying bets as to who would die first. Because you had a bad leg the Captain of the Guard put money on you."

"I wish they were here to kill again!"

"We are Vikings. We can expect no other death than a cruel one. They are terrified of us. I spoke with them. They accuse of everything from eating babies to drinking the blood of babies. It is what happens to people who are terrified. They exaggerate the fear."

85

Night fell and I sent Thrand and Finni to relieve the others. I heard horses moving up the river banks and saw the flicker of fire as they used torches to hunt us. Sigtrygg began to moan in his sleep at one point. I lay with my hands over his mouth to dampen the sounds. The noises vanished up river. They had missed the island in the dark but dawn would rectify that error.

Dawn brought us no relief. We had eaten the last of the food. We had river water but Sigtrygg needed a healer. I was also worried about Erik Long Hair's leg. That too looked to be inflamed. It was Dream Strider who warned us of danger. He did not whinny but he stamped his foot. I knew my horse well enough to react quickly. I crept to the north bank. Einar had fallen asleep. I shook him awake and pointed to the shore. There were ten or twelve men on horses and they were pointing at the island. More riders were coming from the east. There were also men with crossbows and spears. They had found us.

"Keep watch."

I hurried back to the camp and grabbed my bow. "Leave Sigtrygg here, put a dagger in his hand. His wound may not kill him but the Franks will. Bring your weapons. One of you bring the shield from my horse. The Franks are come."

They nodded and followed me back. I had precious few arrows left. I would have to use the last ones judiciously. When I reached Einar I saw that the horsemen were preparing to enter the water. There were four crossbows waiting for us to raise our heads. The river was wider on this side; eighty paces and it was deep in the middle. I knew that from when I had left the drekar all those days ago. There was plenty of water beneath the drekar's keel. I sheltered behind a willow. I could see the river through the curtain of leaves and thin branches. If I did not move then I would be hard to see. They would have to swim. I saw that they had two men who might be leaders. One had a plume in his helmet. His oval shield had a design upon it. It was red diamonds on a white background. The same design was on another warrior but he did not have the plume.

I waited until the noble with the plume was fifty paces from shore and I sent an arrow through a gap in the leaves and into his face. He rolled off his horse which continued to swim. Four bolts thudded into the tree. They were wasted missiles. It would take them time to reload. I took my second arrow and aimed at the man who urged them forward. As he raised his right arm my arrow hit him in the side and he clutched at the wound. With only two arrows left I chose the two closest targets. They would be the bravest. I hit one in the shoulder and the second in the thigh. My bow was useless now. I slung it over my shoulder and drew my sword. I turned to the others, "Stay hidden. When the horses try to land the crossbows will be unsighted. Charge the horsemen when they try to struggle ashore. Listen for my order to fall back."

They nodded. The looks on their faces told me that they would not run. As I had found, landing on the island was not easy. The water was as deep as a man's leg close to the island. The riders had to try to keep control of their horse as they did so. Two of them had managed to clamber up when I rushed forward between them. Their hands were on their reins. I used my new sword with two hands and I hacked at the leg of the horseman to my right. I cut through to the saddle and into the leather of his girth. His horse reared and pulled them both back into the water. The horseman to my left tried to draw his sword. I brought my own diagonally in a long sweep. I hacked into his arm, sliced along his leg and then cut his horse. It reared. I saw that another eight warriors were half way across the river. The crossbows would have a clear target.

"Fall back! Now."

Karl had the shield and he backed off last. Two bolts smacked into the shield and one penetrated it. Karl grinned, "I shall have to be Karl the Lucky now!"

I hoped that he would live long enough to be given the new nickname. "Move closer to the camp and take cover. Stay hidden until we can spring an ambush." I contemplated mounting Dream Strider but that would be cruel for my new comrades might think I was abandoning them. We would fight and, if necessary, die together.

I heard the Franks calling to each other. "Spread out in a circle! We know there are just eight of them." I did not translate for it would sap whatever courage they had left. The horses made a great deal of noise as they moved through the undergrowth seeking us. We had no mail to speak of and they were well armed, well fed and mounted. The odds were in their favour. Thrand broke first. He raced out to attack a horseman who was just four paces from him. Although his sword hacked into the leg of the Frank another appeared behind him and thrust his spear into him. Thrand roared and, even though mortally wounded, turned and drove his sword into the side of his killer.

That seemed to be the signal for the rest to become berserkers. They charged from hiding and I was forced to follow. I heard a Frankish horn. It seemed to be in the river. I knew that meant reinforcements. We would have a glorious death. Olaf the Bear used his axe well and smashed it into the skull of a horse. As the horse was falling Olaf leapt on its corpse and began to hack at the rider. I swung my sword sideways into the leg of a horseman. It seemed the most effective blow for they wore no mail on them. As he tumbled from his horse I saw a warrior raise his spear to strike into the back of Erik Long Hair. I smacked the rump of the horse before me with my blade and it leapt between the spear and Erik. I ran after. I jumped in the air and brought my sword down to cut through to the backbone of the spearman. The horn sounded again and the Franks who remained turned to flee. We had blood in our heads and vengeance in our hearts. The wounded Franks were butchered. I looked around and saw that Karl lay unconscious and Knut nursed a badly bleeding arm.

"Ready! They will rally and come again. Put the wounded with Sigtrygg."

Finni asked, "Can we hold them again?"

Olaf snorted, "Why would you surrender?"

The two wounded were pulled to safety and then the five of us who remained stood in a tight circle. I heard noises as men came through the bushes. They were not using horses this time. They were on foot. I braced myself for the strike of a bolt.

"Ready! Let us sell our lives dearly!"

A face appeared through the bushes and I prepared to bring down my sword. Siggi White Hair laughed, "Not yet, Hrolf the Horseman, not yet. We are late but we are come!"

Chapter 6

The wounded were taken on board first. There were questions to be answered from all sides but the priority was to escape the horsemen. The crossbows had been driven off by our archers but as the horsemen had ridden in the direction of Nantes I knew that there would be trouble ahead. Thrand's comrades carried his body on board. He would be buried on Raven Wing Island. My priority was loading Dream Strider. He could not leap aboard as he had disembarked. Ulf and Siggi White Hair helped me to fell six trees and, after stripping away the branches and tying them together, we made a gangplank for him. He boarded as calmly as you like and I led him to the prow.

"Cast off!" The level of the river was lower this time and Sven was unable to sail around the island. Instead he had to turn the drekar around in the river. It was not as hard to do thanks to the excellent crew who worked together. Once we faced downstream Sven shouted, "In oars! Unfurl the sail!"

The Jarl shouted, "Arm yourselves!" The river would take us to the sea without the need for oars but we would need to protect ourselves from the bolts.

I found my shield and I grabbed a handful of arrows. Ulf picked up his bow and joined me. "You did well my young friend. I thought I had seen the last of you when you left the drekar."

"You did not have confidence in me?"

"You are a fine scout but even I thought it was too difficult a task. No, that is wrong, I thought it an impossible task. Your skill with words must have helped you."

I pointed upwards, "I think the Norns did more."

Just then we were interrupted. Nantes was a mile away from us. I saw four ships leave the shore. They were all smaller and slower than we were but just as small dogs can pull down a cow so they would do the same. The Jarl shouted, "All those without a bow, back to the oars. We will try to break through this wall of ships."

He did not need to give those of us with bows instructions. We would all aim at those steering the ships. Ulf nodded to my bow, "I shall have to get one of those. I have seen you use it before."

"It cost me hard earned gold but this raid showed its worth. Had I had another bow then I would be dead and the seven men I rescued would still be prisoners."

"Use your arrows well. You can use your weapon long before we do."

As I was at the prow I was the closest to the enemy. I could send an arrow over three hundred paces but that would not guarantee I hit the target. Sometimes, however, you could do as much damage by not hitting the target. Ulf nodded, "The nearest ship. See what you can do."

I pulled back and aimed just aft of the mast. The sail was furled and they were just using oar power. I released. I knew I would hit the ship, it just depended where. I watched it rise high and then arc. It was helped by the wind. It plunged down and must have hit someone for the ship turned slightly as though they feared more arrows cascading down. I quickly sent another arrow in their direction. This time my aim must have been guided by the gods for it struck someone close to the steering board. The ship made a deliberate move away from us.

"Well done, Hrolf!"

The oars were already run out and I felt the power as the wind, the current and Viking backs added to our speed. The other ships were now within range of our archers and emboldened by my success they sent flight after flight until their arms ached. It was not the fact that they hit men; our arrows only struck a few but it was the random nature of them which caused the problems. Those rowing had no protection and shafts struck indiscriminately. The rowers spent too much time looking up and not enough propelling the drekar.

One captain was bolder or perhaps luckier than the others for he managed to close with us. He made straight for our bow. Siggi White Hair began to sing at a faster beat.

> *A song of death to all its foes*
>
> *The power of the raven grows and grows.*
>
> *The power of the raven grows and grows.*
>
> *The power of the raven grows and grows.*
>
> *A song of death to all its foes*
>
> *The power of the raven grows and grows.*
>
> *The power of the raven grows and grows.*
>
> *The power of the raven grows and grows.*
>
> *A song of death to all its foes*
>
> *The power of the raven grows and grows.*
>
> *The power of the raven grows and grows.*
>
> *The power of the raven grows and grows.*

We seemed to surge through the water and I realised that the Frankish captain had misjudged his attack. I aimed at the helmsman on the steering board. If I hit him in the wrong place then the Frank would cross our bows and both ships would be sunk. He began to adjust the steering board when they were eighty paces from us. I loosed and hit him. I held my breath and only released it as he fell to his right and the bow of the ship turned away from us. When Ulf hit the captain then the heart went from them. They waved their fists at us as we headed towards the wider mouth of the estuary. Siggi White Hair and his chant had saved the day!

"In oars! Well done!" I could hear the pride in Sven's voice.

By the time the oars were stored we were in the choppy waters of the sea with the wind with us. We would not need to row again and the wind would take us to Raven Bay. We gathered around the mast as the Jarl questioned the survivors of his brother's drekar. I knew some of their story but that had been told from the Frankish viewpoint. It was Erik Long Hair who spoke. Perhaps he felt guilty as it had been his fight with Eystein One Eye which had helped to create the rift between brothers.

"We sailed at night and lay up during the day. It was just as we had done when we had sailed with you, Jarl. It meant we arrived at Andecavis in the middle of the night when they should have all been asleep. We headed for the gate but suddenly the gates opened and we were surrounded by armed men. They used crossbows from the walls and they surrounded us. We had no time to form a shield wall. When the Jarl was killed Sven Dragon Arm ordered us back to the drekar but it was too late. More men had come from the hill above the town while others came in boats from across the river. We fought hard and we slew many. Our swords broke and bent. We eight," he suddenly saw Thrand's body, "we seven and Thrand the Bold were overpowered. They wanted prisoners or so it seemed. I think some of our men got away. I did not see Sven Dragon Arm die but Hrolf here said that he saw his body."

I nodded, "I found it some way downstream. I thought he had been decapitated like the others but perhaps he died fighting. I would like to think so."

"Then we were stripped, bound and whipped. They made us mix concrete for their church and the lime burned our hands. We could not understand what they said to us. And then Hrolf came."

Everyone looked at me expectantly. "I was lucky." I saw Siggi White Hair and Arne Four Toes exchange a grin. "I happened upon Sven's body. I knew what that meant and I headed through the deep forests. I was able to travel unseen through them for few men used the trails that were there. I came upon bandits attacking some merchants. I was going to leave them and then I thought that this might have been put in my way by the Norns and I went to their aid."

Ulf asked, "How many bandits?"

"Seven, eight, nine? I cannot remember. I slew all but two; one was wounded and then they fled. In gratitude the merchant gave me a sword and a purse of coins. Most importantly he gave me the chance to enter the town without suspicion. I spied Erik and the others and I let them know I would help them to escape. I got a boat, rope, food and weapons. Then I used my bow to slay the Captain and two of the guards. Erik and the others killed the rest. We went to the boat and they sailed downstream."

The Jarl asked, "How did you get the boat, weapons and food? Did you steal them?"

"No, Jarl, I used the purse the merchant had given me. That is why the Weird Sisters sent the merchant my way. I did not have to steal them. I paid for them."

The Jarl shook his head as though he could not believe my words.

"And your escape?" Ulf Big Nose had a professional interest in this.

"I hid in the woods until they found me and then I swam the Liger. When they tried to cross I slew all but one and I took his horse. I fled down river and then I found the island."

The Jarl strode up to me and held me in his arms, "Once again we are in your debt; the crews of two drekar. You make me feel shame that I did not take my drekar to rescue them myself."

"It would have been a waste of men, Jarl. This was a task for one or two. I would not advise raiding the Liger again. I think it is cursed."

"You would not advise a vengeance raid?"

"They did what they did because we burned their abbey. Besides it is far upstream and I fear they will improve their defences even more."

"Perhaps you are right. Our raid yielded far more."

We were closing in with our home and men began to gather their belongings. I said to Siggi, "Why were you late?"

"The winds and there were ships watching in the estuary. We tried."

"I was not accusing you, Siggi White Hair. I was curious."

He shook his head, "If I had the words then I would make this into a saga. It is an act worthy of Freyj or Thor. I cannot believe that you are the same stripling who came to us all those years ago. I thought you were like a piece of straw and would break but you are not. You are like steel. Thank you for you have given the clan much honour with this act."

To thank me for my efforts Sven and his ship's boys sailed me around to my bay so that I could land Dream Strider easily. I had few treasures to bring back but many memories. As I led my horse up the path to my home I knew that I had learned much. Ulf's lessons had been learned. I now knew how to change my appearance so that I could be invisible. That was magic.

Erik One Hand was at my home. He smiled when he saw me. "My wife baked some bread today using yeast from the beer. When she saw the drekar's sails she told me to fetch you a loaf. It is good bread."

95

"Thank you Erik." I opened my gate and let Dream Strider in the pen to see his mares. It was touching the way that they put their heads together. They were almost like a human family.

"We brought another barrel of ale the other day. It is a good brew."

"Thank you. How much do I owe you?"

He laughed, "Nothing. My wife has a soft spot for you Hrolf. She swears you are no Viking for you have manners, kindness and good looks! I think she is saying you are the opposite to me."

I disliked praise and I changed the topic, "How are the new slaves? Has there been any more trouble?"

"No but Seara says that Mary cries at night. None of the other slaves will talk to her and Seara is so deaf that she cannot keep up a conversation."

"Perhaps we should have left her. We rarely have an unhappy female slave."

"Aye well two pretty ones, Hildegard and Emma both have men taking an interest in them: Knut One Eye and Beorn Fast Feet. They seem happy enough." Not all of the crew had sailed. The drekar had not been expected to have to fight.

I could see now why this daughter of a noble was so unhappy. She had been the one who had everything and now she had nothing. Those who had nothing before now had happiness. Perhaps this was her God punishing her for pride. Aiden, back in Cyninges-tūn, had told me of the way the God of the White Christ punished men because of their nature. It did not seem fair to me. After Erik One Hand left me I went to the sea leading my three horses where I stripped off and swam. The three horses galloped in the shallows. Dream Strider rolled in the surf and Nipper raced around barking. It was the bark of joy and not warning. My family were content; I was home.

The next day I saddled my two mares and rode each around the island. It was important that they continued to be used to the saddle. Dream Strider, I allowed to rest. He rolled on the turf and chased Nipper. I know it was selfish but I did not want to go to the village. I wanted to be alone. That was one of the problems of what I had done. You began to prefer your own company. I knew I was luckier than most for I lacked for nothing. I stayed away for two days until Siggi White Hair and Arne Four Toes sought me out. It was getting towards noon and I had done all the jobs around my home that I needed and was preparing to go for another ride.

"Have we offended you, Hrolf the Horseman?"

"What do you mean, Siggi White Hair? No one has offended me."

"Then why do you stay alone? The Jarl wishes to honour you as do the men you rescued. Hiding away here is not the answer."

"Arne I was not hiding away. I ..."

"Then what were you doing?"

"I had my horses to see to and my home..."

"You are making excuses. We are taking you, by force if we need to, to the village. Two of the clan are to take women to their hearths and the Jarl is throwing a feast. It was supposed to be in your honour but if you are too good to join us then at least wish your shipmates good fortune."

"I am not too good!" I shook my head. I was getting nowhere. "I will feed my animals and then I will come."

The two of them helped me to fill the water trough and pen the chickens and the horses. With Nipper on duty they would be safe from vermin. With no foxes on the island rats were the only danger. I combed my hair and donned a clean kyrtle.

As we walked I asked, "Who is to take women?"

97

"Knut and Beorn. They have paid the Jarl their worth. There are just their homes to be built. Your hands will make the work go much faster."

When we reached the village I saw that the work on the two huts was half finished. The wooden posts were in and the dry stone walls laid. The men were putting the beams for the roofs while the women were cutting and laying the sods which would help hold up the walls. Arne waved a hand, "See we have left the easy task of clambering on the roof to lay the turf for you, Horseman!"

As we were seen a cheer went up. The men shouted good natured insults to me. That was to be expected and actually made me feel more comfortable. Knut One Eye walked over to me and clasped my arm, "I am happy you have come. You will bring us good luck and besides I have you to thank for my wife! Emma told me that you rejected her advances! A one eyed man cannot be as choosy. Your loss is my gain."

I saw that Emma was unabashed by the revelation. "I am happy for you, Knut, and now that the Eriksson brothers are husbands we will soon have more young warriors who do not know the word, caution!"

The warriors all laughed. The two brothers were renowned for their recklessness. It had cost Knut an eye.

Siggi White Hair shouted, "Come, we have the guest of honour now. The sooner we finish the sooner we feast! And I am too old to wait too long for food!"

When the clan worked together it was a thing to behold. All took part. There were no bystanders. Seara and the other older women fetched ale for those working. The other women and their children cut and brought turf to lay against the walls. Those men without skill carried the timbers for the roof while those like Ulf Big Nose and Rurik One Ear straddled the roof and hammered the long nails made by Bagsecg into the timbers. I was one who could both balance and hammer and I was soon into the rhythm of Rolf Arneson who helped me. The only one who was not working was Sigtrygg Red Hair who had been laid besides the fire. Even the Jarl and his hearth-weru worked.

I had to smile as I worked. If they had really needed me they would have fetched me earlier. We were finishing off the houses. It did not take long to finish the framework and then hazel was laid on the beams and the two of us laid the turf on the roof as the sods were passed to us. I clambered down the ladder and as Rolf joined me there was a collective cheer. The houses were finished.

The ceremony was a simple one. First a fire was laid in the middle of each hut and then Knut and Beorn took in a brand from the village fire. This burned all year round and was a symbol of life as well as a symbol of the clan.. They started their fires and stepped out. At first the fire would smoke but soon bright flames would appear. In that time the two men each went to the Jarl and handed over the price agreed. Then they went to their brides, picked them up and took them inside their huts. That was it. The ritual was a clan one. Until I had joined the clan I had never seen it done that way but I had been brought up in a Frankish village where the White Christ ruled. In Cyninges-tūn they had a similar ceremony but there was no price to be paid.

The departure of the two couples to their new homes was the signal for the feast to begin. Horns of ale were fetched and the women brought out wooden platters laden with food. If the weather had been foul we would have eaten in the Jarl's hall but the sun shone and the ground was dry. Our tables and chairs were crude things. There were roughly hewn logs nailed together and placed on stumps. The chairs were small versions. The children, and there were now an increasing number squatted on the ground. They did not mind the discomfort besides they were rarely still for long.

Usually men sat where they chose but this day I was guided by Siggi White Hair and Ulf to the Jarl's right hand. His hearthweru were sent to the ends of the table. I had the place of honour. As we waited for the two couples to return Siggi rubbed his hands. "I am looking forward to this feast. It seems a long time since we celebrated the feast of Eostre."

Ulf used his horn to point to Siggi White Hair, "I fear the fare will not be as good as it might. There is precious little left to hunt on this island. The seas are filled but we have taken both the trees and the animals."

His words made me think and then to look around. He was right. When we had first come the island had been largely covered with trees. Our buildings and the repairs to our drekar had taken many of the larger trees. There were saplings but if we took those for firewood or building then we would have nothing. They would need to be husbanded.

Siggi White Hair nodded, "You are right. Pig is good meat but it cannot compare to wild boar and a fine young doe is food the gods would relish. It is one of the things I miss about the Land of the Wolf."

The Jarl laughed, "You are getting soft, Siggi White Hair. When we lived on Ljoðhús it was seal or fish we ate!"

"You are right Jarl but we chose this place to live and it is a good one. Ulf is right. We need to do something about it."

"What do you suggest?"

His horn refilled and his platter filled Siggi said, "I will eat first and then think."

He set about his food like a wolf after a lean winter. He did not eat, he devoured. Ulf smiled. He and I ate slowly. "Tell me Hrolf how was the food in Andecavis?"

"It was different. They like their ducks and their beans. They use the spices from the east more. I liked it for it was different." I patted my stomach. "However it took some getting used to!"They all laughed. "I also found it hard to get used to drinking the wine. They water it but it goes to your head if you are not careful. Four or five horns leave a man unable to mount a horse. Beer and ale are safer."

Siggi White Hair had finished one platter and he wiped his greasy hands on his breeks. "The food has fed my mind. We should hunt on the mainland and use the trees there as we first did when we were repairing *'Raven's Wing'*." He waved his horn to the north. "There are places on the coast where we can land and harvest the trees and the animals. We know of many places where there are no people."

I could see that the Jarl was dubious although the recent loss of his brother must have been on his mind too.

Sven the Helmsman had been listening. "I think that is a good idea, Jarl. Our drekar is not getting any younger. Had we hit those Frankish ships on the Liger then we would have had to repair the drekar. Where can we get the right wood if not on the mainland? We should have a store for it must be seasoned."

Ulf nodded, "We could look upon it as a raid. Instead of gold and slaves we seek meat and wood. Hrolf and I could scout out a place and then we could spend a day hunting and hewing. If we make a raft from the logs then we can tow them back to the island."

I could see that he was coming around to the idea. "Aye and it would give the new men, Gunnstein's crew, the time to heal. We need to raid again soon so that they can exorcise their demons."

The seven of them were not sat at the table but around Sigtrygg who was still unable to walk unaided. They seemed to cling together as though separation might be their end. Captivity was a hard thing for a Viking to endure. All of them felt guilty about not dying, as their comrades had done with a sword in their hands. Unless they were to waste away we had to raid so that they could have success again and regain their confidence. At least the maggots had eaten the badness in his wound. When we had taken away the moss they were all dead and there was no smell.

The two new couples emerged almost simultaneously from the huts. They looked almost embarrassed. Brigid and the other women ran to them, made an arch, and began to shower them with wild flowers they had picked. They also began to ululate. The men took out their daggers and banged the hilts on the table. We started to sing our song.

Through the waves the oathsworn come

Riding through white tipped foam

Feared by all raven's wing

Like a lark it does sing

A song of death to all its foes

The power of the raven grows and grows.

Through the waves the oathsworn come

Riding through white tipped foam

Feared by all raven's wing

Like a lark it does sing

A song of death to all its foes

The power of the raven grows and grows.

The power of the raven grows and grow

Knut and Beorn swelled with pride as the war chant began. As they took their place opposite the Jarl everyone gave a mighty cheer.

The Jarl rose and spread his arms. The noise died down apart from three of the children, all toddlers, who continued to cheer and bang sticks against a hollow log. Their mothers silenced them with a blow and the Jarl spoke. "Today we celebrate and we mourn." He turned to raise his horn to Erik Long Hair and his companions. "We mourn the loss of a fine drekar and her crew. I mourn a headstrong brother. Gunnstein I wish you were here now and that we had not parted with words we cannot take back. I will see you in Valhalla! Sea Serpent!"

Everyone stood and shouted, "Sea Serpent!"

The Jarl allowed the silence to wrap its arms around us as we remembered the dead. The Jarl was now the last of his family. His father and brothers were all dead. He was looking at his own mortality. I saw Erik Long Hair and the survivors close their eyes and clutch their amulets. They were saying their own goodbyes.

The Jarl forced a smile as he said, "And now we have mourned we can celebrate living. There is no better celebration than warriors making more warriors." Knut and Beorn beamed at the words. "Raven Wing Clan!"

Raven Wing Clan!"

"And lastly we have a brave warrior to thank. Hrolf the Horseman risked his life to go deep into the land of the Franks and somehow rescue those who survived the ill fated attack. He has helped to mend the bonds that were broken. Now the men of the Sea Serpent clan can join Raven Wing. We will be stronger and better because of this. Hrolf the Horseman!"

"Hrolf the Horseman!" This time the cheers were even louder and when the Jarl sat down it was the signal for the feast to really begin.

He turned to me. "I meant what I said, Hrolf. Had you not journeyed to the land of the Franks we would never have known the fate of my brother and his crew. We would have had haunted nights as their spirits came to haunt us."

"I am just repaying the kindness I have been shown."

103

Siggi White Hair leaned over, "But we are all worried that you spend too much time alone."

"I am not alone! I am with my horses and animals. Each day I learn something more."

Sven the Helmsmen shook his head, "We are sailors not horsemen!"

"There you are a wrong Sven for I would be both. When I am mounted on a horse I feel the same power as you do when you sail the drekar. The difference is you have to stop when you reach the land. You are subject to the winds and the tides. I ride where I like; even in the sea and the rivers. That is true power." I saw them take all of this in. "One day we shall live on the mainland. This is not Norway where a man has to scrape the soil from the stones just to survive. Here we can make enough so that we can trade. One day I will live on the land. I will still sail and raid but I will also ride and raid. I saw nothing to fear in the Franks that I met. They use not the bow and even half starved and beaten men can beat them. Erik Long Hair and his men showed that."

Ketil Eriksson shook his head, "You think too much Hrolf. I have food, ale, a good sword and a woman. I have enough gold to buy more warrior rings. What else do I need? When the Jarl thinks it is right then we will raid again. I will hew more heads and I will be rich again. What more is there?"

That appeared to be the way that most of the young warriors were. I suspected that I was different because of my upbringing amongst hoses and the time I spent with the Dragonheart. I knew that a man could change his destiny. The Weird Sisters might shape the events in his life and put obstacles in the way but a true warrior could adapt and change. It was what had kept me alive in Frankia.

Soon the feast degenerated into arm wrestling and drinking contests. That was not what I enjoyed and I thought about heading home. I spied, seated outside her hut alone, Mary. She was in

Seara's doorway. Something made me go to her. She appeared like an injured animal and I would never leave such an animal to suffer. "Why do you not join them? It is a celebration."

"I have nothing to celebrate. I am far from home and I have to work long hours."

I laughed, "And are you working now?" She shook her head, "Then celebrate that fact. The horn is not half empty, Mary, it is half full." She looked up at me with curiosity written all over her face. "When I was a slave I was beaten every day. Sometimes I might have deserved it but most times I had not. The days I was not beaten were the happiest days I spent as a slave and enjoyed each one which brought neither blow nor lash. Are you beaten?"

"No."

"Do you have food, shelter?"

"Of course."

"There is no of course about it. When I rescued Erik Long Hair and the others they were fed the scraps the pigs would not eat. They were whipped and they were slowly being poisoned but they never gave up hope."

"What hope have I?"

Your people might rescue you."

I could see that thought had not occurred to her. She brightened and then her face clouded. It was as though the sun had gone in. "They would have come before now. Besides with my father dead my brother will be the lord and he did not like me."

"Good."

"Good?"

"Aye for you now know that your old life is gone and you should make the best of your new life." I pointed to Brigid, she was laughing with her husband and Emma. "Brigid came as a slave. She makes ale. She has her own business and she and her husband make coin. There is only old Seara who can sew well. That is why she is no longer a slave. The Jarl knows she will sew better if she is free. Become the new Seara or be like Brigid; find a warrior and bear children."

"I hate this island! It is so small!"

"It is bigger than you think. When we were attacked some years ago Rurik and I led our enemies all over this island. When they thought they had us we sheltered in a cave which the gods directed us to. We were safe. This island offers most of what we need. It gives us security."

"There is but one God!"

I nodded, "That is your belief. We are born to believe that the land, the forests, the seas and the animals all have a god who care for them. The Allfather, Odin, watches over all. Perhaps your one god may be Odin. I do not know. You do not believe strongly enough to know of the others. Had they not shown us the cave in the north of the island then we would have perished."

I could see my words had had an effect. "I do not like Vikings. They are both hairy and smelly."

I laughed, "And in that I cannot disagree. Then become a seamstress and rule your own future."

She nodded and, reaching up, kissed the back of my hand, "Brigid is right. You are kind and I am sorry that I appear so ungrateful."

"You need not apologise. I know exactly what you feel for I felt it too. Be strong and if your god helps then believe in him too."

Chapter 7

When Sigtrygg Red Hair and the others were well enough the Jarl decided to sail to the land of the Bretons and hunt. We left in the middle of the night so that Ulf and I could scout while our drekar sailed back to our island. We would not fall into the same trap as Gunnstein. We would find somewhere without walls or people. We did not want a war with our nearest neighbours. Some day we might but, at the moment, they protected us from the Franks and allowed us to raid.

Sven knew of two narrow channels which would allow us to get inland. They were ten miles from any settlement and the land around was covered in trees. They had not been cleared for farming. There would be animals to hunt, trees to fell and, hopefully, no people. We guessed that it might be the best place to land. Ulf and I would travel inland to see if there were any settlements there. With no horses to land and no shields to carry we slipped ashore and had disappeared before the drekar had time to turn around. We had landed at the eastern channel. Ulf led us up the river bank. We had discussed this and if there was to be a settlement then it would likely be along the river. We ran, in the short time before dawn. It was neither a road nor a greenway. It was an animal path. As the sun came up and we saw no houses before us Ulf took the first path we saw.

We were silent as we moved swiftly under the canopy of green. Suddenly Ulf stopped and held up his hand. I had my bow ready in an instant. I had neither heard nor smelled anything but I trusted Ulf. Then I caught the musky smell of deer and I heard the soft sound of animals grazing. Ulf grinned and waved me on. This was a good sign. As we moved upwind of the deer they caught our scent and we heard them as they raced off into the undergrowth.

We stopped again a short while later. Ulf sniffed and pointed north. I sniffed too and smelled wood smoke and a faint smell of horse. We left the path and headed north. The moss on the trees guided us. We had travelled about a thousand paces when I saw the forest thinning and fields showing where they had cleared the trees for farming. There was an animal fence and a half stone building. Smoke came out from the roof. Ulf gestured for me to stay where I was and keep watch. I had an arrow ready just in case. He disappeared. I saw a servant or slave come from the house and pour something from a pail. I knew what it was when I heard the snuffling of pigs. There was an animal pen. As short while later Ulf returned and led me back to the path. We kept going until the land descended to another river. We knew of this one. It was a few miles from the large settlement they called An Oriant. It had a wall made of stone and a tower. We would not attack this stronghold. It would take half a dozen drekar to capture such a prize. Ulf nodded. We went to the river, cautiously. We could see no one and so we drank. It tasted slightly salty and I knew we must be near to the sea. There was neither path nor road. Ulf said, "The farm we passed is not a danger. There is a family with four slaves there. I am surprised you did not smell the horse."

"I thought I had but I saw no sign."

"They have it in a pen like you. " He pointed west. "We will head back directly and go west. I am confident now that we will not see any more people. If there were any we would have smelled smoke when we sailed north."

"The trees look good and straight."

"Aye they do. I think this plan might work. Come we have a long way to travel back." He led us towards a hunter's trail through the forest back to the place where the drekar would be.

By the time we reached the two channels it was getting on to dusk. We had seen tracks and spoor of wild boar and more deer but not the animals. We would do that when we returned.

The drekar slipped up the channel when the last light had gone from the west. Sven must have sailed during daylight and stayed well out to sea. Ulf gave a whistle and we waded out to the drekar. We spoke when the oars began to pull us home. Ulf was the leader and he told the Jarl all.

He pointed astern to the river we had just left. "We can land at this channel or the one further east by An Oriant. Both are secluded. We saw deer and signs of wild boar. The trees are perfect for us and they are close to the river. We found one farm and that is some miles to the north. The only danger that we could see was the path which cut through the forest. It may be used by their hunters. We saw no recent sign of them but they must use the path."

"You have done well. We will take a chance. If we stumble upon any other hunters then it is *wyrd*. We can only plan so far but at least we will not be going in blind." He left it unsaid but we knew he was thinking of his brother.

We set sail days later. We had more axes than swords and more bows than spears. We had plenty of rope and a full crew. We were confident. There were four groups of us. Two would cut down the trees and they would stay close to the river. They had the axes and the ropes. Two groups, made up of archers and men with boar spears, would travel into the forest to seek our prey. We needed as many animals as we could get. Their skins and bones would be as useful as their flesh. Some would be smoked and some salted to be preserved until hard times during winter while others would be eaten fresh. A third of the deer meat would be dried for that would be useful when we sailed. I was with Ulf's group of hunters. The Jarl led the other with his hearth-weru.

Having done the voyage twice, Sven was confident about timing our arrival correctly. We left not long before dawn and sailed in the darkness to arrive from the west. It was still dark when we landed. As Ulf and I had been there before we took the northern route to hunt. It was the one which would take hunters further from the drekar. We were barely four hundred paces in the forest when we heard the axes as our men began to cut down the trees. We had brought boys from the village to chop off the smaller branches and they would not go to waste. They would be taken back as firewood. If we were lucky enough to find any yew or ash, however unlikely, then they would be taken back too. They made the best bows and spears. As the noise receded in the distance we looked for signs.

Siggi White Hair, Arne Four Toes and Rurik One Ear were amongst the men Ulf led. Ulf, Arne and I had the bows while Rurik and Siggi White Hair would take on any boar we might find. There were another two archers and two more men with spears but we five were acknowledged as the most skilful of hunters and we led the way. In many ways I hoped we would not find boars. They were the most dangerous of prey and could eviscerate a man with one swipe of their vicious tusks. But I agreed with Siggi White Hair; the meat was the best there was.

Ulf halted and sniffed. He knelt down and when he rose he pointed to the trail. I could discern the marks of cloven hooves but it was the droppings which drew our attention. It was early morning and there was still heat in them. The animals were close and they were upwind of us. Ulf pointed to the other two archers to flank the three of us. Siggi White Hair organised the men with spears behind us. It was almost as though we were going to war. We defended each other; that was what brothers did. We could have moved faster but that might have risked making a noise and scaring the herd. It was obviously a herd for we saw broken branches and the slightly damp ground retained their prints. The herd was heading for a clearing where they could graze. I knew from the previous visit that there were many small streams feeding the two small rivers. The herd was heading for one. I had no doubt that they would stop close to one to feed.

I saw Ulf's famous big nose sniff the air and then I caught the smell of deer ahead. Instinctively I pulled the arrow back a little further. In these situations you often had to release quickly or lose the kill. We were moving so slowly now that time seemed to stand still. I caught a sight of reddish brown with white spots. It was a doe's hindquarters. I did not release. I was not alone. We were a band of hunters and we wanted as many animals as we could get. I moved further to my right behind a hazel tree. I saw the antlers of a stag. We would not take the stag. He was the future of the herd and we respected him. A Jarl or a chief might hunt for the honour and the trophy but we sought food. Then the herd all moved and we saw them. A large stag led a herd of six females and four young. When Ulf pulled back on his bow then we all did.

I aimed at a slightly older doe. She suddenly twitched and, as Ulf's arrow was released so was mine. My doe had moved as I was loosing but the arrow struck her in her chest for she had turned slightly towards me as she began to turn away from the danger. She managed three steps before she fell. The herd fled. When we reached them we saw we had two does and one young deer.

Ulf Big Nose glared at the two who had missed with their arrows. The herd had been close together and they should have hit something. . He pointed at a hazel sapling. "Cut down a branch to carry back the kill."

"But there are three of them!"

"Make three journeys. If you cannot hit eleven targets then you are no hunter. We will go on!"

He was a hard task master and I saw Siggi White Hair give a wry smile. Ulf was, however, correct. Had either of them hit the

111

same targets as the three of us then it would have been understandable. But we knew they had missed. We all used different markings on our arrows. I had one raven feather with two goose. I found it helped me to aim. As the two warriors grumbled and cut down the branch they would use Ulf pointed to the south. "We will keep the wind in our favour and head south. Hopefully we will either find another herd or pick up the same one."

We had seen, on our first visit, the trails of many herds. They all appeared to be small ones. With fewer men now to hunt Siggi White Hair and Rurik joined us with their spears. It had not been ordered but both Siggi White Hair and Rurik had been close enough to throw their spear had the deer run back in our direction.

Ulf stopped when we were another three hundred paces deeper into the forest. When he looked up I saw him frown. He whirled around and pointed to the north east. I had an arrow ready and Siggi White Hair and Rurik spun around with their spears held before them. Audun the Unlucky lived up to his name. He looked at us in amazement when we reacted and it was only when he heard the roar and the sound of the charging boar that he turned. It was too late. Even as he thrust his boar spear forward and caught the animal a glancing blow to his shoulder his guts were being torn out by the vicious tusks.

Even though I knew it was too late for him I loosed an arrow. I did not aim at the boar's head. The skin was thick and the skull was hard to pierce. My arrow hit its shoulder. Arne and Ulf also managed two hits with their arrows but it was Arne and Siggi White Hair, working together who brought us victory. They rammed their spears into the tiny eyes of the boar. They pushed hard and the beast twitched and then expired.

Rolf Ragmunsson had raced to the side of his friend, Audun, but he was already dead. Ulf shook his head. "The hunt is no place for those who know not what they are doing. We will have to return now."

Siggi White Hair said, "Aye, Arne and Rolf, make a bier for Audun. Ulf will lead us back and Hrolf can watch our backs."

It was a sad end to our hunt. The day was half over as we trudged down to the river and the drekar. The Jarl was not back yet but the others had felled many trees and already two rafts were almost ready to be towed. Harold Fast Sailing said, "Two rafts of this size are as much as we can tow. By the time we are ready it will be late afternoon."

Sven and Siggi nodded. In the Jarl's absence they made the decisions. Ulf said, "We will put Audun on the drekar. He was truly unlucky. We will bury him on our island. It is right."

The Jarl had been more fortunate than us. He must have stumbled upon the herd led by the boar we had slain. He had three females and two young pigs. With his two deer and ours it had, Audun's death excepted, been a good hunt. We were sombre as we loaded the dead animals and prepared to row home. Ulf said, "Hrolf take Rurik and go and watch the trail. It would not do to be stumbled upon."

"Aye."

"I will whistle when it is time to leave."

We headed back into the forest. When we were a thousand steps from the river we halted and stood on either side of the path, each of us behind a tree. I glanced down and saw a discarded arrow. It was one of Vermund's. He was hearth-weru. He had stained the feathers on his arrows red. He could afford to do that for he rarely used his bow. I picked it up. I would return it. Neither of us spoke because we did not wish to alert any warriors who were out hunting. We had just heard the whistle and were about to return when I heard the sound of steps racing through the forest. I risked a glance around a tree. There was a slave running towards us. I knew he was a slave for he wore a yoke. He looked to be no more than nine or ten summers old. Two men were hurtling after him. There was no way we could avoid being seen for they were coming straight down the path towards us. I nodded to Rurik. We stepped out after the slave had passed us and sent my red fletched arrow into the chest of the leading warrior. Rurik slew the other. All our plans to avoid detection had failed. *Wyrd.*

The boy had stopped and he stared at us. I smiled, "What is your name?"

The fact that I spoke in his language seemed to put him at his ease; that and the fact that I smiled for he answered, "Guillaume."

"Why were you running?"

"Hrolf!"

"Patience Rurik. Carry one body back to the drekar and I will follow." Rurik picked up the warrior he had slain and his weapons.

"They whipped Theobald."

"Theobald?"

"The horse I tend. I took a hot poker and burned my lord's hand. I was angry that they hurt the old horse. He sent his sons after me."

I made a decision there and then. "Would you come with us and be free?"

He nodded, "Aye, lord!"

"I am no lord. Pick up their weapons and come with me."

I slung the dead man over my shoulder and headed down the path. When I reached the river the Jarl and Siggi were on the bank with Rurik. They did not look pleased. "What happened?"

"The boy was pursued by these two men. If we had not slain them then they would have stumbled upon us. There was no way to avoid it but it was not of Rurik's doing. This was my choice." I pointed to the boy. "This is a slave and he would join us as a free man."

The Jarl nodded, "*Wyrd*. Get on board. We will dispose of the bodies at sea."

I turned to Guillaume, "Climb aboard. I will follow."

The man was literally a dead weight and I was glad to drop him next to the other dead warrior. I had to take my place at the oars for with the logs we were towing the sails needed all the help they could get until we reached the open sea. As we rowed Siggi laughed, "Only you could turn a simple sentry duty into something like this."

"What else could I have done?"

Rurik said, "Hrolf is right. They would have seen us or you. A hundred paces from where we slew them they would have seen the drekar's masts. This was the work of the Norns."

Siggi White Hair nodded, "It was *wyrd*."

The Jarl and his hearth-weru stripped the bodies. Ulf sliced off their heads and threw them and their bodies over the side. The odds that any part of either would return to shore were slim. As we neared our island the wind was strong enough for us to stop rowing for a while. I took the opportunity of going to Guillaume who stood fearfully by the mast. I took out my seax and his eyes widened. I smiled and said, "I am freeing you that is all," as I cut him free from his yoke. His neck was red raw. I pulled his loose shirt from his back and saw the criss cross of healed scars. I did not doubt that I would be in trouble for my actions but I had done a good thing. I would stand by my actions.

The Jarl said ,"What will you do with him?"

"I told him he is free."

Siggi shook his head, "If he lives on our island how is he free Hrolf? Is he free to starve? Who will look after him? He is too young to fend for himself."

I had not thought of that. I had stopped a slave being hurt. That was my sole intention. Ulf Big Nose said, "This was *wyrd*. You are clever Hrolf. The Norns sent this boy into your path not ours. There must be a purpose to it." He suddenly frowned, "Why were they chasing the boy? Had he escaped?"

"They wished to punish him. He had attacked his master."

Jarl Gunnar shook his head, "Then he may not be trustworthy. Perhaps we should just land him on a beach in Frankia."

I shook my head, "No, Jarl. He fled because they hurt the horse he tended. He stood up for the beast."

The three of them all smiled and then Siggi started to laugh, "I have never known such a clever warrior as you, Hrolf the Horseman and yet sometimes you cannot see what is plainly before you."

"I do not understand."

"He cares for horses. He is a Frank. You are the horseman and the one who speaks his language. The Norns could not have been any plainer. They have sent him to you. Prove it to yourself. Ask him if he wishes to care for your three horses."

I beckoned over the boy. He looked apprehensive as he made his way through the Raven Clan warriors. We were a frightening band especially to someone who had never seen one and only heard the stories of what they did. I could see in his eyes that he wondered if his fate was to be the same as those who had chased him. The only words he understood were mine. I smiled, "Guillaume they call me Hrolf the Horseman. I live alone but I have three horses. When you are free would you tend my horses for me? I will pay you."

His eyes lit up and his face broke into a broad grin, "Master I need no payment. I will care for your horses and gladly."

116

Siggi White Hair had not understood one word but he clapped me on the back. "His face tells all. The Weird Sisters use him and they use you. Hrolf the Horseman, you walk a precarious path."

Sven sailed the drekar into our bay. It was dark by the time we lowered the sail but our work was not yet done. Not only did we have the dead animals to be taken ashore we had the monumental task of making sure that the logs were well above the high water line. It would not do to have a sudden storm undo all the work of the axe men and take the wood as a sacrifice to Ran. We were bone weary when the last logs were pulled high up the beach. I would have to bring my horses the next day and we would haul them to the village.

We carried the animals and Audun's body up to the village. Guillaume walked close by me. This was a strange dark place to him. I did not blame him for being fearful. As we neared the village Erik One Hand came to greet us. "Jarl, the slave Mary, she has run away. We cannot find her."

"We are weary and it is dark. She can go nowhere. When we have fetched the logs tomorrow then we shall search for her."

I remembered my conversation with her. She did not know the island and, noble born, she did not have the skills to survive for long on her own. "But Jarl there are dangerous places. She might have fallen to her death on the rocks!"

Siggi White Hair said, "Then if so it is *wyrd*. She may have decided to take her own life. She was not happy."

I shook my head, "She is a follower of the White Christ. She would not do that."

"Hrolf we search not this night. That is my command. We will search tomorrow. She is a slave. Take the boy and get some rest."

Siggi nodded, "The Jarl is right, Hrolf. The boy needs his rest."

117

I was defeated. I nodded and took the boy by the hand. His grip told me of his fear. He needed reassurance. "Where were you taken as a slave?"

"I lived on the Issicauna with my family. My sister, mother and I were taken by the men of the Count of Vannes. I was given to my master. It was he gave me the name Guillaume."

"That is not your name?"

He shook his head, "I know not my real name for I was the youngest and teased. It may have been Gille but I cannot remember it was so long ago but Gille was the name of my father. My mother called me 'sweetheart' and my sisters, 'runt'. They meant it not unkindly."

"Did you know that we are Vikings?"

"I guessed that you were. The others all look fierce and frightening."

"They are not. They are men like any others but they fight hard. We give each other names. The one with the white hair, the older man is called Siggi White Hair. Erik is One Arm. You will have a new name. For now it will be Gille. That may be the name that your mother gave you and is shorter than Guillaume anyway. What say you?"

"I like Gille. Thank you master."

"And I am not master. I am Hrolf." I heard barking. "And that would be Nipper."

He looked up, "Nipper?"

My dog bounded out of the dark. He had grown since I had first had him and was now a powerful dog. He stood before Gille and bared his teeth. "Nipper! Sit!" He obeyed but his teeth were still bared. I reached into my pouch and took some dried meat I kept there. I took out a piece and gave it to Gille. "Put this on the flat of your hand and present it to the dog." He looked dubious. "Be brave. This will make him your friend." The boy extended his hand slowly. Nipper stopped baring his teeth as he smelled the meat. He sniffed and then took the treat. He licked Gille's hand. "Now you are friends. He will watch over you as he watches over me and my horses."

We walked the last hundred or so paces to my home and the horses whinnied. Gille let go of my hand and ran to the sound. I let him greet them alone. They would judge him as they had me. If they liked him then all would be well. By the time I reached them Freyja was licking his head and he was stroking Dream Strider. "Thank you Hrolf! It is as though I have died and gone to heaven. This is perfect."

"I know, Gille. It is *wyrd*."

I did not sleep well that night. After I had finally persuaded Gille to leave the horses and curl up in my home I tried to sleep but I worried about Mary. Had I done enough? I was the only one she could talk to and I had walked away and left her. I must have fallen asleep but I woke myself with a jerk before dawn and rose. I walked down to the sea, stripped off and swam to clear my head and my thoughts. Nipper ran with me. He enjoyed the water too. It is strange the way the gods and the Norns shape our thoughts. The icy cold of Ran's world helped me to clear my head. It swept away the fog and the mist, the doubts and the uncertainties. I knew where she would be. I thanked Ran and then waded from the water. I picked up my clothes and ran up to my home. Nipper shook himself and then ran off to hunt himself some food. I was about to dress and then ride off to find Mary when I remembered my new charge. Gille slept still. I could no longer think only of me. I had a child to care for.

After drying myself and dressing I lit the fire I used outside my hut. It was still dark. Dawn was still to break. The boy would be hungry. I put some water and oats in a cooking pot and placed it on the fire. I tossed in some salt and then went to my horses. They would be worked hard this day. They neighed as I

119

approached. I stroked them all, Dream Strider first, and spoke with them.

I looked around and saw a yawning sleepy, Gille. "You should be asleep."

He shook his head, "The horses called to me."

I nodded. "Then dress yourself. I have some food for you. I must leave you here with two of my horses. I have a task to do."

He was young but he nodded, "I can do that, Hrolf."

"Good."

We ate the porridge and then I showed him where the brushes were. The two mares had not had a good comb for some days. I saddled Dream Strider. I had sudden doubts. "Are you certain you will be all right here?"

He grinned, "I do not understand men, Hrolf, for they are cruel but horses are simpler. I will be safe. My father was a horse master. He had a way with them and he taught me, young as I am, how to care for them. I am content."

Nipper led us as we headed down the trail. He must have found something tasty to eat for he did not pester me for treats. I was going north. If I was wrong then Mary would be dead. If I was right then the Norns had guided both of us. By the time dawn broke I was at the trail which led from the village north. We had fought Hermund the Bent's men close to here. Nature had reclaimed where their bodies had fallen. Nipper stopped and sniffed. I dismounted and I looked. I saw, in the grass, a flattened part. Someone had stood here recently. This part of the island was lonely. No one had a reason to come here. This was a sign that Mary had come this way. I hoped she had come in daylight. There were cliffs at this end of the island.

"Nipper! Find!"

My dog loped off and disappeared in a golden flash. I tried to follow her trail. I knew it was Mary. I dared not take my eyes away. If she had run then I might lose it. So long as she kept heading north then I would find her for the island ended a mile hence. Nipper came back. He had lost the trail. I began to fear the worst. The cave in which I thought she might have sheltered was to my left but her trail led north towards the cliffs. Has she done as Siggi White Hair had suggested? Had she thrown herself to the rocks below? I reached the edge of the cliff and dismounted. Fearfully I peered over the edge. There was no sign of a body on the rocks below. It was but twenty paces to the rocks but that would be enough to kill someone. The lack of a body proved nothing. Her corpse could have been taken out with the tide.

Suddenly Nipper sniffed to my left. I grabbed Dream Strider's reins. "Find, Nipper, find!"

He moved along the rocks at the edge of the cliff. Hope soared when I saw an indentation on the left of the rocks where a foot had stepped. I looked ahead. The cave was just two hundred paces from me. I kept at the same speed as Nipper. If she had gone along the edge I had to keep looking down in case she had fallen. We were twenty paces from the cave. Its entrance was still hidden by a fold in the land. Nipper raced ahead barking and he disappeared. I heard a scream and knew that he had found her.

Chapter 8

I tied Dream Strider to a scrubby bush and headed down to the cave. I stepped into the narrow entrance and saw that Nipper was wary of the girl. She was cowering at the back of the dark and damp hole in the rocks.

"Nipper, out!" The dog obeyed. His tail wagged as he passed me. The girl had passed the test for I had not told him to get her. There were two kinds of people to Nipper, my friends and all else were enemies. I spoke quietly to her as I held out my hand, "Come Mary; this is not the place for you. You will be safe."

Her eyes were wild and staring; white against the dark walls. She stood but said, "I will not go back to the village! I would rather die."

I shook my head, "No, you would not. The fact that you sought shelter shows me that no matter how unhappy you are, you cling to life and that is good, now come into the sunlight and I will take you back to my home."

"It is not in the village?"

"No."

"I will not submit to the insults of those others!"

"Come, give me your hand."

Her hand reached over and took mine. I gave it a reassuring squeeze as I led her out. She had been in there some time for she had to shade her eyes against the sun. When they became accustomed to the light she stared around her to see if others waited for her.

"There is no one but me and my horse. Come, Dream Strider will carry you to my home."

"Dream Strider?"

"I dreamt of him before I found him. It was *wyrd*." I helped her into the saddle. "You just hang on and I will lead him. He is gentle."

"I can ride. My father had horses."

"Nipper, home!"

Nipper raced off and we walked in silence. Eventually I broke it, "What was it made you run?"

"Hildegard had some of the slaves spit in my food when they brought it to me. Seara did nothing."

"Seara is old."

"What will happen to me?" I did not answer. "If I am sent back then I will run away again!"

"And they will put a yoke on you. They will tether you like an animal at night. You cannot win." Her face fell as she realised I was right. This was not the world she knew where she got what she wanted. Here she had to obey others and it was hard for her. "I will speak to the Jarl." I was not confident that he would listen to me for I had already used up my favours by bringing Gille to our land. I could only try.

When we neared my home Dream Strider whinnied and the mares answered. Gille ran to me, "Master! Master!"

I shook my head. He would insist on calling me master. "What is it?"

123

"The young one, Gerðr, she is going to have a foal!"

A foal? How do you know?"

"My father knew horses and I have grown up with them. He was a horse master and he taught me the signs. I am certain that she has a foal within her. If you do not believe me I will show you where to touch her as I was taught."

"I believe you!" Now I knew why the Norns had sent me the slave. We had both forgotten Mary and I dropped Dream Strider's reins as I ran to the pen.

Gille put his hand underneath her and waited. Then he smiled, "Put your hand here. You will feel the heartbeat! It is the foal!"

I put my hand there. I knew it was not close to the mare's heart and, faintly at first, I felt the beat of another living being.

Gilles said, "You can only feel the heartbeat a month after a mare has been covered by a stallion."

I almost laughed at this young boy who seemed so knowledgeable. "Is this why you were kept as a slave?"

"Yes lord. I have a gift and the master recognised it but he did not like me for I was foreign." He suddenly noticed Mary. "Who is this, mas... Hrolf? Your sister?"

Mary had dismounted and was wandering over with a bemused look on her face. "No Gille this is Mary. She was taken as a slave from the Issicauna like you. She will be staying with us for a while."

He nodded as though that was perfectly reasonable.

I turned to her. "We will leave you here. We have work to do. I will not take the young mare. There is food inside the hut. Help yourself. Do not let the fire go out. If you wish to bathe the sea is close." I gave her a wry smile. "I hope you are here when I return."

She smiled, "I will be here."

We rode the two horses towards the village. Gille did not need a saddle and Freyja seemed happy to bear him. I knew that we had been expected just after dawn and I saw the disappointed looks at our late arrival. As we approached I said quietly, "Do not mention Mary yet. Let me do that in my own time."

Siggi White Hair asked, "Where have you been! We have brought the firewood and small branches up but you knew we needed your horses for the heavy work. Where is the other?"

"That is why we are late. Gille here discovered the young one is in foal. We will have to make do with these two."

"Gille? I thought his name was Guillaume?"

"It is Gille." I said it firmly to end the debate. "And we waste time here. Come Gille let us see how you are at leading a horse!" The path down to the beach now had flat stones upon it. We had used wood to make steps down the slope so that it was now much easier to haul objects from the beach. The men were preparing to lift the logs and carry them by hand when they heard the clatter of stones as we descended the path. They gave an ironic cheer.

"Finally risen!"

"Did you eat well?"

I smiled at the banter. They meant no harm and all of them would be glad that I had brought the horses. It would make the job much easier. Erik One Hand was there. He often helped me with the horses. They knew him, for he fed and watered them when I was absent. We took off Dream Strider's saddle at the foot of the cliff. I waved Erik over. "This is Gille. He will be helping to look after the horses. He can help you."

Erik, who had also been a slave, nodded and smiled. "That is what a one armed man needs, Gille, a strapping boy to help him. Come I will show you how we tie the traces to the harness we made." Gille did not understand Erik's words but the task was clear and he followed him.

We had two leather harnesses which fitted over the chests of the horses. Two long reins allowed us to attach heavy objects to them without injuring the horses. Once done we handed them to the men with the logs and they tied them on. We used a halter to guide the two beasts up the slope. We did not hurry and it took all day to move most of the logs. We stacked them where they could season and we arranged them in piles of girth and length.

Siggi saw that both the horses and men were flagging in the late afternoon. "We have done enough," he shouted, "and besides we have an errant slave to find."

"No you do not." My voice silenced all the conversation for it was news.

"Have you found her? Is she dead?"

"I have found her, Ulf. I discovered her this morning in our cave. She is alive but she is fearful of returning to the village. She is at my home."

"Will she stay there?"

"I know not. We must speak with the Jarl."

Siggi nodded, "I am pleased you have found her. It would be bad luck if she killed herself. It is bad enough having a haunted farmhouse without haunted waters. Until we have a volva or galdramenn we can take no chances on ill luck befalling us."

We ascended slowly to the village for the horses were tired. Poor Gille was almost out on his feet. He had been up as early as I had. The sooner we got home the better. The Jarl heard us out and then sent for Hildegard and the others. The looks on their faces showed their guilt even before they had spoken.

"I want to know if you spat in Mary the slave's, food and abused her. I want to know if that was the reason she ran away."

The youngest of them was Anya. She was a little older than Gille. "We meant no harm. Emma said it was good for it would pay her back for being born noble."

I said, "And if she died; what would your god think to that?" They were all Christians and each had a wooden cross around their neck. They clutched at them and a couple mumbled something. I suspect it was a prayer. "It is no thanks to you that she lives. Had she taken her own life then the sin would have been yours just as much as hers!"

A couple began to weep as I spat out the words.

The Jarl was angry. "Go! Those who are slaves shall be beaten and as for you two," he pointed to Emma and Hildegard, "I hope your husbands show good judgement and punish you for wilfulness. Mary is the property of the clan!" he turned to me. "She cannot return here yet. Can she stay with you?"

"She can have a home there. I now have Gille. She can sew there and contribute to the clan. She will be happier."

"Then make it so."

Wyrd.

As we went back Gille was quiet. "How was your first day as a Viking!"

"It is not what I expected. They laughed more than I expected. I liked the man with the one arm. He spoke to me as though I knew his words but I did not. I liked the way he smiled at me and he was gentle with Freyja. I wish to know the words of your people, Hrolf."

"And that is good, Gille the Thoughtful. I will teach you and Mary."

He brightened. "She will stay with us?"

"She will and she is a Frank. You can speak with her."

"We will be like a family."

"We will indeed."

"I miss my family."

Wyrd. The three of us had all had our families taken from us and had found each other. We were a clan within a clan.

There was a well kept fire going when we reached the house and a pot simmering upon it. Mary looked nervous. However the first thing I noticed was that she had used my combs to comb her hair. She might even have washed it for it looked lighter than it had.

"I collected shellfish from the shore and found some sampiere and some greens, master. I think there is some bread left although it is a little stale."

I nodded. "If we break it up and put it in the bowls then it will not matter."

"You have not many bowls, master."

I nodded, "We will have to gather some clay the next time we are on the mainland and make them. Until then we can take it in turns."

"Until then, master? Does that mean I can stay?"

"For the time being it does. And I am Hrolf, not master. You will continue to sew and we will have to travel to the village to collect your work." Her face clouded over. "Gille and I will accompany you. The Jarl has punished those who abused you." The relief was clear. "You will also keep house for Gille and I. I will make a screen for your modesty. At night I will teach you both our language for now you are both part of the Raven Wing Clan."

For some reason that made them both happy. "Master, I mean Hrolf. If you get me material then I can make garments for us. I do not like being dressed in rags and poor Gille here has more holes in his clothes than cloth."

She was right. "I will bring some in the morning."

The difference in Mary was astounding. She became happy. She worked hard. She and Gille giggled and laughed like a brother and sister and yet all that I had done was to smile and give them a roof. It showed me the true lot of a slave.

The food she had prepared was tasty but it was hardly filling. I decided that as soon as possible I would go hunting. They would be small animals but they would augment our share of that which the village had from our hunt. I knew that we would only be given a very small proportion. That was to be expected. I had chosen to live apart. We would have to make the best of it. We had our first language lesson but Gille fell asleep half way through. I gently picked him up and carried him to his bed. Mary found a spare fur and covered him. As she did so she saw the scars on his back and her hand went to her mouth.

I led her to the door of the hut, "His master, a noble, whipped him and beat him."

She understood my point. "I did not know."

"Perhaps you understand now why those from your village treated you as they did. I am not saying your father mistreated them but you do not know. I have suffered at the hands of enough overseers to know that much is done in a lord's name."

"I begin to see. Thank you, Hrolf the Horseman. It is true what Brigid calls you. She says you are the most gentle of men."

The next day we finished hauling the wood from the shore. I was pleased for it had been hard work for the horses. I had checked Freyja and she was not with foal. I knew that, with the end of summer approaching, it would be unlikely that she would be in season again. Perhaps that was for the best.

As I was about to leave the village the Jarl called me over. "Hrolf, you did not think we had forgotten that you used your own coin that you had earned to rescue my brother's warriors. It speaks well of you that you have not mentioned it since you returned from the Liger."

129

"It was nothing Jarl. We can get more gold. We cannot replace brave warriors with such ease."

"Nonetheless you deserve recompense." He turned to Vermund who handed him a bag of coins. They had been taken when we had captured Mary and the others. "I hope this compensates you."

"Thank you Jarl. It does."

He put his arm around my shoulder. "I thank you too for what you have done to bring peace to the village. By taking away the troublesome Mary you have made the village fill with harmony."

I was not certain that it was Mary's fault but I nodded. "It is my clan and I share the island with its people."

"We have goods to trade from our raid and I am taking the drekar to Dyflin to trade with Gunnstein Berserk Killer. Some men are staying on the island." He shook his head. "I think Ketil and Beorn wish to spend more time with their young wives."

"And I have two horses to school as well as Dream Strider to care for. Mary will still sew. I will be bringing her to the village to collect any work required. She can sew just as well in my home."

"She can."

I left and sought Siggi White Hair. "Are you going on the trading expeditions?"

"I am, Hrolf. What is it you need?"

"Material for clothes."

He laughed, "And is that work for a wizened old man like me?"

"No but I can trust you. And I would have something else, another Saami bow if you can buy one."

130

"But you have a bow."

"It is not for me. I would like it as a gift for Ulf. He has done much for me and I would like to repay him."

"If I can I will do so." I handed him a large number of coins. "This is too many!"

"Then you can return what you do not spend. Better too much than not enough."

"You are very trusting."

"If I cannot trust you and the rest of the clan then whom can I trust?"

"Aye you are right."

The traders were away for half a month by which time the weather had changed as nights became longer and the winds changed and became a little colder as they swept in from the north and the west. Mary and Gille could now speak to others apart from me. We had visited the village and Mary could now travel there in safety so long as she was with us. Gille had grown in the short time he had been with me. I think it was the food which Mary cooked. She proved to be a good cook. When the material came she was delighted although Siggi was uncertain if he had made the right choice.

I decided to give Ulf his present in private. He lived in the warrior hall. He had not taken a woman and I did not think he ever would. He was sat outside the hall and working on some bone he was carving to make fish hooks. I had the bow in a sheepskin.

"Now, Hrolf, we do not see much of you these days. How is life by the haunted farmhouse?"

"We get on well. I feel like I have a young brother and sister. With the mare in foal it is a good place to be. I have begun to build a small house for Mary. It is not right that she has to share with Gille and I."

He laughed, "You are the strangest Viking I ever met."

"I came here to give you this, Ulf Big Nose. It is to thank you for giving me the skills I have. I have a small part of your skills but I am improving."

He unwrapped it, "This is a mighty gift. I cannot accept it."

"Why not?"

"You have spent your money on this!"

"I spent the coin which the merchant gave me on the Liger. I would not have been able to help him but for the skills you gave me. Consider this payment for my life."

He stood and clasped my forearm. "In that case I accept it and thank you. No one, the Jarl included, has ever given me such a gift."I could see that he was touched by the gesture but I had meant what I had said.

I had thought that the year would end quietly. Samhain was not far away. The fields were being harvested and we were preparing for winter. Stores of wood and dried fish were being prepared. The women and children would soon gather the bounty which the land had produced. We planted, on my land, the beans which would grow and give us food for next winter. Gerðr grew and each day the three of us would feel the foal as it moved. It was our own miracle. We were making our own rituals and they seemed to bond us closer together. Life was good. All appeared to be well and then the Weird Sisters must have decided that we had been too quiet for too long.

I was heading to the fish nets to bring in the day's catch. I stopped at the farm for I spied a sail heading towards our island. I went to the headland to watch it approach. Sometimes Jarl Dragonheart sent his knarr to us or even one of his drekar. I knew all of his vessels and I watched as the sail drew closer. Then I saw there were two other sails. They were ships heading for our island. They were neither drekar nor knarr. They were rounder than a drekar and longer than a knarr. That could only mean one thing, danger!

Chapter 9

I shouted, "Mary, Gille. Saddle Freyja and Dream Strider."

"What is it?"

"Mary do not argue! Do as I order!" My tone was harsh and she recoiled.

Gille said, "Come Mary let us see who can do it the quickest!"

I went into my hut and put on the padded kyrtle which Mary had made for me. This would be the first time I had had the chance to wear it. Then I donned my mail. It had been many months since it had hung from my shoulders. It was still oiled and cared for. I put my helmet on my head. I took Heart of Ice, the Frankish sword I had been given and my seax. I put my shield across my back and took my bow and spear. I was a warrior once more.

When I emerged Mary's hand went to her mouth. The last time she had seen me thus dressed was the day she had been captured. Gille led Dream Strider to me. I hung my bow and quiver from the saddle. "Gille, I want you and Mary to ride double on Freyja. You can lead Gerðr. Ride to the village and tell the Jarl or Siggi that I have spied three ships. They look to be heading in this direction. It may be nothing. They might pass us by but I will wait until I know."

He nodded. "Aye Hrolf. I will not let you down."

I gave him the Frankish sword the merchant had given me. "Take this and care for it. Now ride." I whistled and Nipper appeared. I pointed to Mary, "Guard!" As they mounted I went to the animal pens and opened their doors and gates. I shooed the animals out, shouting at them to make them run. There were just a few animals: a couple of sheep and goats we milked and some chickens but if these were enemies then they would have to find the animals. They ran and flew off squawking and bleating and I led Dream Strider to the headland.

When I reached the farmhouse I took off my helmet and hung it from my saddle. I peered out to sea. I could see the three vessels much clearer now for they were heading for the bay. They were three of the ships used by the men of Vannes. They were tubby vessels and unlike a drekar, which sliced through the sea, they appeared to waddle in the water. I knew that they could each hold as many as forty men although most sailed to war with twenty or so. It seemed likely to me that they were heading for us but they could still veer either east or west. I licked my finger and held it up. The breeze was coming from the mainland. They were sailing cautiously. They did not know the bay. There could be rocks waiting to tear their keels. Their slow approach meant that Gille and Mary would have plenty of time to reach the village. I lived the furthest away but there were others who lived outside the walls. Sven the Helmsman lived close by his drekar and others had farms just a few hundred paces from the walls. They would have time to take their families within the walls.

I had time to wonder about this possible attack. Although we had done all that we could to avoid detection when we had taken the animals and the timber the fact that I had slain two men would have aroused their suspicions. In addition our drekar would have been seen. It might have taken the Count some time to gather all the information and then prepare to attack us but it made sense. This was the time to raid. We knew that. Most people would be in their fields gathering in their crops and preparing for winter. Indeed we would be thinking about another raid soon ourselves. The Jarl would want our grain stores filled.

They were now less than half a mile from shore and there was no doubt that they were landing. Had our men been closer we could have disputed the beach. There was little I could do. I was but one man. I wondered if the Jarl would choose to do as he had the last time danger had threatened and stay behind the walls. I doubted it this time for our enemy would punish us by destroying the crops in the fields. There was more than one way to defeat an enemy; starvation was an effective weapon. I sensed movement and turned as Ulf Big Nose and Arne Four Toes ran up. I just pointed. I saw that Ulf had his new bow with him.

Arne was out of breath but not so Ulf. "Franks?"

I shook my head, "They look to be from Vannes. They must have objected to our hunting and logging."

Ulf just nodded, "The Jarl is bringing the clan. We will fight them here. If we are defeated then we fall back to the walls. Come we will go closer and use our bows. There are only three of us but we can slow them up a little eh?"

I dismounted and slapped Dream Strider's rump. He would return to my home and graze. I rammed the spear into the ground and then followed Ulf and Arne. I had left my helmet hanging on the saddle. We would not be fighting here. We stood on the shelf of rock which was thirty paces above the beach. The shingle and stones below us would slow down any who rushed at us.

I pointed to the wooden jetty. "They will land there."

Ulf nodded. He had a good mind when it came to strategy. "Then when men leap ashore to tie them up we aim at them. However, Hrolf, you and I can try to cause a little confusion as they close. Let us make them wary of these bows from the gods!"

136

Arne had an ordinary bow and ours had a better range. Our elevation meant we could release an arrow further and a packed boat was a big target. Ulf was keen to use his bow in anger and he loosed first. The arrow sailed high into the air and then plunged into the middle of the first boat. I chose the second boat. The sound of the sea stopped us hearing any cries they might have made but the outstretched arms told us that we had both hit something. It spurred us on and we released five more arrows each. The jetty was well within Arne's range and he join in as the boats bumped next to the wooden quay. They had to tie up and it cost them four men wounded before they managed to tie up the first one. They were then able to make a shield wall and we shifted our aim to the two which had yet to tie up.

Behind us I heard the sound of feet as our men approached. Rurik One Ear ran up. We did not turn as he spoke. "The Jarl and the clan are just half a mile behind me." He unslung his bow and stood next to Arne Four Toes. As he pulled he said, "Your young horseman is watching Dream Strider for you. He said he would protect his new land and he was a warrior. He has spirit that one!"

Despite our best efforts and emptying more than half of our arrows the three ships managed to tie up and we had no targets for they raised their shields. It would be a waste of arrows. However our presence meant that they had to wait until all of their men were ashore before they could risk dislodging us. It gave us the chance to assess the opposition.

Their shields were smaller than ours. Most had a helmet but not all. They favoured spears for they normally rode to war as I did. As we peered down we saw that almost a third had mail. They had three banners which meant that they had three of their nobles leading them. They would be encased in mail. They did not favour the bow but I saw evidence that they had crossbows. That was confirmed when Ulf Big Nose shouted, "Down!" as a bolt was sent in our direction. It flew over our heads. We rose and Ulf fitted an arrow and sent it towards the crossbowman who was reloading. It was a well aimed arrow for it struck the crossbow splintering it. The crossbowman and two others held their hands to their faces as shards of wood from the damaged weapon tore into their flesh.

I heard a horn and a wall of shields began to advance up the slope. Ulf said to Arne and Rurik, "You two start to throw stones at the slope. It is a hard surface on which to walk at the best of times. Let us see if we can make it more slippery and unstable for them. Hrolf and I will chose our targets."

The two of them began to throw large rocks high into the air. They tumbled and rolled down the shingle slope. They dislodged other stones which rolled and tumbled too. As their aim improved Rurik and Arne were able to throw them closer to the feet of the marching warriors. They were going slowly for they were trying to stay together. Ulf's arrow struck the thigh of the man who threw his shield arm up to keep his balance. I sent another into another's leg. As the two men fell from the formation there was confusion and Ulf and I hit two more. We were not killing but a wounded man was only half a threat.

The shields stopped and then I heard someone below us shout, "Crossbows!" They were less than a hundred and fifty paces from the top now.

"We had better fall back. They will use their crossbows."

Ulf turned, "Aye, we have done enough. The Jarl is here." We turned and dropped into the dead ground below the headland. The bolts sailed over our heads. Had they used arrows they might have hit us but the bolts flew harmlessly above us.

The clan had formed a shield wall. It was fifteen men wide and three men deep. I saw Gille standing to the side with Dream Strider and my spear. Ulf ran to the Jarl to report and I went to Gille. I donned my helmet. I took the spear and said, "Now take Dream Strider to safety." I laid my bow and quiver down.

"I shall fight at your side."

"No Gille. If we lose then we will fight from the walls. I want my horse and you safe. Now go!"

He nodded and, jumping on, Dream Strider galloped off. I swung my shield around and went to the shield wall. Siggi White Hair and Beorn Beornsson made a space for me. We were on the left of the Jarl and his hearthweru. Ulf Big Nose would be on the right. The Jarl shouted his orders as we shuffled into place. "We will drive these attackers back to the sea. March!"

We began the chant which kept us in step.

A song of death to all its foes

The power of the raven grows and grows.

The power of the raven grows and grows.

The power of the raven grows and grows.

A song of death to all its foes

The power of the raven grows and grows.

The power of the raven grows and grows.

The power of the raven grows and grows.

Our shields were locked together and our spears held underhand below our shields. The enemy were a solid line of metal before us. Those in the second and third ranks held their spears over hand. Their shields were held over their heads. I did not know how the enemy fought for we had never gone to war with them. Our way worked. As we reached the top of the rise which the four of us had so recently vacated I saw that the enemy were just twenty paces from the top. They had a column of men ten wide and, like us their spears were held before them. Their shields afforded some protection but they were only half the size of ours.

"Raven Wing! Charge!"

We did not run as we descended towards them. We had no need. We each pulled our shield tighter and stepped forward with our right legs. The men behind us pressed their bodies into ours. The enemy tried to run at us. It was a mistake for although there was some turf there was also sand and shingle. Some men slipped. Beorn thrust his spear into the throat of a warrior who had slipped to his knees. They were not as tight as we were and I saw a gap. I punched my spear head at the mail links as we all stepped forward again. I heard the clatter of bolts on the shields above us as my spear cracked some links in the mail. I pushed harder, aided by the weight of those behind. The warrior was so busy trying to keep his feet that he failed to stop the spear. As the sharp head prised open the mail links it entered his under garment and tore through that. I looked at his face as the head entered his guts. I twisted and as he gave his death scream he spat blood. I pushed harder and felt the head grate off bone. As I pulled it out he slipped beneath my feet. A warrior had to be careful not to trip on the dead. I shouted, "'Ware body!"

Karl Swift Foot and Gunnstein Gunnarson behind me would know what I meant.

The best warriors of the enemy, those in the front rank, were falling for their shields were not stopping our spears. I had seen the banners of the leaders at the rear of each column. That was how they fought and so their nobles would be able to give orders. Our Jarl fought at the front. If he fell then we would all die defending his body. That was our way.

Now the danger was that we had to keep our footing. Siggi's voice, not the Jarl, gave us the command. "Hold and steady your feet."

It was the sensible order for we had the slope. The enemy did not know our language and they took our halting as a weakness. I heard an order shouted from the rear of their lines, "We have them! Charge!"

I shouted, "They are charging!"

"Brace!"

We all put our right legs behind us and leaned into our shields. With Karl's shield above me I was in a dark world but, through the gap I saw red and yellow painted shields punched towards us. I watched a spear heading for me and I easily moved my head out of the way. It slid along the side of my helmet. I would have repairs to make! Karl and Gunnstein pulled their shields tighter and the spear was held between them. As the warrior tried to pull it out for a second strike I punched blindly up with my spear. He was not mailed. I looked into his face. He had a scrubby beard; he was young. He suddenly looked surprised as my spear tore into him and the light left his eyes. We pushed against our shields. Others had slipped as they ran to attack. They had been slain and there was a wall of bodies before us.

Before us the sky became lighter as the enemy withdrew.

"Forward!"

We knew our land and from the body littered ground beneath our feet we knew where we were. The wooden quay was less than a hundred and fifty paces away. The ground we moved over was flatter although still treacherous. Perhaps it was even more treacherous for wounded men had dripped blood upon it. Others had trailed guts upon it as they crawled away to die. We stepped carefully as we headed down to those who had come to attack us.

A song of death to all its foes

The power of the raven grows and grows.

The power of the raven grows and grows.

The power of the raven grows and grows.

The chant helped us and we moved towards the wooden quay. I would have been tempted to lower the shields but I saw the wisdom in their use when a bolt thudded into my shield. I risked a glance in the gap between Karl and Gunnstein's shield. The enemy were boarding their ships.

141

"They are fleeing!"

The Jarl shouted, "Break wall!" He led his hearth-weru to attack one of the nobles and his bodyguards. They hit each other in a clash of metal and wood.

I held my shield before me as the ones above were removed and then I ran towards the wooden jetty. Two bolts hit my shield. I saw a crossbowman kneel to reload his weapon and I hurled my spear at him. He was thirty paces from me and he took the spear in his chest. He pitched between the ship and the dock. I drew Heart of Ice. The jarl had hurt their leader although I saw two hearth-weru lay with the enemy dead. The oathsworn of the enemy leader were trying to protect the men carrying his wounded body aboard. Siggi White Hair and I ran together towards them. We were reckless but the joy of battle was in us. We wanted to hurt as many of the enemy as we could. If we did that they might think twice about returning.

I had space now and I brought my sword high over my head as I punched at the mailed warrior with my shield. His eyes were drawn to my shield as the boss came towards his face. He did not see the sword which angled down across his neck. His mail was good but the blow was so powerful that he dropped his shield. I rammed the hilt of my sword towards his eye. He screamed as the hilt took his eye. I punched again with my shield and his nose erupted in blood, bone and cartilage. I ended his suffering by ramming my sword into his screaming, open mouth. He fell backwards into the sea for the ship was already drifting out. As more bolts thudded into my shield I held it tightly to me. We had won. Now was not the time to die!

As the ships pulled away we began to cheer and to bang our shields. We had defeated a superior number of men. They were not better warriors! Those in the third rank turned and began to walk back up the slope despatching the enemy wounded. We too had suffered. But three of the hearth-weru lived. The Jarl had a wound too. His cheek was cut to the bone. Harold Haroldsson and

Gunnar Stone Face would fight with us no more. Others would have wounds which would bear testament to their courage. The three ships rode higher in the water as they sailed north to their homes. They would lick their wounds and consider the rashness of their action. If they had thought to quash us with a sudden attack then they had failed.

I took off my helmet. Bagsecg would earn more coins for the spear had gouged a line in the metal. Rurik said, "You were lucky, Hrolf. You could have lost an eye. That helmet was a good investment. It has saved you again."

The Jarl shouted, "Strip the bodies and pile them on Hrolf's beach. Let us make a pyre that can be seen from the land. I want our enemies to see the folly of attacking the Raven Wing Clan. They will know what happens if they venture here again."

We took off our own mail for it was a hard task stripping bodies and taking the treasure to the farmhouse. It took some time. Using some of my precious kindling we lit the fire and watched as the smoke drifted east on the breeze. We piled the enemy dead on the fire and there was a smell of burning hair and flesh. The smoke rose higher. The sails had long disappeared but they would see the thick smoke nonetheless and they would know what it meant.

The Jarl went back with the other wounded to the village. Siggi White Hair put his arms around Ulf Big Nose and me. "The Saami bows proved to be vital! I know the Jarl will thank you when he has got over the loss of his hearth-weru. Had the four of you not slowed down their landing we would have had a harder time." He pointed to the stones. "The land helped us again."

Ulf said, "If we had more boys trained to use the bow we could have done more damage to the enemy. We have perilously few warriors as it is and now we have lost more. It is good that the winter storms will be here soon."

We were the last to leave the beach. The others had headed to the village already. As we made our way back up to my home

Rurik One Ear said, "If any complain about your living alone, Hrolf, I shall beat them myself!"

I stopped, "Do people complain?"

Siggi and Ulf hesitated and then Siggi nodded, "It is those with wives and the younger warriors. It has become more vociferous since you took the Frankish slave. To them it looks as though you think you are better than they are."

I knew who it would be. "Ketil and Knut." The Eriksson brothers had always been more than a little envious of my success.

Siggi White Hair nodded, "They are amongst those who complain."

"I can live with their complaints but if I am causing a problem then I will leave the island altogether and take my horses to the mainland."

Siggi shook his head vehemently, "Do not even contemplate such an action!" He glared at Rurik, "If this had not been mentioned..."

"Do not hide anything from me. I am aware that I am an outsider to some. It is in my nature."

"We meant for the best."

We reached my home and I took my mail inside. Ulf said, "We will leave the treasure here until the Jarl decides what to do with it."

"I will come with you to the village. I sent Mary there for her protection but I will fetch her and my horses home." Knowing the attitude in the village I did not want her to spend a moment longer than necessary there.

As we walked on, Ulf and I striding ahead, I heard Siggi White Hair and Arne berating Rurik. "I would that you had lost your tongue and not your ear! Can you not control your mouth!"

"I did not think. I was praising Hrolf for what he did. Had he not given warning then we would have been destroyed. We need him to live where he does."

Arne Four Toes said, "Aye you are right and I think it is time we had words with the Erikssons. Since they married they have become too full of their own self importance!"

I shouted, "Do not. They have their views and it does not bother me. I now have my own family and my life is good." I knew now that my decision to live where I did was meant to be.

Gille was standing protectively with Mary and the horses when we reached the village. Nipper was on guard. As soon as she saw me I saw relief fill Mary's face. I said, "I will take my horses home now."

Siggi said, "Stay and feast with us. We have much to celebrate."

Shaking my head I said, "No."

Siggi saw the looks on the faces of Gille and Mary and nodded. "Aye you are right. You do have a family now and like any father you put them first. We will come on the morrow and sort out the treasure."

"I will make sure it is protected in case we have rain." I turned to Mary, "Do you wish to ride Freyja or walk?"

"I will walk."

Nipper waited until we had left the gates and then raced off. I turned to Gille, "You are brave Gille but until you can use weapons stay safe. I will teach you how to use a bow and a sword but you would not last a heartbeat on the battlefield."

"I want to be as you, Hrolf. Everyone says you are fearless."

"That is not true. I am as afraid as the next man but I will fight for what I hold dear."

145

We had long left the village and Mary said, "And you hold us dear do you not?"

I nodded, "I do."

"You could have stayed and been celebrated as a hero by the whole village but because you thought we were unhappy you left."

"I enjoy the peace of my home. That is all." I hated lying to them both but I did not wish to give them false hope.

However that night, as we sat in my home with a fine fire burning I did feel content. Gille carved adornments for Freyja's bridle and Mary worked on a sheepskin. With Nipper gnawing on a bone I felt truly happy. Perhaps this was all that I needed.

Chapter 10

When the Jarl and the others arrived the next day we sorted all of the weapons and mail out. Siggi wished to give me the mail from the warrior I had killed but I shook my head. "I have a fine byrnie. I can wear it while I ride. There must be warriors who do not have one. Let them have it. I need little."

The Jarl turned, "But it is right that you, who were in the front rank and slew so many of their warriors with spear, arrow and sword, should be rewarded."

"Then give me the coin when we trade with the men of Dyflin. I have enough mail and weapons. There are other things I need. I need tools to help me make harnesses for horses. I need to know how to make horseshoes. I need an anvil. Do not worry Jarl. I am content."

I saw Siggi shake his head. For him the acquisition of weapons and mail was all.

We left for Dyflin a week after Samhain. Mary and Gilles were happy to be left alone. We had made the house secure. The crossing to Hibernia was atrocious. We had to row for most of the way and when the wind was in our favour we had to shelter beneath an old sail to keep the rain from us. It was as though we were being punished and we knew not why. It was all made worse by the low spirits of the Jarl. The last battle and the loss of three hearth-weru had disturbed Jarl Gunnar Thorfinnson. It was not that he was sad but he was restless. He confided in Siggi as we sheltered from another westerly squall. I was seated near them taking shelter beneath my wolf cloak.

"I am the last of my line. When I die who will carry on my name? All of my father's sons but me are dead. I do not even have a wife. If I had fallen in battle like Olvir or Alf who would remember me a year from now? I need a wife and I need children. The Allfather wishes us to carry on our blood into the next generation. He wants strong warriors. I have not done as was intended."

Siggi and Ulf both shook their heads and Siggi spoke for them both. "We have had women. I dare say there are children we have fathered I know not but when we die then I hope that men will remember us for our deeds."

"Siggi is right. I am content with my life, Jarl."

The Jarl looked thoughtful, "And I am not. Gunnstein died and we parted on bad terms. I cannot go back and change that but what I can do is change my life now. I look at Hrolf. He is not yet a father but he has a family. You just need to look at Mary and Gille and see the esteem in which they hold him. That is not because of any title but because he is the man he is. That is what I would have."

Neither Siggi nor the hearth-weru could cheer him up. I hoped that the lively city of Dyflin would effect a change in our young jarl. I had brought all of my coin and I had also been promised another purse when the Jarl sold that which we did not need. I was not worried. He was fair. While many of the crew wished to stay ashore I chose the drekar. It would suit me. Ulf Big Nose and Rurik did the same.

We were all expected to go with the Jarl to speak with Gunnstein Berserk Killer. He ruled Dyflin. Had it not been for the Dragonheart he would still be the captain of a drekar hiring his sword out. He was however an honest man and I liked him. He greeted us as friends. I noticed that he was now a heavy man. The last time he had drawn his sword in anger had been when the Dragonheart had driven Hakon the Bald from Hibernia. He showed off his wife. She was overweight and over painted but she was a happy enough hostess and he brought forth his son and two daughters. His son looked to be what he was; a spoiled young lord who thought the world owed him a living. He had two daughters and they were both as pretty a pair of maidens as I had seen in a long time.

In all the years I had followed Jarl Gunnar Thorfinnson I had never seen him show an interest in any woman save the whores who frequented these places. Yet he was suddenly attentive towards the two young women who were the daughters of the ruler of Dyflin, Hallgerd and Hlif. I saw Ulf Big Nose shake his head and roll his eyes. Siggi White Hair just shrugged.

Gunnstein Berserk Killer raised his hands and said, " We will hold a feast this night in honour of Jarl Gunnar Thorfinnson!"

It was a wild night for it was a chance for the warriors in the clan to enjoy themselves but I drank little. I had seen too many of these feasts degenerate into fights and even deaths. I sat with Ulf and Siggi. We watched an awkward Jarl as he tried to court two sisters. Ulf shook his head, "When you hunt you choose one prey and make that your target. He turns from one doe to the next. The Jarl will lose them both!"

Siggi laughed, "So speaks a man who has never spent a whole night with a woman!"

"Aye but I know what is right!"

I just watched. I knew what was in the Jarl's head. He wanted children to carry on his name and to do that he needed a wife. He did not care which one. In many ways I felt sorry for the two young women. Dyflin was a lively and exciting town. Raven Wing island was a backwater where the most exciting event was when Brigid changed her brew! If one chose the Jarl she was choosing a totally different way of life.

I left when Erik Green Eye and one of Gunnstein Berserk Killer's men began to fight. This could only end in blood and anger. I slipped back aboard the drekar. Sven the Helmsman and Harold Fast Sailing had broached a barrel of beer and were seated on the quayside.

"Come and join us, Hrolf the Horseman."

I took the proffered horn. "Things are becoming a little lively back there!"

"Aye well, that is why we stay here. There comes a time when waking up black and blue is not as enjoyable as it might have seemed. We grow older and I hope a little wiser."

"The Jarl seems set on a wife."

"That is as it should be. A Jarl with a wife is less reckless. He has something to tie him to the land. Young Gunnstein showed that recklessness is a danger."

We chatted amiably until Rurik, Arne and Siggi returned carrying an unconscious Ulf. Sven laughed, "What happened? Did Ulf put his nose where he should not?"

Rurik, a little drunk himself, nodded, "Aye he spoke out of turn about the Jarl and the young sisters he was chasing. Vermund felled him. If I were Vermund I would be wary. Ulf does not forgive easily."

Only a handful of us slept on board. As we had less to drink we were up and about early and I was able to go to the market to buy what I needed for my home. In a few short months I had gone from just thinking of myself to worrying about two others. I bought a fur: it was a bearskin from a Swede. It was expensive but it would be needed in the depths of winter. I also bought six woollen blankets. They would be for both us and my horses. Gerðr would need cosseting. I did not want her to lose her foal. The young animal would be part of my herd. The other items I bought were also domestic. I bought more bowls and another cooking pot. I was laden when I returned to the drekar.

Rurik laughed as I stepped aboard, "Are you seeking a wife too? You have enough there for the clan."

I took the banter in my stride. "When you have two others and three horses to worry about, Rurik One Ear then you may comment. Until then give me a hand to stow these."

After they had been placed in and on my chest I asked Sven, "Do we sail today?"

"I know not. The Jarl did not say. I doubt it, Hrolf. If you two are staying aboard then Harold and I will go and buy some more rope. They have a good rope walk here. The women make them on the island but they are not as good as those from here. As we have the coin it would be foolish not to buy that which we need."

Ulf came to. He walked to the side and pulled up a pail of Liffey water. He poured it over his head. "That Vermund has a fist like Bagsecg's hammer."

Rurik said, "You were being a little critical of the Jarl. Vermund was not happy."

"He has lost three of his brothers has he not Ulf? It was to be expected that he would take it out on someone."

"Aye. I suppose you are right Hrolf. I will let this go but the next time he will feel the edge of my blade!"

Siggi was the first to return not long before noon. Rurik had lit a fire on the stone quay and we were cooking some river fish we had caught. Siggi rubbed his hands, "I have timed it well. Is there enough there for an old man who has news to pay for his food?"

"News?"

151

"Aye."

"Then sit. Does this news tell us when we leave?"

"It might Hrolf. The Jarl is speaking with Gunnstein Berserk Killer. He wishes to marry Hallgerd the Fair."

Ulf asked, "Which is she for they were both pretty?"

"She was the one who has seen fourteen summers, Hlif is a little younger. Gunnstein and the Jarl are discussing the bride price."

"Then we leave?"

"Then we leave but there will be another feast first. I am guessing another two or three days here. The Jarl will have things to buy for his home and his new bride. He has already sent Erik and Vermund of his hearth-weru to the slave markets to buy slaves for his bride and his house." Siggi turned to me, "Erik suggested Mary as a suitable slave for Hallgerd as she is noble born." For some reason I did not like that thought but I said nothing and kept my face as stone. "But the Jarl said he would not split your family after the service you have done us."

"Service?"

"You must know how grateful he is, how we all are for your timely warning when the Bretons came to our land. He has had little time to tell you but I know that he values you." He smiled, "I can see changes in our future."

Ulf laughed, "So, Siggi White Hair is now a galdramenn!"

Siggi gave an enigmatic smile and took the fish which Rurik held out for him, "We shall see, we shall see."

It was the next day when the news was confirmed. The Jarl was to be married that day. Vermund came to tell us that we were all invited to the hall of Gunnstein Berserk Killer for the feast. Sven and Harold were not happy about leaving the drekar unattended and they armed the ship's boys and gave them strict instructions to fetch us if there was danger. We then had to prepare. We had to be presentable. We combed and plaited our hair. Those like Siggi, Ulf and Rurik who had long beards, plaited them too. I was luckier than most. Mary had made me some new clothes. I had a fine kyrtle and new breeks made from doeskin. Rurik teased me, "Hlif will be casting her eye out for a husband now that her sister is to be wed. Watch out Hrolf, you would make a fine catch in your new apparel. You look like a young jarl yourself!"

We arrived at the hall and saw that it was packed with all those of importance in Dyflin. We were relegated to a long table some way from the Jarl but we did not mind for we were closer to the ale and the food. We did not need to see the great and the good. Hallgerd did not look unhappy nor did she look joyful. Having seen Mary and her experiences I guessed why. She would be leaving Dyflin with all which that civilised place had to offer and exchanging it for a remote and exposed island which was surrounded by enemies.

Jarl Gunnstein had entertainment laid on. It was a safer way than allowing the various warriors to provide their own. A Pict had a dancing bear which performed before us. There were some dark skinned acrobats and tumblers. After they had finished the Jarl took Hallgerd to his wedding bed. As they went we banged our daggers on the benches and chanted. Then Hlif and her mother left too. When they had gone those from the town began to drift off leaving just the warriors in the hall. Sven and Harold left too for they both fretted about the drekar. We were following when Jarl Gunnstein Berserk Killer waved Siggi, Ulf and me over to him.

"Jarl Gunnar has told me of your exploits. He is lucky to have the three of you." We nodded. A warrior does not mind praise but we all knew that no one praised you if they did not want something in return. "Should anything every happen to the Jarl or you wish to leave his service then know that I can offer you not only a place in my hall but your own drekar." He waved a hand towards the river beyond the walls of his hall. "I have a newly built threttanessa on the river and thirty warriors to sail her but I need a captain who has experience and men I can trust to lead."

That was unexpected and not to be rejected out of hand. A drekar was not cheap and gave a man power.

Siggi White Hair spoke for all of us. "We thank you Jarl for that is a generous offer. However we are all oathsworn of the Jarl and you would not wish us to break our word."

"No I would not. Consider my words then and as a token of my promise take these." He waved a hand and one of his oathsworn produced a box. He opened it and took out three daggers. They were pointed and double edged. The hilts had a dragon carved into the wood. They were an expensive looking gift. "These were given to me by a Moorish trader in return for trading rights here in Hibernia. I thought to give them to you so that should the Jarl fall in battle and you do not then you would return here and speak again of my offer."

We looked at each other. There was no loss of honour in agreeing. He was right, the death of Gunnstein Thorfinnson had showed us all that death was just a mistake away. We nodded and Siggi spoke, "Aye, I shall speak for us all, Jarl. We are honoured."

As we went back I said, "I can understand why he wants you two but I am but a youth."

Ulf shook his head and smiled, "Siggi would be captain of the drekar and I would be scout. That is why he chose us but you have something in you which neither Siggi nor I have. The favour of the gods. That is something which you cannot buy and you cannot earn. They like you Hrolf. When we sit around our fires in the village there is often talk about how you disappear into a host of enemies and emerge not only alive but covered in gold and glory. I can scout better than you but if I had gone down the Liger to find Gunnstein Thorfinnson then my bones would lie with his. The Jarl is buying the favour of the gods."

I had much to occupy my mind as I curled up amongst my new furs and blankets. The chests and boxes began arriving soon after dawn the next day. The Jarl and his bride followed. Hallgerd looked much happier and she clung nervously n to the Jarl's arm. He looked slightly embarrassed by the whole thing but that may because of our grins. Sven the Helmsman helped Hallgerd aboard and seated her by the steering board. The slaves were fetched from the slave pens and brought aboard along with the servants she would be bringing. The servants looked a little happier than the slaves who just had resigned looks on their faces. One master was much the same as another.

Finally, when we were loaded the Jarl stood on the quayside waiting. We wondered why until Jarl Gunnstein Berserk Killer arrived with ten warriors and his own hearth-weru. "I come to say farewell to my daughter and my new son." He clasped the forearm of the Jarl and Hallgerd went ashore to hug her father. "And I come with ten warriors. These would crew my new drekar but as it still wants a captain they are anxious for adventure. They would all serve you, Jarl Gunnar Thorfinnson, if you will have them. I have released them from their oath to me and I swear that they are all honourable men. These are not like Harald Black Teeth or Hermund the Bent. When these swear an oath they will keep it."

The Jarl looked at them. Only one had a mail byrnie but they all had swords, shields and helmets. More importantly they were all young. Young warriors were always keen to fight to get better weapons and mail. The Jarl spoke. "You would all serve me and live on Raven Wing Island?"

They all chanted, as one, "Aye Jarl."

"Then come to the raven prow and swear!"

They all marched to the bow and laying their hands on the carved black raven, swore to be the Jarl's oathsworn until death. As we headed out to sea Siggi and Beorn Beornsson had the task of allocating oars. We were crowded with the servants, slaves and cargo. The new men meant we would not be rowing smoothly but

155

the voyage south would show them both the worth of these new members of our clan. As I sat on my chest and took my oar I was happy for a full crew meant we could raid once more. I had spent all of my coin in Dyflin. I needed more to make my new family comfortable.

The rough early winter weather was a good test for our new men. It took us until we had turned east for Siggi and Sven to be happy with the balance of the drekar. Of course when we went to war it would be different. We would not have the slaves and the chest but it was important that the crew pulled together. The extra men proved their value when we were able to row through quite stormy seas. We had more men on the oars than we had had in some time and the drekar seemed to enjoy the extra power which their arms provided.

We had all done so much rowing that we were exhausted by the time we hove to in Raven Wing Bay. The Jarl himself carried his young bride ashore. It was a terrifying experience for her. When she had boarded it had been from a stone quay. What she thought as we ascended the path to her new home I know not. The island did not look its best. It was bleak with waves crashing on to the shore. It took me two trips to take my goods up to the village and I watched Hallgerd as she saw the crude huts and her new hall for the first time. It was not Dyflin. She was young and did not disguise her shock. Perhaps she thought that the home of such a famous jarl would be more imposing.

I left my supplies with Erik One Hand where they would be kept sheltered from the weather. I strode through the rain and mud to my home. I would return with my horses and Gille later. As much as Hallgerd might not like the island and preferred Dyflin was how much I loved the island and disliked towns. Nipper must have smelled or sensed me for he came bounding over when I was still a mile or two from home. His barks brought Mary and Gilles out.

Their beaming smiles made me forget the weather. "Gille, saddle the two horses. We have goods to fetch."

He ran off eagerly. Mary said, "Did you buy all that you sought, master?"

"I did. We will be warm this winter and tomorrow I will build you your own hut."

"I do not mind sharing yours with you and Gille. I am happy."

"You were not born to that. I cannot change your state but I can change your surroundings besides it will still be within my home." I pointed to the western end. "I will take that end out and build your room. It will be safer for Gille and I will guard the entrance. It will be warmer too for it will abut the stables. The horses keep that as warm as a fire does."

"You are too kind, lord."

"I told you that I am not a lord."

"You have no title but you have the bearing."

Gille's voice came from the outside. "Ready!"

I hurried to Dream Strider. I was anxious to get my goods back to my home and then I would be dry again. The weather was a sign that winter would be upon us before we knew it. No one even noticed our return. Hallgerd was the centre of attention and most were gathered in the hall. Vermund was trying to organise quarters for the new servants and slaves. The old slave quarters were no good for they were too far away from the hall. Like me the Jarl would have to do some building. Erik and Brigid helped us pack our goods on the horses. We laid the blankets and furs across the neck of Freyja and Erik loaned us a seal skin cloak to cover them. I hung the pots and bowls from the saddle of Dream Strider. It mattered not if they became wet. We slipped away and headed for my home.

Mary was delighted with the pots and the bowls. She immediately washed the pot for she was determined to use it. I took the furs and blankets in to the house. "Gille, three of these blankets are for the horses. I would not have the foal come to harm because of the cold this winter."

He nodded, "I had them in the stable at night while you were away. We had much wet weather. I will take these to them now."

Mary went to the corner and brought out a cloth covered bowl. "Brigid taught me how to do this when we lived in the village. Here is my first cheese, lord." She took off the cloth and there was a fresh sheep's cheese. I cut a piece and ate it. She had flavoured it with nettles and it was delicious. "This is good."

She gave a little curtsy and smiled, "It is easier than I thought." She then began to babble on about all the other things she had learned and the improvements she would make in the house. It showed a different Mary from the one I had found hiding in the cave. This Mary was content.

The next day was cold but the rain stopped. After examining Gerðr, Gille and I set to work on the new room. I had built my home in the style of the houses of Cyninges-tūn, It was oblong with stone at the base and wattle and daub beneath a turf roof. In Cyninges-tūn they used the local slate to make the roof even more watertight. Here we had to make do with turf. We had been gathering the stones from the beach for some time and that was ready. I had already brought back timber and so we began.

I planned on using the buildings we had. The room would extend from my hut to the wooden stable I had built for my horses. The new room would give protection to both the stable and the house. We would all be warmer. It was simple just to extend two walls. That would give Mary plenty of room for her trade as well as somewhere to sleep. First we laid a floor of the largest and flattest stones over pebbles and small stones. We used sand from the nearby beach to bond it together. We had the new walls up by noon. I say noon but it was impossible to see any sun behind the grey clouds. The roof timbers and the brush upon which the turf would sit was also easy to construct. The wattle and daub, however, was both messy and time consuming. We were aided by the recent rain and by the time night had fallen the framework was complete. The last job we did was to make a small entrance for Gille. He crawled in and lit a small fire which he kept feeding. It would drive any insects from the roof and start to dry the walls. The hard part would come the next day when we added the turf.

The fire was out by morning. When I felt the walls they were not totally dry but that did not matter. It would become drier when the turf roof was added. Laying the turf was both a messy and a tiring job. Gille was small and lithe. He was able to lay the turf on the roof. Then we began to put the turf against the stones. It would make the new room warmer and wind proof. We had just finished it when the rain began again. It was another storm from the west. We went indoors and began to carefully remove the stones from the adjoining wall which would allow us to make a door. We placed the beam I had cut from a solid log above the door and then hung an old blanket from it. When time allowed we would make a door. With the fire lit again we were cosy. We could settle in for the winter. We had food in our store room and I had fish nets in the bay. We would not starve. After the raid by the men of Vannes we had gathered our animals again so that we had milk once more.

Mary moved in to her new room two days later. It suited Gille and I for we had far more room. We had not thought we had been crowded but now that Mary took her things to her own room we saw how much more room we had. I envisaged us rarely leaving my farm for some time to come but that was not to be. A week after our return from Dyflin the Jarl arrived with his hearth-weru, Siggi and Ulf.

Mary peered fearfully from behind the door to my home.

"Welcome, Jarl. I had not expected a visit."

159

"I have to speak with you. We are going to raid and your skills will be needed."

I turned around. Mary could now speak enough of our words and she had heard the word, 'raid'. She disappeared inside the house.

"Pray come into my home. Mary, Gille, fetch beer and cheese. We have guests."

Mary had recovered her composure and brought out the food and drink. The hearthweru stood in the doorway which was just as well. I had only made four crude chairs! The beer was Brigid's but the cheese was Mary's. This one had been soaked for a few days in sea water and had a pleasant salty tang to it. She served up some pickled fish to go with it.

"This is good, Hrolf. You have a fine home."

"Thank you Jarl."

"Before we plan the raid I would tell you that we have decided upon the best way to reward you. You are now Hersir of this farm and this bay. Mary will no longer be the slave of the village but your slave. We all think that would be better."

Hersir! This was an honour. It was but a step away from being a Jarl. "Thank you, lord."

"It probably means little yet but I know that some in the village would live close to this bay for the fishing is easier. If they came here they would be yours to command in my absence." He handed me a small bronze raven on a chain. It had been cast by Bagsecg; I recognised his work. It had been painted black. "Here is the sign that you are Hersir."

I knew that Mary had no idea what a Hersir was but she recognised the gesture and could not conceal the joy on her face.

The Jarl looked pleased with my response. "Now we come to the raid. We had a Thing. We would have invited you but Siggi said that you would be busy and I can see that you have. I will ask you now; do you object to a raid?"

"No lord but I would ask where you would raid?"

Siggi and Ulf exchanged a smile. The Jarl said, "These two said you would say that. Where would you choose?"

"The land to the east of us is in a state of readiness for our attacks. Your brother raided the Liger and we the Issicauna. I am not certain what we would get from it. The men of Vannes will be wary of us and expect a revenge raid after their attack on us. I think we head north to the land of the Saxons or even the Cymri."

"The Cymri are poor and their land filled with mountains."

"True Jarl but not so Ynys Môn. It is flat and there are many beaches that we can use. Aiden, Dragonheart's galdramenn, told me that it is the bread basket of that area. It is rich."

"True but it is a long way to travel and it is winter."

"Then I say the Saxons are rich and they are almost as close as the Franks."

"You agree with Siggi White Hair and Ulf Big Nose then for that was their choice too. Where?"

"Cent. It is rich and the warriors who live there do not use the bow. The Medway and the Temese are both easy to sail and we could raid deep in the heart of the land. Ulf will tell you of the churches there."

"It is true Jarl. They have the largest churches in the land close by those rivers. There are many abbeys and nunneries too. I think that Hrolf is right and we have not yet raided there. The Danes make incursions but they come by land. We would come by sea."

"Then you have persuaded me. We will raid in six days time. That will allow Sven to fit his new ropes." He stood. "Thank you Hersir."

After they had gone I told Mary all that we had said. The words I had taught her were not the words of war but those that she would need to talk to others in the village. "You leave us to go to war?" I nodded. "But it is dangerous. When you went last I heard it was because a whole boat load had perished."

"Some survived."

"But not all. Why must you go? We have all that we need here, lord. I can sew more. "

"I will return."

"You cannot promise for you do not know."

"No I cannot and I will not promise but I tell you that I will come back. You must have faith in what I do. I am confident that the two of you can look after my horses and my house." I stood. "It is not a matter for discussion. I go to war. Come Gille and I will show you how to sharpen my sword on the wheel. Then you can sharpen your own sword when I am gone. Go fetch the weapons." As he went out I said, "And tomorrow I will build you a bread oven. When we took up the turf for your roof I found a patch of clay. It is not large but it is enough to seal an oven. Then you can bake your own bread. It will mean less visits to the village."

She brightened at that. "And perhaps I can get Brigid to teach me how to make ale too."

I worked from dawn until dusk on the farm and then in the house each night fletching my arrows. I had learned how to do it and I trusted my own work. When the time came to leave I was as ready as I could be. The bread oven was made and we had tried it twice. Gille knew how to grind the grain and I left my home confident that the two would survive until I returned.

I called Gille and Mary together just before I left. "The Jarl made me Hersir. He also gave you to me, Mary, as my slave. I will have no slaves here. You, Mary, have your freedom. What say you?"

She dropped to her knees and, crying, began to kiss my hand.

I raised her up, "No, Mary, you are a slave no longer. You do not have to kneel."

She looked at me and I could see that the tears were tears of joy, "No, Hersir, I kneel because I wish to. There is a difference. Take care."

"I will but I leave knowing that the two of you will be safe here together."

Once again we were fully crewed. Our new men took their places. We had a new hearth-weru. Rolf Arneson was a fine warrior and had asked the Jarl if he could join his remaining three. The Jarl accepted his offer. The Jarl would now have four men to watch over him in battle. That was good.

I was the last to board and I received a wry cheer. Rurik and Arne Four Toes gave me mock bows and touched their hair at the front. "We are privileged, master that you will sit with us! We are honoured to have a hersir with us!"

I knew the banter and the mockery would come. It meant nothing to me for it was a title only. It would only mean something if others came to live close by and then they would be my bondi. They would be warriors who would fight under my banner; if I had a banner. Until then I was still Hrolf the Horseman who lived with his horses. The banter went on until we had cleared the island then Siggi started our chant. It was he who chose the one we would use and he picked one which silenced the humour at my expense.

The horseman came through darkest night

He rode towards the dawning light

With fiery steed and thrusting spear

Hrolf the Horseman brought great fear

163

Slaughtering all he breached their line

Of warriors slain there were nine

Hrolf the Horseman with gleaming blade

Hrolf the Horseman all enemies slayed

With mighty axe Black Teeth stood

Angry and filled with hot blood

Hrolf the Horseman with gleaming blade

Hrolf the Horseman all enemies slayed

Ice cold Hrolf with Heart of Ice

Swung his arm and made it slice

Hrolf the Horseman with gleaming blade

Hrolf the Horseman all enemies slayed

In two strokes the Jarl was felled

Hrolf's sword nobly held

Hrolf the Horseman with gleaming blade

Hrolf the Horseman all enemies slayed

The new men had not heard the chant and it took a couple of renditions for them to learn the words. When the wind came to our aid and we shipped our oars they asked about the battle. Rurik told them all. He did so without exaggeration but I could see that the newly acquired warriors were impressed.

Although it was risky we were going to raid the Medway. We knew from earlier voyages along the eastern coast that there were many small, deserted islands where we could lay up. There were settlements there and we would raid the ones by the coast. If we were not discovered then we would venture further up the river. One of the new men thought that there was a bridge from the times of the Romans but we did not know. What he did know was that he had heard there was a large church there. It was a start. The danger in the raid lay in its proximity to Lundenwic. King Egbert hated Vikings and he had appointed his own Jarl to that walled city.

I asked Siggi about the Jarl's new wife. He laughed, "She has settled down. For the first few days she cried and she roared. She hated the village. It was only when the Jarl had new quarters built for her servants that she stopped howling the nights away. Now she seems happier. She enjoys the attention the Jarl gives her. He seems besotted with her. Perhaps when she is with child she will have better things to occupy her."

I knew that we still did not have enough women. We had more single men than those with women. Our clan could only grow if we had more children. Many children were born but not all grew. I did not have too long to think of such things for a storm came up out of nowhere. We had mighty seas which towered over our tiny drekar. It was all that we could do to keep the ship together. In a lull in the storm Harold Fast Sailing commented that this was a good thing as no one would expect raiders out in such weather. He was probably right but it did not make for a comfortable voyage. I was glad that my byrnie was in my chest and wrapped in a sheepskin. I did not want to have to clean rust from it before we raided.

After two days at sea we saw the coast of Cent to the west of us. It was late afternoon although the sky was so dark that it was difficult to tell what time of day it was. We took to our oars for we had used the wind from the south west all the way north but now we would have to use our backs to take us into the shelter of the estuary. We could see nothing as we rowed. We were dependent upon the eyes of the ship's boys and the skill and experience of Sven. He was sailing into unknown waters at night. That was never easy.

Chapter 11

It was a pitch black and cloudy night. There was a faint mist which limited our view as we edged into the estuary. We did not chant and we rowed slowly for Sven took us gently between the mud flats of the mouth into the wider basin which could be seen ahead of us. As soon as we had passed the mouth we noticed that the wind was less strong and the motion of the ship was easier. He held up his hand and Siggi lifted his oar. It was the signal to stop rowing. Sven left the steering board to Harold Fast Sailing and he walked the length of the drekar to stand at the prow. He sniffed as he peered into the gloom. When he returned he nodded to Siggi who slid his oar out and we all copied him. We rowed but I noticed that we had changed direction. We headed south and west. When Sven raised his hand again I knew that we had reached the land. I felt the keel as it slid over mud and then the ship's boys raced ashore to secure us to the land. I could see nothing. There was no sign of where the land began and the sea ended.

As the boys tied us up so we prepared. Ulf and I would need our mail for we would go from scouting to fighting. I put my shield over my back. I left my bow on the drekar. Haaken, one of the ship's boys said as he passed, "It is muddy. Beware." I saw that his breeks were covered in black and sticky mud.

Sven came up to us, "This is not a good place to land but I need you two to find us somewhere better."

Ulf nodded and we went to the side. We lowered ourselves over the strakes of the drekar. Haaken had been right. There was mud and it took us some time to make it to more solid ground. The ground upon which we could stand was three hundred paces from the drekar. Once on the spongy ground Ulf sniffed. I did too. I caught a faint scent from ahead of us. It was the smell of plants. He pointed with his sword and we trotted across the grass. The water was to our right. There were few trees and the bushes were very small. Then I smelled animals or their droppings at least. We reached a path of sorts and I saw that we had been on a narrow strip of land.

Ulf said, "See if it is muddy here. I will check the farm yonder."

I nodded, amazed at Ulf's skill. I had known there was something nearby but Ulf knew exactly where and what it was. I would never be a scout as good as him. I walked towards the water. There was mud by the narrow strip of land but there was a shingle and sand beach which headed north west. I returned to where I had left Ulf.

"It is a better landing site."

"Go and fetch the drekar I will meet you back here."

I ran back until I reached the mud. I did not have to cross it again for the Jarl had Erik Green Eye on guard. I knew that I was far enough from the farm not to be heard and I hailed, Erik, "There is a better place to land. This is a thin strip of land attached to the shore. It is less than two thousand paces to an easier landing. Follow the water around."

"Aye."

I turned and made my way back to where Ulf had been. There was no sign of him and so I headed inland. I would not go far but I had been taught to find out as much as I could. I had gone barely twenty paces when trees loomed up. The ones at the edge were spindly and thin. Most were stunted but as I went further in I saw that they became sturdier. I returned to the meeting point. Ulf loped back. He was out of breath. Behind me I heard the faint sound of oars gently cutting through the still waters.

Ulf said, "There is a village just along from here. There is just a farm in the opposite direction. You watch here and I will tell the Jarl where the village is."

The raven prow appeared out of the dark as the keel grated gently up the shingle. It disappeared as Sven backed water and turned our ship beam on to the shore. It would make for a faster departure and enable the clan to land faster. I peered into the dark looking and listening for signs of an alarm. I heard feet as they splashed in the water and then moved along the sand and shingle. Ulf appeared next to me and nodded. We headed off into the dark. From now on we would use hand signals. We ran in the direction in which Ulf had said that the village lay. Ulf gave me the signal for us to go around to the other side. We would stop any escaping and raising the alarm.

The ground started to rise slightly. Ulf took us off the track and into the woods which grew to the left of us. I doubted that we could have been seen but this path guaranteed that. Ulf had never been here before but he took us unerringly in the right direction. He put his hand up and we stopped. He led us towards the sea again. As the trees thinned I saw that there was a slight rise which had a wooden palisade. It was too dark to see the top but we knew where the village was. We moved back into the trees and this time walked with the small hill to our right. When we had passed the hill Ulf squatted. We would now wait until the Jarl attacked the sleepy settlement. I took the opportunity of taking off my shield. I sat on that. We waited.

As our ears became attuned to the night I heard the sounds of the woods behind us as well as the sea as it surged back and forth. Animals skittered back and forth. Leaves moved as roosting birds prepared for their dawn chorus. When I heard a faint sound from the east which was not natural then I knew the attack was beginning. Ulf and I stood together. I saw him smile approvingly. I slung my shield over my left arm and silently slid my sword from the sheepskin lined scabbard. Ulf's weapon was already in his hand. We moved from the shelter of the woods and, crouching, headed towards the track. There was a shallow ditch along both sides. I guessed this low lying land flooded frequently and the ditch kept the path drier. Ulf went to the one on the river side and I took the other. We crouched down.

Then we heard the clamour of battle as the clan attacked the gates. They must have been poorly made for we heard a crash and then the gates which lay just a hundred paces from where we hid opened. We had not seen them until their opening showed the braziers of the night watch within. A rider burst out. Ulf and I stepped out of the ditch when the horse was just twenty paces from us. We both held our shields out and the startled horse stopped. Ulf's sword slashed at the rider's side and as he tumbled from the back of the saddle I grabbed its reins. A riderless horse galloping into the next town would be as disastrous as a messenger.

I sheathed my sword and stroked the horse's neck to calm him. I led him to the woods and tied his reins to the lower branch of a tree. I returned to Ulf and we stood side by side on the track. The screams and cries from within told us that our men were winning but we saw nothing for they had closed the gates again. Ulf tired of waiting and he led us down to the gate. There was no sentry on the walls. I wondered if Ulf was considering entering the town when the gate opened. As it opened inwards we walked with it. The three warriors and the handful of people who stood there were not expecting two mailed Vikings to be standing there. I think they must have been preparing to flee.

We reacted first. I lunged at the nearest Saxon with my sword. He wore no mail and my sword bit into his stomach. The people who had been with the warriors fled back to the huts. As I pulled my sword out a second warrior hit his axe against my shield. I brought my sword over my head and it struck him in his neck.

My sword bit down into flesh and blood spurted. Ulf had slain the third.

"Close and bar the gates."

I pushed the heavy gates back in position. I had to sheathe my sword for the bar took two arms to lift it and drop it back in position. We were stood together with the three dead Saxons before us when Siggi, Beorn and Rurik raced up. They looked relieved to see us. Siggi nodded, "We wondered if any had escaped."

Ulf spat, "We were told to stop any who tried to escape. Did the Jarl not trust us?"

Beorn laughed, "Nothing would get past you two!"

The drekar was brought down to anchor closer to this village which, we learned from the captives, was called Gyllingas. The men of the village had died fighting. They had grain and, as dawn broke we began to load it aboard the drekar. A cow was slaughtered and put on a large fire to cook. The Jarl came over to Ulf and me. "The captives tell me that there is a larger place just down the river. It is called Hrofecester. We cannot get further upstream because there is a bridge there. I think there is a small huddle of huts between here and this large town. It is called Cetham. Take six men and capture it."

Ulf turned and went into the village to choose the men. I took the opportunity of returning the horse to its stable. Ulf had chosen young men who could run. Beorn Fast Feet, Ketil Eriksson and his brother Knut One Eye were three while he also picked Karl Swift Foot, Sigtrygg Red Hair and Gunnstein Gunnarson. "We have to take a small village. We will run there. Hrolf take Beorn and Karl run around the village and attack from the far side. No one escapes."

I slung my shield over my back and we began to run. We did not have far to go. It was low lying land and the village was slightly raised above the surrounding land. It was still misty and

171

we saw shadows not houses. We crossed a shallow beck and I smelled the fires from the huts. I led my two men up stream and we ran again using the muddy, swampy, folds in the land to hide us from the huts I knew were not far away. When I thought we had gone far enough I turned and moved cautiously through the trees to the fields I saw before us. Cetham was a miserable little place. There were four huts. It was still early but I saw two men by the shore examining their nets. Even as we moved towards them one of them glanced east and saw the mast of the drekar. He shouted the alarm and we hurried to meet them.

Karl Swift Foot and Beorn Fast Feet lived up to their names and they reached the two men before they could get to the huts. They slew them. Our arrival drove the other villagers towards Ulf and the others. They were soon stopped. The mist lifted, almost as though it had been pulled up by the gods, or the Norns. I turned and saw, less than two thousand paces from us, a walled village on a high piece of ground. It was bigger than Gyllingas and I saw, rising above the walls, a tower. It had a well made church. It had to be Hrofecester. Here would be treasure. I ran back to Ulf.

"I think I have found Hrofecester. It has a good wall and a church but it is close enough for them to see us here. From the tower they might be able to see the drekar."

He turned to the Eriksson brothers, "Take the captives and the animals back to the drekar. Tell the Jarl we have found Hrofecester but we need to strike now before the drekar is seen." As the brothers herded the captives to travel the mile and a half back to the drekar, Ulf waved us towards the woods. "If there is a bridge then we need to stop any from escaping that way. Come."

He was not daunted at the prospect of four men holding off however many warriors were in the town. We were Raven Wing Clan and we were warriors. I could see, from the land over which we travelled, that this Hrofecester had water on three sides. I guessed that there would be a ditch before it. We needed to get to the branch of the river which headed west and approach the bridge with stealth. I had seen Roman bridges before. They were made of stone and not wood. Climbing one would be very hard and so we would need to sneak along the river bank. I hoped that the four men we had with us were able to do what I knew Ulf and I could do- disappear. The people of this town had cleared the trees and farmed the land for a hundred paces around. We used the woods they had left for cover.

I followed Ulf and the other four walked behind me. Suddenly Ulf stopped and held up his hand. I sniffed as I had seen Ulf do many times. I could smell men. They smelled differently to us. Once I could smell them I heard them as they walked towards us through the woods. I silently drew my sword. We could not see them and we used our ears and noses to tell us when they were close. I left my shield over my back. Ulf lunged forward and I went to my left. The surprised hunter had good reactions and his bow was coming up even as I ran him through with Heart of Ice.

Ulf turned to the others, "Strip the bodies of treasure and then hide them. Follow Hrolf and me."

When I had smelled the men I had also smelled the river and thirty paces from where we had slain the hunters we saw the river. The tide was heading out and there were mud flats. It would make our approach difficult. We found a good vantage point from which to view the bridge and the town while we waited for the others to hide the bodies. The walls, some two hundred paces from us were made of wood but they were substantial. I could not see it but I knew that there would be a ditch around it. The tower of the church was clearly visible. I saw no watch on the walls and, being winter, no one worked the fields. The pillars of the bridge could be seen and they were stone. This was a Roman bridge.

The other four joined us. Ulf led us to the river. There was a bank and we slid down it. We had cover from the town walls and we moved along the river treading the narrow line between the bank and the cloying mud. As it was winter there were few river birds which might be startled by our approach and we headed towards the bridge. I could see, at the far end, a wooden gate. There would be guards there. I hoped they would be looking north. As we neared the walls I saw that the only way we could ascend the bridge was by climbing the stone pillar close to the land. It was as high as two men.

Surprisingly we reached the bridge unseen. Ulf pointed to Gunnstein Gunnarson and Karl Swift Foot when we sheltered close to the end of the stone bridge. They took Karl's shield and held it between them. Ulf slipped his shield behind his back as I did and we sheathed our swords. Ulf climbed on the shield and the other two raised him into the air. He leapt up to grab hold of the parapet and plant his feet on the stone ledge which supported the bridge. I jumped on the shield and was propelled upwards. Ulf had vacated the ledge and slipped over the top. As I followed him I saw that the gate to the town was still open. Just then I heard a bell tolling. Had we been seen? When no arrows came in our direction I guessed that the drekar had been seen or the clan, advancing down the road. Even as we hurried the twenty steps to the gate two guards saw us and shouted something. The door slammed shut. I saw Sigtrygg and Beorn as they began to help Karl to clamber up. A spear clattered into Beorn's shield across his back.

Ulf and I ran back to help. We held our shields above our heads and then over our comrades as they climbed up. The worth of our shields was shown that day as arrows and spears tried to penetrate their defence. They failed. With all six of us on the bridge we had a decision to make. Ulf took it. "We run to the middle and stand back to back. If they want this bridge then they have to take it from us. Pick up any spears that you can. Perhaps we can return them to their owners eh?"

Ulf was enjoying himself. I saw an unbroken spear which had hit the metal boss of my shield. I picked it up and, still holding the shield behind me I ran to the middle. Ulf said, "Hrolf you Sigtrygg and Karl watch the far end."

The bridge was just a little wider than our three shields but not by much. The six of us were a barrier. We were far enough from the two ends to be safe from spears and all but the most accurately aimed arrow. If they wished us removed then they would have to winkle us out and that would take men from the defence of the town. I saw that there were six men at the far end of the bridge in the gatehouse. They had a dilemma. Could the six of them attack us and remove us? They obviously thought not for they stayed where they were. Their problem was that the gate on the bridge was designed to stop an enemy getting on to the bridge and not from it. I saw the men as they peered at us. They were town watch. They had no mail and crude leather helmets. They had spears and shields. The shields I could see were just made of wood.

"Ulf, I think we can take the six men at the far end of the bridge. If we held the far end then it would help the Jarl."

"You can do it?"

"I think so but in any case we can whittle their numbers down. I see no mail."

"Then go. May the Allfather be with you."

I turned to the others. "We walk as though we are in the shield wall."

Karl said, "Let us chant then. It will fright our foes."

Raven Wing Clan goes to war,

A song of death to all its foes

The power of the raven grows and grows.

The power of the raven grows and grows.

The power of the raven grows and grows.

As usual the chant kept the beat and our shields were as one. The end of the bridge was just thirty paces from us. I did not understand the words of the men there but someone shouted orders and spears were hurled at us. They were wasted; they should have saved them for when we struck. We saw the missiles coming and ducked beneath the trim of our shields. When they hit we raised our heads again. We did not slow as we marched. They would have been better going for our legs but they saw our shields and aimed at them but they did no damage. Their leader quickly stood with three of his men ain a line with two more behind. Their shields were smaller than ours. Having hurled their spears they were unarmed. Sigtrygg reached around with his spear and broke the shaft of the spear which was embedded in his shield.

It was we who held spears. Even though they had been used they would strike the enemy before they could fight back. I had to time this right. "Charge!" When we were four paces away we charged with our spears above our shields. I punched with my spear a heartbeat before our shields clashed. My spear entered the eye of the one who gave orders. The two behind were splattered with blood, brains and gore as the head of the spear smashed through the back of his skull. They both ran. Opening the gate they fled towards the road to Lundewic.. Karl had also wounded his man and the last two, realising they were outnumbered also ran. These were not warriors. This was the town watch. As Sigtrygg despatched the last man I shouted. "Close the gate!" Karl obeyed and then I turned and shouted, "Ulf, we have this gate!"

Even as I shouted I saw that the gates to the town had opened and warriors were coming towards us. Had the Jarl's attack failed?

Ulf and the other two ran towards us. They picked up the spears as they passed them. "We will hold them here. You did well Hrolf. It is our turn now. Shield wall."

There were just six of us in the shield wall. I stood behind Ulf and held my shield angled to protect his head and me. I pushed my spear through the gap to rest on his shoulder. We started to sing

176

as they approached. This time it was not to help us march but to put fear into their hearts. We sang a little louder each verse.

Raven Wing Clan goes to war,

A song of death to all its foes

The power of the raven grows and grows.

The power of the raven grows and grows.

The power of the raven grows and grows.

It worked for they slowed. This was not the town watch who approached but some of the warriors from the town. The leader had a full length byrnie but he had a white beard. He was an old man. Only Ulf had a full byrnie in our front rank but the other two had mail shirts which covered their bodies. Our shields and helmets would protect us. Those alongside the old Eorledman had smaller shields than us and open helmets. Their spears shook a little as they approached. They outnumbered us but we were the wolves from the north. Their priests told them tales of us to inspire fear. Before they had even met us we already held an advantage. The fact that we stood and did not move was worrying for our enemies.

"Brace!" When Ulf sensed that they were going to charge we all stepped forward on our left legs and locked shields.

The Eorledman shouted, "Charge! For King Baldred!" I knew enough of their language to understand most of the words.

We needed no orders to use our spears. We had done this before. We punched them at the faces. Mine went into the cheek and tore a hole in the side of the face of the warrior who faced me. Their spears clattered and banged against our wall of wood and iron. They were not using the advantage of weight of numbers. The ones behind were waiting for their chance to fight rather than pushing behind their warriors in the front rank. As the man I had hit reeled from the line Sigtrygg, in the fore stabbed at the unprotected middle of the man revealed by the fleeing warrior.

177

Karl next to me saw his chance and plunged his spear into the side of the man nearest the edge of the bridge. He punched with his shield and the man toppled into the river.

Ulf shouted, "Forward!"

We were all using spears and it was hard to use them properly. I saw Ulf, as he stepped forward, head butt the Eorledman in the face. I was pushing into Ulf's back and the Eorledman lost his balance and tumbled backwards. Ulf had fast reactions and his spear stabbed into the thigh of the leader. As blood spurted his oathsworn dragged him from our spears. As we stepped forward into the gap Sigtrygg, Beorn, Karl and Gunnstein Gunnarson took advantage and their spears came back bloody. There are moments in battle when you seize your chances. This was one such opportunity. Ulf yelled, "Charge!"

I hurled my spear at one of the oathsworn who was helping the Eorledman to his feet and drew Heart of Ice. My spear struck him in the leg. I roared, "Heart of Ice and the Raven Wing Clan!" I brought it across the side of the head of the wounded warrior. It bit through to bone and he fell dead. The last two oathsworn used their shields to protect them as the Eorledman was helped back to the gates of Hrofecester. Some of those from the town were so afraid of us that they panicked and fell as they fled. They were quickly slain. We halted twenty paces from the gates for arrows and javelins as well as lead balls were hurled at us.

Ulf shouted, "Hide inside your walls but it will avail you nothing! We are Raven Wing Clan!" We all joined in the chant.

" Raven Wing Clan!"

" Raven Wing Clan!"

" Raven Wing Clan!"

There was silence after the third chant and Ulf said, "Let us go back to the other end!"

We walked backwards as missiles slammed and cracked into our shields and pinged off our helmets. Had we worn helmets such as the Saxons wore then we would have been hurt but each of us had invested his money wisely in well made helmets and leather caps beneath them.

When we reached the other end we slipped inside the chamber which the guards had used. There was bread, cheese and ham as well as beer. "Hrolf, keep watch while we eat. We will save you some!"

I walked back onto the bridge. Below I saw the body of the man who had plunged to his death. I lay my shield down and sheathed my sword as I climbed the ladder to the walkway above the bridge. I peered north west. I could see the Roman Road headed towards Lundenwic. Were the guards heading for there or was there another burgh closer? I did not think it mattered. It would take time to get here and if our encounter on the bridge was a measure of the defenders of this town then we would be gone before they would find us. I turned to look at the burgh at the other end of the bridge. There did not seem to be many men on the gate and I could hear, in the distance, the sound of fighting. The Jarl and the rest of our band were attacking.

"Hrolf!" I descended as I heard my name called. Karl stood there. "I will watch now. The cheese is good but the beer is like cow's piss!"

I was thirsty. Combat always made me so and I drank the horn down without even tasting it. I took my seax and cut a hunk of bread and smeared it with the runny goat's cheese. I pointed with my seax towards the town, "I think the Jarl is attacking. There are not many men on the gate here." I began to eat.

"You think to attack the gate?" I nodded. "With six men?"

I swallowed and washed it down with some beer. "Some of the Saxons had axes. When we chased the guards into the open gate I saw that the wooden walkway would given an attacker

179

shelter. They would have to use arrows from the corner towers and we have shields to protect two axe men."

The others nodded and Ulf said. "I would rather do that than sit on my arse and wait for the Jarl to take the burgh. Besides it might draw more men to this gate." He pointed to the bridge. "Gunnstein Gunnarson, Beorn Fast Feet go and find some axes. Sigtrygg find as many undamaged spears as you can."

There were four good axes. Sigtrygg and Gunnstein Gunnarson were the biggest warriors. We called down Karl and explained our plan. Ulf said, "Karl and Beorn use your shields to protect these two. Use the axes to break down the gate. When one is blunt take another. Hrolf and I will use the spears to keep their heads down." He shook his head, "I knew we should have brought our bows!"

As we marched down the bridge, with shields held before us, the defenders began shouting. They sent arrows our way but Saxons are not the best of archers. Their bows are poor and their arrows badly made. Those that struck us found only our shields. While the other four ran to the shelter of the walkway Ulf and I began to throw the six spears we had each found. We chose our targets. Ulf managed to hit one warrior. I feinted each time a head peered over. After Ulf's fine hit they were wary. When I had feinted three times one archer raised himself above the wooden palisade. This time I did not feint and my spear plucked him from the walls. I heard his body crash to the ground below. The two men with axes were making deep gouges in the door. They were striking at the join so that they would be able to hack the bar eventually.

Ulf hurled a second spear. It did not kill the archer but he managed to hit his arm. I heard arrows striking the shields as men loosed from the corner towers. They were beyond our range. Suddenly one struck my helmet and made my head ring. I turned to the right and saw the archer. I would remember him. I turned and hurled my spear at the gate for I glimpsed a face. My spear cracked into a helmet and the man fell, stunned. The archers on the towers had become emboldened now and were directing their arrows at us rather than the four at the gate. When an arrow hit Ulf's helmet too he said, "To the gate, Hrolf. They are almost through."

As we ran to the gate I could see that a gap was appearing. Soon they would be able to strike at the bar. I dropped my spears and took out my sword. It was Gunnstein Gunnarson who struck the last blow. We were ready and the four of us still holding shields hit the gate as one. The other two picked up their own shields and we ran into the town. Those who had been on the gate began to clamber down to fight us. Karl ran at a ladder and hit it with his shield. The ladder and the three men who were descending crashed to the ground. Beorn and I were amongst them and with swift strikes with our swords they were slain.

"Shields!"

We joined together and locked shields. This time Ulf and I were in the centre with swords held above them. A dozen warriors had gathered to attack us and when they ran at our wooden wall they discovered how hard it is to kill a Viking. My sword darted out and plunged into the chest of a screaming Saxon who had made the mistake of raising his axe as he moved his shield to allow him to strike at my head. I twisted as I pulled it out and felt it grate along his breast bone. Six blows meant six of our enemies either dead or wounded. Our weapons were far superior to those of the defenders and they had poor mail.

Ulf knew that we had taken the initiative and we had to exploit it. We would not wait to be attacked, we would attack them! "At them!"

Their attack broken we burst upon them. My sword was longer than those which the Saxons and Jutes before us held. They hit my shield; I hit their shoulders, their helmets and their upper arms. I whirled my blade around so quickly that I mesmerized those I fought. Then I felt a blow to my back. I turned and saw the archer who had hit my helmet. I ran at him. He had been so confident that he had killed me that he was already looking for another target. Even as he loosed one at Sigtrygg's back I brought my sword down so hard on his unprotected head that it was cracked in two and my sword buried itself in his throat. I pulled it out. Sigtrygg had an arrow in his shoulder. I suspected I did too but I felt as though I could still fight and there were enemies before us.

Ulf shouted, "To the front gate!"

I pulled my shield around and gritted my teeth. I would ignore the blood I could feel seeping down my back. I said to Sigtrygg as we tightened into a wedge, "You have an arrow in your back!"

He laughed, "As do you! It does not hurt much and we have a chance for glory! We can win the gate for the clan!"

Sigtrygg and I were close behind Ulf. The others had seen our wounds and they were tight behind us. I heard cries and screams as Karl and Beorn slew any who approached as we ran through the huts and houses of the burghs. It was not a large town. As we passed the wooden cathedral I saw the gate ahead. Men had propped wood against it but, even so, it was bulging and I could hear the sound of axes upon it. Once again we were outnumbered but, as Ulf Big Nose shouted, "Charge!" there was a collective wail of despair as the defenders realised that we had breached their walls and they were being attacked from two sides.

We threw ourselves into the Saxons who defended the gate. They were not mailed and my sword raked down the chest of a warrior who turned in surprise as Ulf took the head of the man next to him.

"Hrolf, Sigtrygg, open the gates. Shield wall!"

Our four comrades turned to face the Saxons and Jutes who had rallied to eject us from their burgh. I dropped my shield. My shoulder was aching and I sheathed my sword. I began to throw the beams and timbers to the ground. I felt myself weakening. Sigtrygg and I reached the bar as I heard Karl Swift Foot shout, "Hurry!"

Sigtrygg managed to lift the bar from the gate but, as we threw it to the side he fell to the ground. I pulled on the door but my head felt light and suddenly I saw blue sky and then I saw nothing. I saw blackness.

Chapter 12

I was in a black drekar with a dragon prow and the ship was sailing down a long black tunnel. I could almost touch the sides. There was no wind and yet it moved. I was alone on the boat. I heard a roaring and the boat began to move faster. There was a light at the end of the tunnel and I prayed to the Allfather that I would see daylight again. Suddenly the drekar pitched over the edge of the world and I was thrown from the drekar. My arms flailed as I tried to regain my balance. I went round and round; over and over. The ground rushed up at me. I noticed that it was rich green grass. Surely I would be crushed and then, as I landed, I found myself on the back of a golden stallion with a blond mane. With a sword in my hand I galloped across the grass and behind me I saw a line of Vikings, also mounted on horses. Each bore a lance and a long shield. As I turned to shout I saw Siggi White Hair. He was seated upon a rock and he shouted to me, "Hrolf! Come back! Hrolf! Come back!"

I opened my eyes and saw Siggi. His face was creased and frowned with worry. He smiled as I opened my eyes. "I thought you had gone to Valhalla." His fingers took Heart of Ice from my hand. "I gave you your sword in case the Allfather had need of you. You gave us a scare. You had lost much blood."

I tried to speak but no words came out. Siggi poured beer into my mouth. I was parched. "How long have I lain here?"

"You opened the gate two days since. We have captured the burgh and we have much treasure. We awaited only your awakening. The drekar is ready to leave. The priests and nobles from Cantwareburh paid ransom so that we did not destroy their cathedral nor slaughter their priests. We have no need to sell the books of the White Christ for they bought them from us. We are rich. However we have no slaves and no women. We must seek them elsewhere. " He turned and I closed my eyes. I heard him say, "You four pick up his bed and carry him to the drekar."

When I felt movement I opened my eyes as the memory of the last fight entered my head. "And Sigtrygg Red Hair?"

Siggi shook his head, "It seems he did not wish for life as much as you. He died soon after we captured the burgh. He lost more blood than you had. Perhaps the wound from Andecavis never healed properly. He is with his Jarl now. You gave him a longer life and the chance to die with a sword in his hand. You sent him to Valhalla and he will be forever beholden to you."

I looked up and saw that the four who carried me were Erik Long Hair and three others from Gunnstein Thorfinnson's crew. Even Olaf the Bear carried me. Erik looked down and said, "Sigtrygg knew he owed you a life. It was his greatest honour to fight alongside you." He nodded to Ulf Big Nose. "Ulf told us what you all did at the bridge. That is an end any Viking would be proud of. We were in your debt before, now we too owe you a life."

I closed my eyes. They were happy with Sigtrygg's death. I wished he was alive. I had been proud to fight with him. When I opened them I said to Siggi. "Can we leave safely? Will not the men of Cent try to stop us?"

"They may for we took much gold but they would have to capture our ship. Do not worry. There are others in the clan who have much to do to equal the achievements of the six of the bridge." He shook his head. "I wish I had been there. That will be a tale told around the fires all winter. Six of you took three gates and a bridge. The Eorledman will never fight again and the Saxons and Jutes speak of the clan with fear. What a fight!"

I was carried gently aboard and laid by Sven at the helm. I think they must have put a draught in my beer for I kept drifting in and out of sleep. I woke in the dark of night and the drekar was rising and falling like a fiery stallion. I looked up and saw Sven at the steering board. "Fear not Hrolf for the Norns and the Gods watch over you. They sent this storm when four Saxon ships tried to close with us. Two were sunk by the fierce winds and strong seas and the other two fled. Men say it is you and your luck which brought the sea to our aid. I care not so long as my drekar is safe. Now sleep. We have far to travel."

Each time I woke I was given beer and told to sleep. The drekar smelled of animals for we had ransomed the people and the books but not the animals. The grain also lay in our holds. The men of Cent would speak of us in fear for years to come. I would have been happy to rise but I was kept in my bed until we reached the bay of the haunted farmhouse.

I was carried ashore and the Jarl himself accompanied me. "We will not raid again this winter, hersir, you can rest and care for your family and your animals. When Spring comes we will plan raids for we need women. We have brought your share of the raid and Mary and Gille watch it for you. Your wound should be healed but Siggi has said that you should not exert yourself for the arrow went deeper than we thought. We have your mail and Bagsecg will repair it for you." He clasped my arm. "I am honoured that you are in my clan."

When he had gone Mary and Gille rushed back in, "Your are hurt! I knew it! I had bad dreams while you were away!" Mary threw her arms around me and sobbed.

Gille nodded, "It is true, lord. She woke me with her screams."

Mary stood and pointed an accusing finger at me, "Ulf Big Nose told us that you need rest. You shall not stir until Siggi White Hair says that you are well. We almost lost you!" She rushed out.

"Do you think she is a volva, Gille?" He did not know the word I could see that. "A witch? Can she foretell the future?"

"I think she is happy here. When you went away she cleaned our house and tried to make it perfect for you then she had the dream. I know not if she is a witch. I did not think that Christians had witches."

"Nor did I but I have heard of the power of dreams. I have dreams which seemed very vivid but I have never had a dream which predicted an event. We will get life back to normal now. I shall tell Siggi when he next comes that I am well and she will be happy then." He nodded. "How is Gerðr?"

"She grows large and each day I feel for the foal." He frowned. "I have only helped a mare to foal once. I am not certain that I will be strong enough to birth her on my own."

"If you tell me what to do then I will use my strength. Your father birthed many horses?"

"He did. It was not just the horses of our lord he birthed but those who lived close by us. I learned everything from him. They called him the horse master."

"You have never told me of your family."

187

"We lived on the Issicauna, the southern shore and the men from the south came to raid. They came for the horses and, I think, my father, but he fought them and hurt the lord who captured me. They slew him and took me instead. I think that is why they whipped me to punish me for my father's actions. They wanted him to care for their horses and they were left with me; they called me the whelp. My father was a good man and I think of him each time I groom the horses. I see his face in every pail of water I fetch for them."

It was some time before Mary returned. I think she had been calming and cleaning her face. She brought in some bread. It was still warm. She had some cheese; it was flecked with wild herbs. "Here is food. You need you strength building. Gille, empty the fish traps." She was running my home now. Where was the timid slave who had cowered in Seara's doorway? Then she smiled at me. It was the start of my life getting back to normal.

Siggi did not come for two days. We had the first hard frost of the winter followed by an icy wind. Only Gille braved it to see to the horses. When Siggi arrived and examined my wound he sniffed it and seemed satisfied. "There is no smell to the wound. You can move from your bed. If I were you I would not rush to use your left arm. There will be no more raids until the new grass comes."

As Mary walked in with bread, fresh from our oven his eyes lit up. "Why, you live as a prince here! Fresh bread and goat's cheese too. I may well have my own hut built nearby and call you hersir!"

"I found some clay and it enabled me to make an oven. This is a good island but it does not have all that we need."

As he ate the bread and cheese he said, "You would still live on the mainland?"

I nodded, "Not yet for we are too few in numbers but when we outgrow this island then we should." I pointed north. "Even the rocky land to the north of us has vast empty areas with timber and game. The Issicauna is even richer and more fertile. It is even better than the land of Cent for the climate is gentler."

"That is something, perhaps, for the future but for now this will do." He stood, "Sigurd and Skutal have asked the Jarl if they and their families can move here when the new grass comes. It makes sense for they are fishermen. The seas to the south are more dangerous than your sheltered bay and as you are here they do not fear the ghosts of the dead."

"They are welcome for there is space here." Although I said that I did not feel it in my heart. I enjoyed the privacy we three had.

"Jarl Gunnar Thorfinnson said that they would have to acknowledge you as their lord if they did so. You are hersir here."

I fingered the amulet around my neck, "So it is not merely a title?"

"No, you will be responsible for guarding this bay. It pleases us in the village for you are like a rock. And now I must go. I fear the Allfather will be sending us a harsh winter. I feel it in my bones."

We had no Aiden, the galdramenn, or Kara, the volva, but we made do with Siggi White Hair's predictions when it came to weather as well as healing our hurts. Most of his weather predictions proved to be accurate. This one was. We had snow. In all the time we had been here we had only had a covering of snow for a day and then it was gone but this snow fell for four days and it lay. The blankets I had bought proved to be a good investment and the horses were comfortable. The stable was warmer as my house and Mary's quarters protected it from northern winds. The horses seemed quite comfortable. As Mary could no longer do work for those in the village she made items for the three of us. I had brought material back from Dyflin. It was not the most colourful but it would suit our needs. Gille seemed to grow each day. I think his mistreatment had held him back but now that he was well fed he grew rapidly. I had no doubt that by the end of the year he would be the same size as Mary. She had done her growing but now her body was blossoming too.

While we could not go far I taught Gille how to make and fletch arrows. We had made him a bow for I had found a yew tree at the north of the island. When the weather improved we would go outside and I taught him to use a bow and a sword. We also made his first shield. It would not be as big as mine for he was not yet fully grown but it would protect him if we had to fight. We would die to defend this land. He had no helmet and so Mary and I made him a leather cap. I had worn one when I had first gone to Cyninges-tūn. Mary wished to use a bow for she wanted to protect herself but she had not the strength and so Gille and I taught her to use a slingshot instead. She became so good that she was able to bring down seabirds, pigeons and doves. We ate better.

That winter was the best of times. We were alone and we were happy. My horses also prospered from our improvements and with the grain we had brought from Cent, they ate well in the winter. On the shortest day we celebrated Mary's god. It seemed his birth was in the depths of winter. I did not mind. She called him the one god as did Gille. I called him a god and we all celebrated the birth of a god.

The earth and the soil were warming when Sigurd and Skutal came to speak with me. Forewarned in time before winter I had been expecting their visit. I knew that the new grass would bring changes but I did not wish our idyll to be spoiled.

"Hrolf the Horseman we ask permission to live here in this bay."

Sigurd Einarsson was the elder of the two brothers. Their father had been a warrior. He had died in battle not long after we had come to the island. The two boys had taken up fishing to provide for their mother. She had died the year after Einar. Now the two were married with young wives. The brothers were pleasant and hard working. They had both been on raids with us as ship's boys but since we had our new warriors from Dyflin they could stay at home and fish. They both seemed to enjoy fishing more than fighting. Our clan had many parts.

I nodded, "Siggi White Hair has told me that the Jarl has sanctioned this. I am happy but I ask that you build your huts closer to the sea. I have no doubt that the two of you and your wives will have children. I have horses and I hope to increase the herd."

Skutal nodded, "That suits us, Hrolf for we wish to build our homes by the water. We know that the bay is quieter and we would be close to our boats."

"I have fish traps there. You would need to avoid them."

"We know." Sigurd smiled, "We sailed around during the winter. We think that we have a place in mind. It is on the opposite side of the bay from the ghosts. Our wives are fearful of the dead."

"They have never bothered us but I understand their fear. I am afraid there is little turf there."

"I know. We intend to bring some from the huts we now have."

And so it was settled. The first settlers came to my bay. The small settlement became known as Hrolfstad. I did not name it; others did. They are always the best names for it shows that it is *wyrd*.

Before spring had truly arrived the Jarl held another Thing. We all remembered the acrimony of the one when he and his brother had parted. It was for that reason that Siggi pressed me to attend. I had not attended one and it was seen as discourteous to the rest of the clan.

"You may not give much thought to your title but it holds sway. Ulf Big Nose, too, has been made hersir for he now lives in the north of the island. Already there are two other families who wish to go with him for there is good pasture in the sheltered dells for sheep."

"You should be hersir, Siggi White Hair. You are the one the people respect and listen to. The Jarl relies on you more than his hearth-weru."

"And I will continue to advise him. I am happy living in the warrior hall. Ulf Big Nose likes to be alone as do you. I prefer the company of people. It is in my nature."

"Then I will come and I will bring Mary and Gille. They have hidden away here long enough. I wish the people to know that they are my family."

I told them both that we would be travelling the following day to the village. Surprisingly Mary seemed content. However I noticed that she spent most of the afternoon and evening preparing for the trip. She had a new dress she had sewn. She went to the sea and bathed and then used water soaked with rosemary and thyme to make her smell sweetly. She washed and combed her hair until it shone. When we were ready to go she rode Freyja while Gille walked behind. I rode Dream Strider. The three of us looked well dressed compared with those in the village.

When we arrived I saw that Hallgerd was now with child and she had a large bump before her. She had not met Mary before and when we arrived she asked Mary about the clothes she wore. When Mary told her that she had sewn them herself then the two of them sat closeted together. Now Mary had two women in the village to whom she could speak, Brigid and Hallgerd. It made me happier.

When all had arrived and were seated the Jarl began, "It does not seem but a moment ago when we stood discussing our raid and much has happened since then. I am married and to be a father. Ulf Big Nose and Hrolf the Horsemen are the first of my hersir. But amongst that joy is the sadness that I have lost a brother, most of his crew and some of my hearth-weru. So when I ask do we raid this year and if so where then I would have each man speak from his heart. Let no one keep silent."

Lars Larsson was one of the new warriors who had joined us in Dyflin. He stood and spoke, "I care not where we raid so long as we do. A warrior needs to raid to show he has skills. Why not Cent? We all made much coin there."

Siggi stood, "And do you not think that they will be watching for us? They were taught a harsh lesson last year. They will have more towers and guards."

"But we are warriors!"

Ulf Big Nose stood, "Look around and tell me how many warriors you see? We have one boat crew. We were lucky last year. Had not Hrolf the Horseman chosen to have us attack the gate then we might still be trying to gain entry and many more warriors would have died."

Erik Long Hair asked, "Hrolf, will you give us your views? I would be interested for it seems to me that you never do anything which is not well thought out."

I stood. I knew that as hersir I had responsibility but I preferred to listen. "I will Erik but I ask the Jarl a question first. What does the clan need?"

He looked surprised, "Need? We need to be richer!" Some men began banging their shields.

I shook my head, "I have been on every raid and I have gold and silver enough. I thought |I needed coin but this winter has shown me that I do not. I can only wear one byrnie at time and I have enough coins to pay Bagsecg to repair my helmet and mail. We took enough grain last year but we will need some more. It is not gold we seek, Jarl Thorfinnson, it is women." I waved a hand around the gathering. "How many men have a woman? Not enough. Lars Larsson would like us to gain some glory by attacking somewhere big. To do that we need another drekar and we need more men. We can buy a drekar but we all know we cannot buy men. At least we cannot buy men we can rely on."

As I sat I saw people nodding. Eiril Jorgesson stood. He too was a warrior from Dyflin. "I think that raiding for women is necessary but I still wish to try my sword against an enemy."

The Jarl stood and nodded to me, "You have come up with a good suggestion, Hrolf the Horseman. I will ask now, who knows of somewhere that we could raid to get women and let our warriors prove their worth?"

It was Sven the Helmsmen who came up with the answer, "The land of the Cymri. The women there are as tough as those from Hibernia and they have grain. We can raid the Sabrina or Ynys Môn. They are further away than Cent but they do not have burghs." He smiled, "They do have fierce warriors and they have archers who will test your armour, Eiril Jorgesson."

Lars Larsson stood, "I have heard of the men of Cymri although I have never fought them. I think this is a good suggestion."

We all looked at the Jarl. We had debated but the decision would be confirmed by him. He stood, "We will raid the land of the Cymri. We will try the Sabrina first for it is close." He smiled at his wife. "Soon my son will be here and I would hold him in my arms, arms which are covered in Welsh gold! We know that they have women but there are gold mines in that land. The Dragonheart found much."

The mention of the Dragonheart was a cause for nods of agreement. He was seen as the one chosen by the gods. If we copied his actions then we could not go wrong. The announcement was a cause of celebration for almost all. The exception was Mary. She did not flee in tears but her face was clouded and covered in frowns.

Sven raised his arm, "First we need to overhaul the drekar. We will do that at Hrolfstad. We can pull her from the water.

Tomorrow I will sail her around the island just after dawn." He looked at me and I nodded.

Siggi put his huge arm around me. "We will bring the beer and the bread. You will not have to feed the army which will descend."

I said, "But I will need to travel back now for I will have to warn Sigurd and Skutal. Their homes are close to the beach and the wooden quay."

"I had forgotten. You take your duties as hersir seriously then?"

"I cannot let the Jarl down. He did me honour with the appointment."

I went to fetch Mary. She was still talking with Hallgerd. I had never seen the Jarl's wife so happy. "I have told Mary that I shall be coming tomorrow. I am anxious for her to make me some fine clothes such as she wears."

I bowed, "We would be honoured to have you as our guest."

We headed for Gille who had already saddled the horses. As we walked he said, "Will I be coming with you on the raid?"

"I think not. The horses will need all of your attention until the foal is come. Would you wish to come?" He hesitated. "Be honest with me Gille as I am with you. I will not be offended whatever you say."

"Then I would rather stay here. I will defend this home with my life but I am no sailor and the thought of sailing close to the edge of the world frightens me. I will guard our home."

I was quite touched that he said, *'our home'*. I had tried to make it so.

"And you Mary? What are your thoughts?"

"I would have you home safe and without an arrow in your body."

I laughed, "That was blunt. This will not be as dangerous. We will choose somewhere which is undefended by walls and I will have my armour."

She smiled, "You will have more than armour!" Enigmatically she said no more.

When we reached the farmstead Gille and I saw to the horses and Gille fed and watered Gerðr. "I will go and speak with Skutal and Sigurd."

The two young fishermen had already been fishing and they were salting some fish. Their wives were both with child and they were gutting a second batch of fish. I guessed that would be cooked fresh.

"We have spare fish lord, if you want some?"

I spied some octopus which lay on the rocks. "What will you do with that?"

"Use it for bait. We do not like the taste nor the texture."

"Then I will have it for I am partial to it."

"You are welcome lord and we will save any more we find for you. We normally throw it back. This bay is rich enough with fish, crabs and shellfish. A man wants for nothing here."

"I have to tell you then the Jarl is bringing *'Raven's Wing'* here on the morrow to clean her hull and repair her."

"That will not bother us. Besides there is another small bay to the west we thought to fish. It might be a good thing to let the fish in the bay alone for a day or two. They will be easier to catch when we return to them."

When I reached my home Gille had his bow in his hand. "I thought I would see if I could hunt some game for the pot." He spied the fish I carried. "Although you have our meal I see."

196

"This is not substantial. Whatever you have will augment the pot. Besides this is good practice. If you can hit a sea bird or a pigeon then you can kill a man."

He loped off west. I took out the sac with the black liquid in and put it to one side. I removed the beak and then chopped up the flesh. I put it in a bowl and went indoors. Mary had a pot already on the fire. I handed the bowl to her. "This can go in the pot with the greens. I have left the sacs on the rock."

She brightened, "Thank you! The Jarl's wife can have colour now upon her new dress. She likes colour." She put the octopus in the pot and then wiped her hands. "I have something for you. I made it over the winter." She went into her chamber and returned with a short kyrtle.

"What is this?"

"One of the lords who visited us when I was free had one. It is worn beneath your byrnie." She held it towards me. "See I have put wool here between two pieces of cloth and sewn them so that they cannot move. It will be padding under your mail. It will not stop a sword but it will cushion you from a blow and may slow down an arrow. I know that you will still be taking risks. This way you may have more chance of returning whole."

She had made me a thinly padded kyrtle when she had first arrived but this was much more substantial. A great deal of work had gone into it and the wool would not shift. I took the garment and smiled, "Thank you. This is a good idea."

"If it works it is!"

Gille returned when dusk was falling. He had a wild duck with him. They sometimes flew over at this time of year as they headed north. He had done well to hit one. "Well done. Be careful when you pluck the feathers for they can be used for our arrows."

Our meal, that night, was filled with interesting tastes. I had learned that anything which stopped food tasting bland was to be appreciated. The octopus went surprisingly well with the duck and we did not even notice the nettles and the greens.

It was a pleasant evening and the wind had died. We sat outside with a fire before us. We watched the moon rise. Mary asked, somewhat shyly, "When you raid the Welsh will you be looking for a woman, lord?"

I shook my head, "The woman I take to my bed will be free and she will come there because she wishes to be the one who will bear my children. She will not come to my bed because there is no one else."

She seemed satisfied with my answer. They both went inside and I stayed there with Nipper watching the fire die. The land to the north of me drew my gaze. One day I would live there. That would be where I would find my woman. I knew that she would be a Frank. My whole life was bound up with the Issicauna, the Franks and horses. I could not escape that. Mary's words had made me focus on that. It was *wyrd*.

Chapter 13

Mary was up in the middle of the night preparing the bread. I awoke before dawn drawn by the tempting smell of fresh bread. I went down to the bay. The Einarsson brothers were also up. They waved to me as they pushed off their long fishing boat. They were used to my naked bathing. The sea woke me up and cleansed me within and without. By the time I had dressed and walked up the slope to my home the sun had risen. Gille was returning from the pen where he had taken the horses. He had a smile upon his face. "What is it Gille? Has Nipper done something to amuse you?"

"No, lord but we have a second foal. Dream Strider must have covered Freyja last month for I felt the foal's heartbeat when I groomed her."

"Then this is a good day." Mary brought out the still warm loaf and the sheep's cheese. It was wrapped in dried nettles and vinegar. "And now it gets even better!"

When Mary heard the news she was delighted as we were. She was very fond of the horses. When they had been part of her father's herd they meant nothing to her. Now she had helped to groom and feed them. She understood them now.

The clan arrived before the drekar. They had pulled carts with the beer, tools, timbers and bread upon them. As we waited for the drekar to appear we toasted the day and asked the Allfather to look kindly upon our efforts. When the prow edged around the headland we stripped to our breeks and went down to the shore. We laid the timbers so that we could haul the drekar out of the water and on to the shingle beach. It was the main reason Sven had chosen my bay for the work. There were more sharp rocks in Raven Bay. Once the mast had been placed on the mast fish we began to haul her sideways on to the timbers. We had greased the timbers with pig fat and sea weed. It made it easier. We pulled until her steering board side lay pointing to the heavens and then we spread out and began to scrape the green weed from the hull.

We sang as we worked and we worked together. The same rhythm which helped us row helped us to scrape and we soon had the weed removed from one side. We wandered up to the haunted farmhouse to have bread and ale while Sven and his ship's boys coated the newly cleaned side of the ship with the concoction Aiden of Cyninges-tūn had devised. It did not stop the weed and the sea creatures from attacking the hull but it kept it a little safer. We did this each year. Many jarls did not bother. They were the ones who disappeared in the vast reaches of the ocean. We then had to lower the drekar into the water, turn her around and do the same on the other side. We had finished by the middle of the afternoon. It was hard work but none shirked their duties. Even the Jarl and the hearth-weru slaved with the rest of us. The Jarl's wife, along with the other women, brought us ale. Most of the clan returned home at the end of the day while a few of us stayed with Sven to help him raise the mast. There were still tasks to be done on the drekar but Sven could complete them in the bay.

My wound ached by the end of the day. I had used my left arm and side more than usual. It was good though for it would strengthen it. I had to be able to use a shield again. I was a warrior and a warrior with a weak side would not last long in combat. I knew that the voyage north would strengthen it too.

When everyone had departed it made my home even more special. We had shared it with the clan but now it was ours once more. We groomed the three horses taking special care of the two mares and spoke and sang to them. They enjoyed the songs which Gille made up. Afterwards we sat outside again with a fine fire. We watched the mainland become darker until it disappeared. To all three of us our home was over there. We each kept our thoughts hidden but the moment was shared.

We left six days later. Ulf and I took our bows for we would be scouting. The drekar had fewer men on the oars. Sigtrygg Red Hair had not been the only warrior to fall. As the year progressed then more young men would be able to come with us and learn to row but it would be at least a year until they were ready to be given their shield and to take their place as a member of the clan.

The seas at spring time are unpredictable. It can go from a flat calm to a wild storm in the blink of an eye. We sometimes rowed and then a pleasant wind would take us where we wished to go. Just as suddenly a storm would erupt from the depths of the sea. The voyage was a lively one. As we had made enemies in Cent, Sven took us north west across the open sea. We hoped to avoid the isles of Syllingar. They all knew that a witch lived there for my journey into the underworld with Jarl Dragonheart and his galdramenn was told to young children to frighten them. I had not felt fear but I was loath to revisit the islands in case I heard something I did not want to hear. The result was a longer voyage as we stood well out to the west before turning north east and heading up the coast of On Walum. It was tempting to raid On Walum but the coast was treacherous and the people there had citadels on high cliffs. I knew that the Dragonheart had fought there and won but Jarl Thorfinnson was not Dragonheart.

The Sabrina is a wide river but it is possessed by the goddess after whom it was named. We pulled in to the northern shore of Wessex. It was an empty beach and there were no settlements close by. We left a strong guard aboard and then took the lamb we had brought with us. The sea here mixed with the Sabrina and the Jarl made a Blót. The corpse of the slain lamb was thrown into the estuary with a prayer to Sabrina to make our venture a success.

We left at dawn and sailed across the estuary towards the coast of Dyfed which lay to the north of the Sabrina. The Saxons controlled some towns but we would avoid their burghs. We saw two fortified towns as we sailed up the river. We avoided them. Just after the second we saw a long beach and fishing boats. We headed in to shore. We were hidden form the fortified town by a headland and the fishing boats were well to the north of us. Sven managed to find a bay where we could leave the drekar and go ashore.

The Jarl waved Ulf and me over. "This looks like a suitable place. The fortified towns make me wonder if we might try Ynys Môn. If we need slaves and grain then it might be a more profitable raid."

Siggi shook his head, "If Ulf and Hrolf find nothing then we can sail north. Let them go ashore."

Ulf agreed, "There is a path up the cliff. If there are fishing boats then there is a village nearby. We can slip ashore now." It was almost as though he had taken the decision for the Jarl.

He and I grabbed our bows and dropped over the side into waist deep water. I followed Ulf who unerringly chose the best path. We scanned the cliff top for any watchers but we saw none. I, too, saw the path which Ulf had spied and he led us up it. I found it hard to breathe. That was my wound. It would take time to totally recover. When we reached the top we crouched and looked for any enemies. We saw none. The drekar had moved into the middle of the small bay. We headed east. The ground fell away before rising again and we approached the top slowly. What we saw is still etched in my memory. A shaft of sunlight suddenly lit up the cliff ahead of us. It was golden. I knew that it was impossible and could not be gold but it looked as though the whole cliff was made of gold.

Ulf said, "Look, a village!" I dragged my eyes from the golden cliff and saw a fishing village nestling by the water. There were at least fifteen huts and, more importantly, there was no wall. However the fishing boats were returning to the village. Ulf said, "Go to the drekar. If Siggi comes with half of the men then the Jarl can sail with the drekar. We can trap them as we did with the men of Essex."

"Aye."

I turned and retraced my steps. Sometimes a warrior forgets where he is and so it was with me. I had seen a cliff of gold and my mind was distracted. The horsemen who suddenly appeared should have been seen by me. I was a horseman! I should have smelled them. They were heading for the village and they saw me just as I saw them. They were riding the small hill ponies favoured by the people of this land. They had spears and they galloped towards me. I cursed myself for my inattention as I slipped my bow around and took out an arrow. They were approaching rapidly. I pulled back and took the first warrior in the chest. He tumbled backwards over his pony's rump. The second whipped his pony's head around as he realised I had a bow. I aimed my second arrow. He was less than forty paces from me and heading along the cliff. My arrow went into his shoulder and through his body. He began to tumble. Holding on to his reins, his dying hands took the pony to its death as it fell from the path.

I walked to the second pony which was shaking. I took its reins and stroked its head as I spoke to it. I could not leave it to return to its stable for it would bring men searching for the two riders. Nor could I kill it. That was not in my nature. I took the dead rider's belt and hobbled the pony's forelegs. I slung my bow and headed down the path. The body of animal and rider were gone. The sea had taken them. Perhaps the goddess would take it as a second Blót. I prayed so. I took every precaution as I headed back to the drekar. I smelled, I looked and I placed my feet carefully.

When I reached the bay I waved and Sven the Helmsman brought her within hailing distance. "There is a village beyond the headland. Ulf says land half the men and I will take them to him. We will attack from the landward side. The fishing ships have returned to the village. We can catch them between us."

I saw the Jarl and Siggi as they spoke close together. After what seemed like an age the drekar closed with the shore. Siggi, Rurik and Arne Four Toes were the first ones ashore. They handed me my byrnie and my shield.

"Is it far?"

I shook my head. "We will be there before dark."

I saw that all of the new men had come ashore. The Jarl was keeping his hearth-weru and the more experienced warriors with him. Once I had my mail shirt on I slung my shield over my back and led them up the path. It was harder going with the iron weighing me down. When we reached the pony I took off the belt from the pony's forelegs and led the beast. I turned to Siggi. "You can ride him if you wish."

"Are you saying that I am old? No, I will walk." He pointed to the body. "You were lucky again, Hrolf."

I did not tell him that I had been more than lucky. The Weird Sisters were watching over me.

When we reached Ulf he cocked a quizzical eye at the pony and then shook his head. "I have watched and they keep no guard. The men have gone into their huts and there are few people about. I think they must be eating."

"Then let us go."

I let go of the pony which was grazing on some long tufts of grass. It would not bolt back to its stable now and we would soon be gone if it did. We ran in a loose formation. Normally I would have been at the fore with Ulf but a combination of my wound, the climb and tending to the horse meant I was in the

204

middle. As we burst over the top of the headland to descend to the village below the drekar could be seen. The walled town was behind us and as soon as the drekar was spotted then the villagers began to run for the safety of the walled town. They came towards us. Their eyes were on the drekar which was approaching from the south and they did not see us until it was too late.

When they did see us we had weapons drawn and we attacked the men. We were after women. Ulf swung his sword almost contemptuously at the middle of the man who tried to stab him with his spear. The women and the children huddled together and then tried to turn back to the village. A handful tried to make their way north over the scrubby, bush covered upland.

Siggi shouted, "Hrolf, take Rurik and Arne, catch those villagers."

There were ten of them ahead of us. Four women and six children. I waved the other two to the side and we set off in pursuit. We were aided by the fact that they stayed close together for protection. There were three small children amongst them and that slowed them up. None of us spoke their language or else we would have told them to halt. Whatever we shouted would frighten them and so we ran. Rurik and Arne were running faster than I was and they began to overtake them. The frightened women and children bunched more and that made it easier for us to catch them. Arne and Rurik pounced. They turned in front of them and held their swords out. The women stopped and one woman shouted something. Another turned and saw me behind them with Heart of Ice held in my hand. Her shoulders sagged in resignation. The children clung fearfully to their mothers. I knew just how frightening we looked. The fishermen in the village did not own helmets and mail. We must have looked like some kind of metal monster to them.

I stood aside and gestured with my sword. Still shouting and, I did not doubt, cursing, they began to trudge back to the village. I saw that there were two sturdy boys in the group. That would please Bagsecg. He needed boys to work his bellows. I looked ahead and saw that it was over. The men lay dead. However the closer we came the more I realised that there appeared to be no one else who was alive. The drekar was tied up and I saw the Jarl striding towards Siggi, Ulf and the others. We were still two hundred paces from them when the Jarl arrived but I could hear the voices which were raised in anger. Lars Larsson and the other new men stood with their heads down. I wondered what had happened to cause this slaughter of women and children. There had been twenty odd women and children in the village. We had less than half.

The Jarl, his hearth-weru and the new men were already marching back to the village when we reached Siggi. Arne Four Toes asked, "What happened?"

"We brought the wrong men. With you three gone Ulf and I just had the new men left. We killed their men quickly but one of the women tried to scratch Lars Larsson's eyes out. He slew her and when her son struck him he was killed. They became uncontrollable and just slaughtered everyone."

"But why? Captives always fight. It is to be expected. You cuff them and they obey."

"You are right Rurik but, it seems, this was the first slave raid they had been on. Jarl Gunnstein Berserk Killer had fought Hibernians but that was in pitched battles. It was why they were so keen to go A-Viking. The Jarl is less than happy with his wife's countrymen."

We herded the captives to the beach. Having seen the slaughter they were cowed. They saw that they were alive at least. The woman who had shouted flashed angry eyes at Ulf and Siggi. It did not bother either of them. Everything of value had been taken from the village. There was plenty of fish and some furs but no grain and naught else of value.

The Jarl glared at the new men, who sat apart as he spoke to us. "We will stay here tonight for Sven has told me that the river and the tide are against us. We will sail at dawn. Had some of the clan not lost their heads we would be sailing home on the morrow but we will now need to sail north. I have learned my lesson. I know which warriors I can trust and which ones I cannot!"

As we ate our dried fish and drank the poor beer I said to Siggi. "We would have had to sail north anyway."

"How so?"

"There was no grain here. Lars and the others made a mistake, a terrible one at that but we would have had to go north regardless."

"You may be right but the Jarl frets over his unborn child. He wanted to be away for the briefest of times. If I am honest he did not wish to raid at all. His wife asked him to stay home."

We all looked at Siggi. He nodded, "It is true. I was there. She said that her father did not raid so why did he?"

"He is Jarl and it is what we do."

"You are right Ulf but his wife does not see it that way. The thought was in the Jarl's head. It is hard to winkle such thoughts out of your mind. It is why we made the sacrifice. He wanted everything to be perfect. This may be the last raid the Jarl makes until his child is born."

As we rowed down the river there was a strained atmosphere on the drekar. I had spoken with Eiril Jorgesson when we had both risen in the night to make water. He asked, "Why is the Jarl so angry? They were nothing which we killed."

"They were the reason we came, Eiril. I have done this many times. The women always fight. Ketil Eriksson almost lost an eye on his first raid. You use your hands. There is no honour in killing a woman."

"True Hrolf, but there is even less honour in being struck by one."

"You will all have much honour if you stay with the Jarl. We win more times than we lose."

"That is why we joined his crew but now I am not certain."

As we walked back I said, "Aye Eiril but now you are oathsworn. You have cast the bones and must play them."

The wind was against us and that helped for we had to row. Rowing brings a crew together. Until we turned the coast and passed the church on the headland even the Jarl had to row. It was the song of the raven clan which helped to heal our rift.

> *A song of death to all its foes*
>
> *The power of the raven grows and grows.*
>
> *The power of the raven grows and grows.*
>
> *The power of the raven grows and grows.*
>
> *A song of death to all its foes*
>
> *The power of the raven grows and grows.*
>
> *The power of the raven grows and grows.*
>
> *The power of the raven grows and grows.*
>
> *A song of death to all its foes*
>
> *The power of the raven grows and grows.*
>
> *The power of the raven grows and grows.*
>
> *The power of the raven grows and grows.*

As we turned north the wind began to push us and we could stop rowing. We slumped over our oars for it had been a hard pull along a hostile coast where every eye viewed us as an enemy. We spent the night anchored off the small island which was inundated with sea birds. A priest had a hut on the island but we did not bother him. We used the island for it was a safe place to stop and the birds and their eggs made good eating.

The Jarl waved over Siggi, Ulf and myself to speak with him and Sven. I think I was included because I had spent so much time with the Dragonheart and I knew the island as well as any. Sven had a piece of wood on which had crudely drawn the island with a piece of charcoal from the fire. The Jarl used his dagger to point out where we should not attack.

"Here in the north is one of their strongholds. Caer Cybi has Roman walls and towers. Here on the south is the Royal Palace of Aberffraw. The Dragonheart has raided both and they keep watch for such as us."

Siggi took his own dagger and jabbed at a point on the northern coast, half way along. "There is a village here. It used to have a wall but it was destroyed when the Saxons attacked. Since the men of the island have retaken it I do not know."

The Jarl nodded. "Here, where the small island is close to the main island is another settlement but it is not large."

It was Sven who found our target. "On the edge of the island. Just across the straits from the holy mountain, Wyddfa, is a small harbour. It is prosperous as it has a ferry to the mainland. I have passed there before. I do not recall seeing any walls. At least none that were made of stone or wood. There may have been a ditch and mound in times past but I do not recall it."

The Jarl stroked his beard, "That is good. We could sail to Dyflin after the raid. I would speak with the jarl there. We might be able to sell that which we do not need and there are other matters I need to discuss."

Siggi looked up, "Jarl, if this is about the men who joined us I would consider your words. They had not raided for slaves. It is as much my fault as theirs. I should have controlled them." He shook his head, "It was almost as though they went berserk."

"Yet they are not berserkers. If they had been we would have seen that at Hrofecester. But I was not going to speak of that. They are oathsworn and my men now. I would tell Gunnstein that he is to be a grandfather."

I think we all breathed a sigh of relief at that news.

"We will land Ulf, Hrolf, Arne Four Toes and Rurik just north and west of the village. They all have skills when it comes to moving in the night. They can dispose of any sentries. We will land on the beach away from the mainland."

The next morning we did not sail due north for that risked the straits and we would be easily seen. The island was small and an alarm would make our task harder. Instead Sven took us towards Hibernia. We had to row for a while but when he turned east we found the prevailing winds sped us east quickly and we were able to prepare for the raid. We would be landing at dusk. That was a good time. The day would be almost over and those within the settlement would be eating, talking and ending their day quietly. Most Vikings raided at dawn or in the night. I thought it was a good plan but it was determined by the winds for they decided when we would reach the island. It was *wyrd*.

Those of us who had sailed often with the Jarl knew the place Sven meant. I had never taken much notice of it for we were normally heading somewhere else and it was just a place on the way. What I did know was that it was almost totally flat. The other thing was its proximity to the mainland. I remembered Aiden telling me how a Roman General had had his army swim it with the horses to attack the galdramenn who lived there. Having swum horses myself I could see how they had done it but it must have terrified those on the island.

The sun was setting behind us when Sven turned the drekar towards the coast. It was just a smudge on the horizon but the wind was taking us there quickly. I would not need my bow. Landing at night meant that I would not get the benefit from its range and I left it with my chest. I would, however, need my wolf

210

cloak. I was not Ulfheonar but I had killed a wolf and I now used its skin when I wished to be harder to see. The head of the wolf went over my helmet. As I put it on Eiril came over to me. "Are you Ulfheonar? I know you served with the Dragonheart."

I shook my head, "I have not the skills they have. I hunted the wolf with them. It brings me luck. I cannot wear it around my horse for the smell makes him nervous but if we land in the dark then I can move unseen."

Sven had the sail taken down while we were still out to sea. Even in the dark its white sail could be seen. The men took to their oars and rowed us in. The ship's boys kept watch. They whistled when they saw the flicker of firelight in the darkening night. Sven put the steering board over and edged us into shore. This side of the island had beaches and not rocks but, even so, we had to land in water which was waist deep. We waded ashore and even as we turned the drekar slipped towards the settlement.

We ran. Ulf led and I followed. We crossed sand dunes and then found fields. They had just been cleared and I knew that it was winter barley. The island was in such a favourable position that it could harvest two crops a year. The kings of Gwynedd guarded their granary jealously. They had fought hard to retake it from the Saxons of Mercia. I could smell the smoke from the fires as we headed closer. I could even hear the sound of animals. Dogs yapped and barked and there were milk cows lowing. There was a hollow and when we climbed from it we saw that they had erected a wall. It was made of wood. Ulf halted while he assessed the situation. The four of us knew each other well. Ulf used hand signals. He had seen a warrior walking the walls. He was just a moving shadow and we knew not if he had mail or what weapon he held. He signalled for Rurik and me to eliminate him and then enter the walls. He and Arne slipped to the right.

I took out my seax. Rurik was shorter than I was but he was both broad and strong. When we reached the wall he stood with his back to it and cupped his hands. The wall was just slightly

211

higher than me with my arms held up. I took three steps away from the wall and crouched. I knew that even if he looked at me the sentry would see nothing for I wore my wolf cloak. I waited until he had passed Rurik and was heading towards the sea before I ran. I planted my right foot in Rurik's hands and he propelled me upwards. I made the top easily and I scrambled over the top, seax still in hand. I crouched so that I would be unseen as the sentry walked towards me. He was not looking ahead but to the side. I was so close that I could smell him and I rose and ripped my seax across his throat. I caught his body before it could fall and I laid it on the walkway.

I leaned over and hissed. Rurik moved away from the wall and then he ran at it. I held out my arm and Rurik grabbed it and then climbed up the wood of the palisade. We were in. I sheathed my seax and took out my sword. I left my shield over my back for the walkway was narrow. The village lay below us. It was larger than the one on the Sabrina. There was a large hall which suggested a noble of some description. We had not anticipated this. Rurik and I were invisible. If anyone saw us they would take us for the sentry.

I headed in the opposite direction that Ulf had taken. As we approached the ladder at the end I looked along the wall which led to the straits. I saw something rising from the end of the wall. It was a tower. I pointed to it and we hurried down the walkway. There might have only been one man on the rear wall but a tower suggested more. With the drekar about to loom out of the dark we had to reach it before the alarm could be given. We dared not run for our feet would have sounded on the wood and the sudden movement might have alerted those below us. As we passed one hut there was a burst of laughter. They did not know what was to be unleashed upon them.

We reached the tower when the guard on the top saw the drekar. There was a ladder leading to a platform some three paces above the walkway. I heard him say something to his companion who came out of the lower part of the tower. In four strides I was

212

at the ladder. The man on the lower platform turned in surprise. I ignored him and clambered up the ladder. It was too late for the alarm was given. He shouted even as my sword plunged into his middle and I pushed him over the wall and onto the ditch below. Rurik had killed the other but there was no time to waste for we had to reach the gate.

Inside the walls there were shouts, screams and cries. Confusion reigned. A voice asked a question which the dead sentry would never answer. Suddenly something struck me in the back. My shield saved me an injury. They were loosing arrows. I saw the gate. Arne and Ulf were fighting a half dozen men. Some were wearing leather armour and had shields. We were above them. I decided to use my body as a weapon. I ran and hurled myself, like a human arrow, at the backs of the defenders from the walkway. I gambled that they would break my fall. Even so it was like my worst nightmare when I was falling through blackness. In my excitement I had forgotten that I still held my sword. As it tore through the leather armour and back of a warrior it was torn from my grasp. I was slightly winded when I landed but I had three stunned warriors of Cymri beneath me. Ulf and Arne quickly took advantage of the surprise and slew the remaining two. As Rurik descended they finished off those on whom I had fallen. I retrieved my sword from the body.

"Open the gate for the Jarl!"

"Aye Ulf!"

I had hurt my knee in my fall and I felt a little unsteady but I managed to lift the bar on the gate. As I pulled it open the clan raced up from the shore. I barely got out of the way as they raced in. I took the opportunity of bringing my shield around to the front. I saw the arrow sticking from it. I had been lucky. Rurik ran up to me, "I thought you were a raven! That will make a tale how Hrolf the Horseman leapt from a wall to strike four men with one blow!"

I shook my head, "It was foolish. I did not think!" I pulled my shield tighter and made sure I had a good grip on my sword. I could not replace Heart of Ice.

"It is time to get back to the battle then. Come."

We followed the others. There was a rear gate and we headed for it. Lars Eiril and the new warriors were trying to make amends for their error on the Sabrina. They fought like wolves. I saw their swords and axes flashing in the firelight. Their hands moved so quickly that they were a blur. Someone must have knocked over a brazier and one of the huts was burning. It was a chaotic scene. Smoke drifted across before us and there was the smell of burning flesh. A dead body lay in one of the burning buildings. The Jarl and his hearth-weru were fighting their way to the hall where the defenders were gathering. I followed Ulf to the rear gate. We reached it as four warriors were trying to open it to allow the women and children who were with them to escape. A woman turned and saw me. She screamed and the others turned. The sight of a human wolf was too much for the women and children. They ran in every direction like chickens without heads as they tried to escape the demons in their village.

The four warriors turned to face us. I fended off a hastily thrust spear and brought my sword towards his head. He brought his shield up but it was a small one. The edge of my sword rattled off his helmet. I pushed his spear aside with my shield and, as I closed with him, rammed my good knee between his legs. He doubled up and I hit his helmet with the hilt of my sword. As he lay at my feet I gave him the warrior's death. The others lay dead.

"Rurik guard the gate with Arne. Hrolf, come with me and we will see if there is another gate."

The women who had fled us were cowering behind a hut. When we padded towards them they screamed and ran back towards the main gate. I think they had decided that their best hope lay in numbers. We found the south and eastern side deserted and we made our way back to the hall. The battle was over. The last of the defenders lay dead and the women and children were resigned to their fate. I saw that the battle had not been all one sided. Lars Larsson had had a glorious death. The Jarl of the settlement lay dead before him but I could tell that the oathsworn had avenged themselves on Lars. Eiril was also wounded although not badly. I counted five of our warriors dead. A high price but we now had plenty of slaves.

The Jarl took off his helmet. "Find any supplies."

I said, "There must be barley. They have just harvested their winter crop!"

"Good! This has been a better day!"

Chapter 14

We left in the middle of the next morning. We were heavily laden and our short voyage to Dyflin seemed now a necessity rather than being a courtesy. We had over thirty women and children. We had left the old and the men who had been captured. We had the sacks of barley and the last of the previous year's wheat under our deck. The mail and the weapons were at the prow making the bow dip alarmingly. It had been a bigger haul than we had expected. We even found some jars of coins buried beneath the floors of the huts.

As we rowed Siggi said, "We will either have to hire a knarr or sell some of the slaves in Dyflin. We cannot sail across the open seas close to home this laden."

I said, "It seems a pity for it cost us five warriors."

He lowered his voice, "Had the Jarl's brother not lost his temper we might have two drekar and two crews. Unless we take gold and go to Bolli of Cyninges-tūn then we shall have to make do with one ship."

Arne Four Toes decided to make up a song about my reckless act in diving from the walls.

The night was black no moon was there

Death and danger hung in the air

As Raven Wing closed with the shore

The scouts crept closer as before

Dressed like death with sharpened blades

They moved like spirits through the glades

The power of the raven grows and grows

The power of the raven grows and grows

With sentries slain they sought new foes

A cry in the night fetched them woes

The alarm was given the warriors ready

Four scouts therewith hearts so steady

Ulf and Arne thought their end was nigh

When Hrolf the wild leapt from the sky

Flying like the raven through the air

He felled the Cymri, a raven slayer

The power of the raven grows and grows

The power of the raven grows and grows

His courage clear he still fought on

Until the clan had battled and won

The power of the raven grows and grows

The power of the raven grows and grows

When he had finished Ulf said, "Not quite the way it happened but I liked the line 'raven slayer'. In your black fur with your arms held out you looked like a raven. Tell me did you mean to stab the mailed warrior?"

I could have said, '*yes*' and received the approval of the clan but that would have been a lie and I did not wish to upset the

Norns. They had guided my arm, I knew that. "No Ulf. I just thought to hit them."

Siggi burst out laughing, "Then that is even more heroic! You save your friends by using your body as a weapon!"

Arne sang it twice more so that he had the words in his head. Siggi decided we would use it the next time we rowed. It was not a battle chant but it had the steady rhythm we liked to use when we had to row a long way. It took some time to navigate the mouth of the Liffey for the dipping bow threatened to take the drekar into the banks. Rurik said, "I will be glad to be rid of the mail and the weapons. I think the Cymri are still fighting us!"

It took so long to reach the quay that a crowd had gathered. Jarl Gunnstein Berserk Killer himself was there to greet us. He waited until Jarl Gunnar Thorfinnson had landed before he went towards him. He looked troubled. "How did you know I had need of you and your men?"

I heard the question in the Jarl's voice as he said, "I did not. We raided and needed a safe port and I came to tell you that you are to be a grandfather."

Jarl Gunnstein gave a wan smile. "And normally that would be news to be celebrated but I fear we will have to wait. The High King of the wild tribes of this island has come to give battle. We are beset by enemies." He turned to one of his men. "Have the slaves placed in the slave pens and guarded. Bring your men, Jarl Gunnar, and we will talk."

I was honoured that I was one of the eight men the Jarl took with him. We went to the Jarl's hall and ale was brought. As we went I saw that the city was an armed camp. There was the sound of weapons being sharpened and the urgent clang of hammers on metal as new swords and spear heads were made. War had come to Dyflin.

"The one who claims the position of High King of Ireland is Conchobar mc Donnachada. He claims it through his father.

Two or three years since he allied himself with Feidlimid mac Crimthainn, King of Munster. He was opposed by Murchad mac Máele Dúin of the Uí Néill clan. The Síl nÁedo Sláine clan helped him and there was a bloody murder when the king invited them to a meeting to discuss peace."

Siggi White Hair shook his head, "I am sorry, my lord, but all these names are just confusing me."

Jarl Gunnstein smiled, "As they do me. The murders and the treachery means that now that he is allied to the King of Munster he feels he can cleanse his land of us, the Norse. He cannot call himself High King, no matter how many tribes he controls so long as there are Norse controlling Dyflin. He is on his way here. I have sent a ship to Úlfarrston. If Dragonheart and his people come then we can defeat them."

"And if not? How many men can you field?"

He looked at Jarl Gunnar, "I have a hundred and fifty warriors. Some of the local tribes support me. The last thing they want is a High King ruling here. We have brought peace and order. With your men and those as well as the bondi I think we can field three hundred men."

"And the High King?"

"He is no fool. He would not attack if he did not think he had more men than us. The walls here are made of wood. We cannot defend them. We will have to meet him on the field. I have sent two of my hersir to arrange where we shall fight. I hope to buy enough time for Jarl Dragonheart to reach us."

Jarl Gunnar said, "Since the death of Wolf Killer I have heard that the Jarl has not left his home. Perhaps he has given up war."

"Perhaps. That is what worries me. We will know soon enough. The knarr I sent should be back by tomorrow."

219

I wondered what Jarl Gunnstein would say if we said we did not wish to fight his battle for him. I knew that the Jarl could not for now, of course, they were blood kin. We were Jarl Gunnar's oathsworn. This was our battle.

"Do we know where the High King is now?"

"The last I heard he was two days away." He pointed to the west. "There is a hill yonder, by the river. I would meet him there. We have not enough men to man all of the walls and there we can make a good shield wall. He comes not to take the town. He thinks it is his by right. He comes to slaughter every Norse he can find. He thinks there are too many of us and he would wrest our grip from this part of his land."

His eyes pleaded with his daughter's husband. Jarl Gunnar nodded, "We will fight."

The relief on his face was clear. We might only have forty or so warriors to his army but thanks to the Welsh most of our men now had mail and we had spare weapons. "Good. We have plenty of food and ale."

Thorgeir Sigurdsson, the leader of his warriors laughed, "And we might as well eat it. For if we lose the Hibernians will feast on it instead!" he was a mighty warrior. He could have been a jarl himself. It was said that he had fought as Jarl Gunnstein Berserk Killer's champion before now. He was a reassuring presence for he had a fine byrnie and many warrior rings on his arms. He had a warrior's attitude. Eat and drink while you can for tomorrow you may die!

"Did you tell him where we would meet in battle?"

"I did Gunnar. I told him we would wait on the hill beneath my standard and now we shall have the raven too. I just hope that we have the dragon and the wolf with us as well. The Dragonheart is the only warrior who frightens the High King. Each time the Jarl has visited the island his passing was marked by

220

a trail of corpses. Irish women frighten their children by telling them that the wolf will come in the night and get them."

"We had better go and tell our men. I would not count on two days, Jarl. If this High King knows you have sent to Dragonheart he will hurry here before his enemy arrives."

"And that is what I fear too."

The warriors, like Eiril Jorgesson, who came from this city were happy to be fighting for its survival. Those like Ketil and Knut, the Eriksson brothers, were less happy about risking their lives. Siggi White Hair heard them complaining as we set up camp not far from where we would fight the battle. He rounded on them. "You two whine and complain about everything. When you first came you were reckless but you had courage. Since you wedded those women you have changed. Then you were warriors and now..."

Ketil's hand went to his sword, "I will not be insulted by an old man."

Ulf, Rurik, Arne and I all stood. Ulf Big Nose said in a low threatening voice, "Sit and apologise before I take your head. Siggi is right but even if he were not remember the oath you swore to the Jarl. If you would break your word and become outlaw do it now for I will not share an oar with someone who is foresworn."

Knut One Eye smiled, "My brother means nothing. He is anxious to get back with his treasures. We will fight and fight as bravely as the next man!"

Siggi smiled, "Good but I will not forget your words Ketil Eriksson. This is not the time but you and I will have a reckoning."

Such conflicts were inevitable. This would be a bloody battle. Our minds were focussed by the impending conflict. I sharpened my sword and seax as well as putting an edge on my spear. I had only used two arrows on the Sabrina and I had a full quiver. My mail had not suffered any damage but I oiled it anyway. My shield had been hit by an arrow. I had left the arrow head in my shield but snapped off the shaft. It was more metal and the broken end could be used as a weapon. Finally I checked my helmet. It had no damage. As I looked at my battle gear I smiled. Mary had made me the padded under shirt without knowing that I would need it so soon. I would be fighting in a shield wall and there was no escape there. If one man broke then the whole shield wall would be destroyed. When I had landed on the four warriors it had not hurt as much as I might have expected. Beorn had examined my wound and declared that it had not opened. I could fight.

The next day the knarr returned and we all watched as it tacked across the large bay to get to us. In our hearts we knew it brought ill news for it was alone. The captain said, "The Dragonheart is abroad with his men, Jarl. We will get no aid from there."

"Then we are alone."

Gunnstein Berserk Killer looked at Gunnar Thorfinnson, "I fear so." He looked sad but then he brightened. "We have an unborn child to fight for! My grandson and your son. We will defeat these barbarians! We are Vikings and we are warriors. If we cannot defeat a bunch of half naked wild men then we ought to become followers of the White Christ and live in a monastery!"

Late in the afternoon we received confirmation from the two men the jarl had sent to the High King. "They come lord. They will meet us for battle tomorrow morning!"

"And how many men does he have?"

"It is hard to tell, lord for they move like a swarm of flies over a dead body but I would estimate five hundred."

He nodded, "I will speak with my leaders."

There were just four of them. There was the Jarl, the leader of his warriors, Thorgeir Sigurdsson, and two local chiefs: Connor Mac Loinsig and Mal mac Rochride. They each led a warband. I could see why they fought for the Jarl. The two of them and their body guards wore the same mail and used the same weapons as we did. They had adopted our style. Their men were wild and had neither helmet nor mail but they were fierce warriors with tattooed bodies and limed, spiked hair. Their advantage was in their speed. I saw them playing some game by the river using a pig's bladder and some sticks. Some of them could move as fast as a pony. They might be dangerous. They also gave me an indication of the sort of men we would be fighting.

The night before the battle we groomed ourselves. We bathed in the river and then combed and plaited our hair. Some, like Siggi, plaited their beards. I saw some warriors crushing beetles to make the juice they would apply to their eyes and faces. Others used the black liquid from the sac of the octopus to the same effect. I took the opportunity to paint parts of the horse's head on my shield. I used the red to make his mouth stand out more and the black to deepen his eyes. I checked my straps but they were relatively new and I knew they would not break. It was what you did before a battle. When you began to fight you needed to rely on your weapons.

When we were all ready we sat around our fires and sang songs of heroes past or spoke of brave deeds we had witnessed. Those who had fallen well, like Alf the Silent and Gunnar Stone Face, were remembered. We knew that some of us would die and that at some future battle we would be spoken of. We would be in Valhalla but we would have immortality on earth so long as the clan lived. I felt sorry for those like Erik Long Hair who had followed the Jarl's brothers. They had sad memories. It would take many battles to clear them.

When the Jarl had returned he had spoken with his hearth-weru and Siggi White Hair. Now, as we sat around the fire Siggi brought the news of our formation. "Tomorrow Jarl Gunnstein fights in a boar's snout. We will be one tusk and the oathsworn of Jarl Gunnstein the other." He went on to tell us the formation for the whole of our army. The rest of the Viking warriors would be

223

led by Thorgeir Sigurdsson. His men would link the two wedges . Our allies would form the flanks of the snout. When he had finished he stood up and smacked one hand into the other as he punctuated his words with actions."We want the enemy to break his back on our spears and shields. When their hearts are broken then we will give them the sword and use our position on the hill to drive them from the field."

It sounded a good plan but like all plans there were many things which could go wrong. Some men tried to sleep. I could not and I sat with Rurik, Ulf and Arne Four Toes. "What do you think, Ulf Big Nose?"

"I think the wild men of this land will see the other wild men and they will charge and attack them. They will be slaughtered and we will have to fight alone."

We had not fought in as many battles as Ulf but we agreed with his assessment. Rurik asked, as Siggi returned having spoken to the rest of the band, "Where do we fight?"

"The Jarl will be the snout with the five hearth-weru behind him. Ulf and I will be on the right in the third rank then Hrolf and you, Rurik, will be on the left. Beorn and Arne will anchor the right of the fourth rank and the jarl will have two of his brothers crew protected by Gunnstein Gunnarson. He wants Erik Long Hair to have the chance, along with Olaf the Bear, to gain some honour and glory."

I asked, "Do they use horses?"

Ulf laughed, "You will be on foot so what does it matter?"

"I am interested in such things."

Siggi nodded, "It is a good question. They have ponies but they ride them bare backed. They do not have your stiraps."

"And if they are ponies then they are easier to kill. Their neck is at the right height for a blow." I was a horseman but if someone was trying to kill me I knew how to defeat someone who

224

rode bareback. I recognised the weaknesses of horses as well as their strengths.

We did eventually fall to sleep but we were awakened while it was still dark and we made our way to the hill and our positions. The Jarl clasped our arms. We were his oathsworn and it might be the last time we saw each other in this life. We did not say much to each other apart from, *'may Odin watch over you'* or something similar. His banner was planted behind Erik Long Hair. It would flap above the Jarl but if it fell then it meant our best warriors were all dead and the banner would mean nothing then.

As dawn broke behind us we saw the enemy form up. Sometimes the kings or leaders would meet in the middle and decide on the rules of the battle. Here there was no need. Whoever stood, at the end of the battle had won. If it was the High King then the days of the Norse in Dyflin would be over. Our brief stay would have ended. If it was us who won then the High King would need to watch his back as the families of those he had defeated plotted his downfall. These were treacherous times and you sought a throne at your peril.

The wild men who were fighting alongside us had been drinking most of the night and they were ready for a fight. They hurled insults at their enemies and taunted them. Four hundred paces away the men of the High King did the same. Some of the enemy had a helmet but it was perhaps only one in ten. One in five had a shield; they were small but I saw few, including the nobles, with mail. Their leaders were riding their ponies up and down before their men exhorting them, I have no doubt, to slaughter us. They seemed to have many leaders. The ponies were so small that some of the rides' feet almost touched the ground.

Ulf and I had brought our bows and Ulf said, "Let us string our bows, Hrolf. We can do some damage as they approach."

I rammed my spear into the ground and strung my bow. I chose my best arrow and I waited to draw. The hill and my powerful bow meant I could send one four hundred paces. If I chose to release when they were in range I could hit one of their front rank. I waited.

Jarl Gunnar said, "Could you two hit one of their leaders?"

Ulf snorted, "We could hit two if we chose."

"Then while they prance around on their little ponies see what you can do."

It was a long way away and with the slight breeze I did not wish to risk a miss. I chose a chief who was not riding up and down but speaking to his men. He was among the others who were also mounted and looked to be chiefs too. There were four of them together and I guessed they were exhorting their men to valorous acts. I was not risking as much for there were four targets. I drew back my bow as far as I could and released. Ulf's arrow left his bow a heartbeat later. Normally I would have sent another straight after but I wished to see the effect. The arrow struck him in the neck and threw him from his pony. Ulf's was an even better strike for he hit one who was riding and the arrow knocked him onto his men. The other two chiefs leapt from their mounts and went to see to the two fallen warriors. Taking heart from my strike I sent another and this one hit a leader in the top of his leg. I must have penetrated through to his pony for it reared and threw him before galloping through the massed ranks. The barbarians scattered before the panicked pony. When Ulf killed a chief standing in front of the High King it prompted a charge towards us. I have never seen men on foot move as fast. We had made them charge before the High King was ready. I wondered if that was an advantage or not.

Siggi said, "That is one way to start a battle!"

I could see that they would not take long to reach us. I released eight arrows into the mass of men who charged us and then dropped my bow. I would have to use my spear. The Jarl shouted, "Shield wall! Up!"

226

I thrust my spear above Rolf Arneson's shoulder through the gap in the shields. I brought my shield over my head to touch Rolf's shield. The sky became dark. The enemy did not use arrows but they had slingers. Another tactic to break a shield wall was for warriors to hurl themselves over the top and to balance on the shields while thrusting down with their javelins and spears. We were, in effect, making a mobile stronghold.

"Brace!" We locked our left legs forward and leaned into the warrior in front of us making a huge, immoveable block of men.

Through the gap I could see the white painted faces of the wild warriors as they raced towards us. They held axes, spears and curved swords. They came so quickly it took my breath away and then it went dark as they hurled themselves at the shields. Had we not been braced then they might have broken it for many of them jumped upon the top.

"Spears!"

We all punched with our spears. Those behind thrust up in the gaps at the warriors who were there. We did so blindly but I felt my spear strike something and I pushed harder and twisted. As we withdrew our spears the weight lessened as men were felled. I heard swords battering at the front of the shield wall and the cries and screams of the dying. It seemed to go on forever but, of course, it did not . The battering began to diminish and the pressure on our shields lessened. When the sound of swords stopped there was silence punctuated by moans.

"Down shields!"

The light was almost blinding when we lowered our shields. I could see a gap and as Einar stepped into the gap vacated by Erik who had been wounded and was crawling away, Erik Long Hair stepped forward to stand with the hearth-weru. Beorn Fast Feet stepped next to me. We had to fill the ranks of the wounded. I could see, beyond the helmets of the men before me, the Irish streaming down the slope. Their first attack had been beaten back. We had held. I looked to the right and saw that those who had been beaten by us had caused those attacking Thorgeir and Jarl Gunnstein to fall back too. They would gather at the foot of the slope and regroup.

Suddenly and to our horror, Connor Mac Loinsig led his men in a headlong charge after the enemy. We had no one left to defend our left flank. I heard Vermund snap, "Fools! Another attack from them and the enemy would have broken." Someone at his feet must have stirred for he raised his spear and stabbed down. There was a scream. "A man should know when he is dead!"

It was hard to see the battle below us unfold but the sudden charge by our allies appeared to have a great initial success. Their speed and momentum carried them deep into the enemy. They carved a path through the disorganized warriors but the High King had not committed all of his men and we heard the crack and crash as the reserves hit Connor Mac Loinsig and his men. All I could see for a while was the rise and fall of weapons but I could hear the cries.

Then Einar, who had a clear view shouted, "That is it. They are broken!"

The Jarl shouted, "This time we give them a wall. They will have to negotiate the bodies before us and they are slippery. Those on the right, beware!"

We all knew what he meant. The warriors on the right of the wedge had no shield to protect them. Our two wedges stuck out from our line and they were exposed. Thorgeir Sigurdsson, who lead Jarl Gunnstein's men, had a great responsibility. If our right side looked in danger then he would have to advance. I looked along the line to Siggi White Hair. He was on the right with no one protecting his sword side. He did not seem concerned with his exposed position.

This time their chiefs were able to extol their men to great deeds for they were not harassed by our arrows. I had no doubt that we had slain many of the leaders but they seemed to have an inordinate number of them. Eventually they came. This time I could see that the main body was moving more slowly although the High King must have sent unused and fresh men for a line of warriors raced ahead of the main body.

"Spears!"

This time I held my spear overhand and rested it on Rolf and Vermund's shoulder. The haft of a spear and a spear head appeared over my shoulder as we became a hedgehog of spear heads. I noticed that many of the spear heads of our rank and the ones before us were bloody. The Jarl's had gone and he had his sword held before him. The fresh warriors ran at us, their faces contorted and wild as they sought to gain honour by slaying the vaunted men of the north. None of those who ran at us had a shield. Most of them had long curved swords without a point. They appeared to be a giant seax. One, faster than the others out ran the rest and he ran directly for the Jarl. He swung his long sword in a mighty sweep. The Jarl's shield came up to block the blow and his sword darted out. I saw the tip come out of the warrior's back and yet he lived still until Vermund's spear punched a hole in his head and he fell.

The rest of the line reached us. It was their own dead who were our allies. Some of the barbarians slipped on the gore and the blood for they fought barefoot. Spears darted out and struck them. Others made our line and slashed with their swords but well made shields held and our blades ended their lives but they had numbers and they began to make inroads along our exposed right. Ulf brought his own spear around to stab over Siggi's head. His spear plunged into the throat of a warrior with white and red paint upon his face. Even though we were killing more of them, numbers began to tell. With no allies on our left we were being surrounded. I heard a sword crash against Beorn Fast Feet's shield and I punched my spear into the chest of the warrior.

Ulf and I were now defending the sides ahead of me. Rolf Arneson was having to stab left and right as more of the enemy filled the gaps of the fallen. Rolf was stabbing to the right as two warriors hacked Erik Long Hair's head from his body. As Beorn Fast Feet stepped into the gap. Gunnstein Gunnarson quickly and seamlessly joined me. However we had lost three men already and our band was shrinking as more of the enemy pressed against us.

A horn sounded from behind us and I heard Thorgeir Sigurdsson shout, "Forward!"

Jarl Gunnar said, "On my command advance!"

"Aye Jarl!" We all roared as one and we took the enemy by surprise at the shout. The warrior who was about to hack at Beorn Fast Feet hesitated and I rammed my spear into his side. The head crunched against ribs and I twisted as I pulled out. These wild men must have taken some potion so that they did not feel pain for the man turned and roared at me. I punched again with my spear into his open mouth and he fell backwards.

As Thorgeir Sigurdsson and his men advanced so the pressure on our right lessened. The Jarl timed it well and he shouted, "Advance!"

We all stepped forward on our right legs stabbing with our spears as we did so. The timing was impeccable. Every spear struck at the same time. Those enemies who were striking us hit shields but all of us found flesh. Gunnstein and I hit the same warrior. He was a huge man with a massive war hammer. When our spears came out I saw pieces of the man's heart clinging to them. He was dead. The potion could not keep him alive! We marched, we punched, we blocked. Jarl Gunnstein Berserk Killer must have planned this with his leaders for the Jarl and Thorgeir Sigurdsson both shouted , "Halt! " at the same place.

This time our boar's snout was not as prominent. Thorgeir's men were now just behind Siggi. The enemy had fled down the hill. I looked to my right and saw that the other snout had also shrunk a little but still held. The two jarls and the front rank were the ones who stuck from our line. Had our allies not fled we could have ended the battle there and then but, despite the body littered field, there were still plenty of the enemy.

Siggi began to sing and we all joined in.

Raven Wing Goes to war

Hear our voices hear them roar

A song of death to all its foes

The power of the raven grows and grows.

The power of the raven grows and grows.

The power of the raven grows and grows.

We sang it two or three times and then banged our shields to show that we were not afraid of the enemy and we were unbeaten. I shaded my eyes and looked into the sky. By my reckoning we had been fighting for a couple of hours. We were all thirsty but the enemy would be feeling it just as badly. Now was not the time to lose your nerve.

I noticed a huddle of nobles on horses. They gathered around the standard of the High King. There appeared to be a heated discussion. Then two detached themselves and approached our lines. Arne Four Toes said, "Perhaps they wish to surrender!"

Siggi White Hair shouted, "I hope not. I am just getting warmed up."

They stopped about a hundred paces from us. They rode directly to Raven Wing Clan. Bearing in mind that we had shown that at least two of us could use bows it was a brave or perhaps foolhardy thing to do. One, the elder of the two, began to shout; he pointed at our banner. We did not understand a word but one or two hurled insults back for we thought it would be insults he was shouting.

231

Thorgeir Sigurdsson came over to our wedge. "They are talking to you. They say that the two archers who killed their father and badly wounded their uncle are cowards. If they be men they should stand forward now and do battle with these two."

Everyone knew who had loosed the arrows. We had been challenged and we could not ignore it. Ulf Big Nose snorted. "If they want my head they can try to take it." He stepped from the wedge. "Tell them that I will face them."

I began to move and Siggi held a hand out to restrain me. He said, "You need not. They look to be experienced warriors, Hrolf. You are still learning how to fight."

I smiled, "Do you have so little confidence in me Siggi White Hair? It was you who taught me how to use a sword. Besides the honour of the clan is at stake. I will go." I turned to Thorgeir Sigurdsson. "Tell them I will fight too."

All my comrades cheered and banged their shields. It made me feel better about my decision. As I stepped forward the two men on the ponies burst out laughing. One said something and Thorgeir Sigurdsson said, "He insults you, Hrolf the Horseman. He says you barely have a beard and there will be little honour in killing a woman."

"Tell him that is the only way he could get a woman to lie with him for she would have to be dead to bear his ugly face."

The clan all laughed and cheered. When Thorgeir Sigurdsson translated the one who had insulted me pointed at me."

My friends all laughed. I had said the right thing and showed that I was not intimidated.

They dismounted and put their cloaks over their ponies' backs. They spoke again and Thorgeir said, "They wish to fight Ulf first. They say they will enjoy watching the beardless one wet himself."

I did not bother with an insult. I checked the straps on my shield and slipped my seax into my left hand. Ulf had walked forward. I would watch and see what tricks these Hibernians used. They were both naked to the waist. I ignored their appearance and looked at their weapons. Their shields were half the size of ours and their swords slightly shorter. They looked to be poorly made. They both had a long pointed dagger in their belts. If their men were anything to go by they would be fast and if they had taken a potion too, hard to kill..

Ulf and the elder of the two circled each other. The barbarian suddenly flicked his sword out and Ulf barely had time to bring his shield across to block it. Sparks flew as it clipped the metal edge. The half naked warrior suddenly spun around and brought his sword across Ulf's back. He broke some of the mail links. Ulf was not hurt and he did not look worried but I could see the noble drawing blood soon. As the Hibernian turned Ulf brought his sword down. The barbarian had quick reactions and his shield took the blow but I saw a splinter of wood come from it. I stored that information. There was no metal on the shields. They could be broken.

He was using his speed to mesmerize Ulf. I had seen Ulf hunting and he had quicker reactions than most men. The barbarian came at him with a flurry of blows. He had quick hands. Ulf took most of the strikes on his shield but a couple struck his mail. There was a danger it might start to weaken. Ulf's mail was making him slower than the Hibernian. Ulf then attacked with his own sword. He was going for the head and body of the noble but the barbarian deflected every blow. It was, however, at a cost. His shield began to show signs of deterioration. There was the first sign of doubt on the barbarian's face. He backed off and then did something I had never seen before. He dived forward and did a roll so that his sword came up under Ulf's shield. Ulf was fast and flicked his shield to the side but the sword bit deeply along Ulf's knee. Blood spurted. It was a deep wound. The edge of the barbarian's sword must have been sharp. I could see that Ulf was hurting and the barbarian sensed victory.

As Ulf squared himself the barbarian charged in with another flurry of blows. Ulf did not retreat. His left leg was not moving. He had been slower before and now he was almost stationary. He pushed his shield forward and, instead of striking with his sword he hooked his hilt behind the shield and pulled him towards him. When they closed he pulled his head back and butted the barbarian. With no helmet to protect his face, his head snapped back and his nose erupted in blood and cartilage. He reeled and this time Ulf put all of his power into a mighty blow to his opponent's shield. It splintered. Not only that the warrior's arm hung down, it was broken. He gamely tried to use his sword to fend off Ulf but Ulf's backhand swept aside the chief's sword as though it was a stick. Ulf's right hand was still fast and he brought it around to strike the chief. The blade bit into his chest and he fell backwards. Ulf limped over to him and, holding his hair he took the man's head in one blow. He held it up. We all cheered. Then he threw it towards the High King. It rolled down the slope and the skull ended looking through sightless eyes at the enemy.

As he walked back, pouring blood from his damaged knee he said, through gritted teeth, "Slippery bastards. Watch for tricks."

It was my turn.

Chapter 15

I walked forward. I had never fought one man before. Normally I fought with others. This time every blow would be aimed at me. The man was older than me and, from the scars and warrior bands, more experienced too. I could see the anger on the warrior's face. He had white on his face with a long red streak down each cheek and running into his beard. I think he thought it would make him more frightening. It did not. He also had his long hair stuck up to make him look larger. If I had been him I would have worn a helmet. As I approached I could see that he thought me young, inexperienced and, with a mask on my helmet likely to be unsighted. He came towards me with an easy, confident manner. He had done this before. He was armed just like his brother; a sword and a small shield. Around his neck I saw a metal cross. He was a Christian. I had to find a way to defeat him.

He danced from side to side and swayed. He was trying to do as his brother had done and mesmerize me too. I was not fooled. I could fight on horseback and I had trained myself to keep my eyes fixed on danger. I decided to try to fool him. I opened my left arm so that my shield was slightly open. I kept my sword down. I wanted to tempt him into a quick strike. It was as though he had fooled me and I did not know what to do. He thought I was a novice and I was playing the part.

I heard Erik Green Eye shout, "Pull up your shield, Hrolf! You invite a thrust!"

I said nothing for I knew what I was doing. As his sword darted towards my middle I brought my shield across sharply and I struck the edge of his sword, deflecting it away from me. More importantly I struck it a blow on its blade and began to take the edge off it. At the same time I brought my sword across the top of his shield. He was moving backwards and it was at the extreme range but Heart of Ice had a sharp edge and it tore across his bicep. Blood flowed and my clan cheered.

It enraged him and he did as Ulf's opponent had done, he ran at me with sudden sharp blows with his sword. I danced away and blocked each stroke, not with my sword but with my shield. I would not take the edge from my sword. I kept moving back up the slope away from the blood spilled in the previous combat. He had to stop to catch his breath. I saw, as he rested, that the edge of his sword was nicked and bent slightly. It was true no longer. The bend meant it had no balance. Although my helmet did restrict my vision at the side I was able to concentrate my eyes on him. He could not see my eyes. When his eyes flickered briefly down I knew what he intended. He feinted to my head and then tried his brother's strike and he lunged at my leg. My byrnie came down lower than Ulf's and the warrior had to aim lower to strike flesh. I jumped as his blade came towards me and I landed upon it. I stepped back quickly as he pulled it out and tried to unbalance me. His sword was now definitely bent. My whole weight, byrnie and all had landed on it. He started to shout at me but I could not understand him.

It was my turn to attack for he had run out of the tricks he could use. His shield was still sound and I saw him pull it tighter to him. That suited me. I feinted with my sword and when he moved his sword to block the stroke I punched him in the hand with the boss of my shield and I stepped closed to him. He had seen the head butt from Ulf and he pulled his shield up to stop me. I had no intention of doing so. As I raised my sword I hooked my right leg around his left and punched again with my shield boss. I was unable to hit his face but I caught his shoulder and he began to stumble. He was light on his feet and he moved backwards quickly; too quickly for he tumbled over down the slope. He rolled just beyond his brother's headless corpse.

I could have run after him but I did not. I wanted him to hear the jeers from my clan and to become angry. He picked himself up. I saw his eyes glance at his dead brother's body and he roared and ran up the slope towards me. I waited. I balanced myself on my toes. I did not move and he came directly for me. The slope sapped the energy from his legs and his left arm bled even more. I saw that his shield was dropping. He raised his sword. He was gambling on his speed allowing him to hit my neck with his sword. Even a bent sword might break my neck. Still I did not move and I saw his eyes widen as he saw his chance to win this fight he had been losing. As he swung I stepped back with my left leg and raised my shield. His sword clattered off the top rim and, as he passed me I swung Heart of Ice in a huge sweep with all the power that I could muster. Without armour, without clothes there was nothing to stop the blade and it bit into his side and then slid across to his spine. The power I had put into the strike kept the blade going and it sliced through his backbone and kept going. Had he not been moving away I would have cut him in two. As it was his body fell just twenty paces from the Jarl. His organs and intestines began to slip from the huge hole I had made. The clan cheered.

As the Jarl nodded I heard Siggi shout, "You must take his head. That way they know he has died."

I nodded and, walking to the body, took my sword in two hands and brought it down cleanly. I picked up the hair. The stiff spikes made it hard to hold. I managed to hold it in the air and turned to show first our army and then the Hibernians. Ours cheered. I brought the head around and threw it. It rolled down the hill and stopped just ten paces from his brother's. I sheathed my sword and slung my shield around my back. The two ponies still stood eating grass. They were prizes and I took their reins and led them to the rear.

237

I heard Arne Four Toes shout, "You are still Hrolf the Horseman!"

Ulf was lying down behind our rear rank and Jarl Gunnstein's healers were stitching him. Seeing me he grinned, "I knew you would beat him! No armour and all tricks are no match for a Viking with a shield and a sword. I will watch your animals for you. With this wound I would be a liability."

I picked up a new spear and returned to my place. Asbjorn Ulfsson had taken Ulf's place. "I am honoured to fight alongside a hero."

Olaf the Bear said, from behind me, "Is it not over yet?"

Siggi White Hair snorted, "No but the two deaths have done much to make up for our allies flight."

Gunnstein Gunnarson said, "They have returned. There are few of them but our left side is now, at least, guarded."

I turned and saw the clan all cheering me.

"Shields!"

Once again we locked shields. Mine was pressed into Beorn Fast Feet's back and my spear rested on his shoulder. I could hear the enemy advancing. And then Siggi and the clan began to sing. It was my song.

The horseman came through darkest night

He rode towards the dawning light

With fiery steed and thrusting spear

Hrolf the Horseman brought great fear

Slaughtering all he breached their line

Of warriors slain there were nine

Hrolf the Horseman with gleaming blade

238

Hrolf the Horseman all enemies slayed

With mighty axe Black Teeth stood
Angry and filled with hot blood
Hrolf the Horseman with gleaming blade
Hrolf the Horseman all enemies slayed
Ice cold Hrolf with Heart of Ice
Swung his arm and made it slice
Hrolf the Horseman with gleaming blade
Hrolf the Horseman all enemies slayed

In two strokes the Jarl was felled
Hrolf's sword nobly held
Hrolf the Horseman with gleaming blade
Hrolf the Horseman all enemies slayed

The words sounded clear and this time they were sung with pride for it was our clan which had defeated two enemy champions and it also drew their ire. As they moved towards us I could see that their attack was aimed at our Jarl. We would have to bear the brunt of their attack. This time they did not run. They had no arrows to fear and the ground was still littered with bodies and covered in blood and gore. They had to pass two headless corpses and it had an effect.

Siggi shouted, "Jarl we have stood and endured enough. Let us end this. Can we not meet them, kill this High King and go home?"

We all laughed and the Jarl shouted, "What say you Raven Wing Clan?"

239

As one we shouted, "Aye! Aye!"

The Jarl timed it well. As the line approached and came close to the top of the slope he shouted, "Raven Wing, charge!"

We did not run but we all stepped together in perfect time. During the lull in the bouts the dead from before us had been laid to the side to make a barrier protecting our flank. The ground before us was clear while our enemies had to negotiate bodies. We were together with shields locked and bodies close together. They were a mass of individuals with few shields and no mail. The Jarl and his hearth-weru ploughed in and through the first two lines of men. We in the third rank had plenty of targets too. To our left our allies joined us, throwing themselves at the enemy who had driven them from the field. We punched with our spears and their swords bounced from our shields and mail. As the slope took over we lost a little cohesion but we were now deep in the heart of them and we spread out. I found myself next to Vermund and Siggi in the front rank. The enemy sought me out. I was a champion and had to die.

My spear shattered on the skull of a hard headed Hibernian. His skull spattered blood and bone on those around him and I drew Heart of Ice.

The joy of battle coursed through my veins. I had slain a chief and I shouted, "Heart of Ice! Allfather give me strength!" I left the line and charged at three warriors who were climbing the slope towards me. I blocked two swords with my shield and brought my sword sideways into the side of the third. His sword caught my helmet but I barely noticed it. The other two pulled back their swords to strike at me again but I stepped forward and punched with my shield. The edges caught on the top metal rim. One broke and I slashed across the arm of the other. I severed it to the bone. As the other looked in horror I plunged my sword into his throat. I knocked the armless man out of the way and ran towards the High King. Only his bodyguard stood between us and I heard my comrades as they called my name and followed me. It

240

was too much for Conchobar mac Donnachada of the Uí Néill and he and his bodyguards fled.

The heart went from his army. Feidlimid mac Crimthainn, King of Munster, fought on for a little while. We were busy mopping up those who stood before us but when Jarl Gunnstein Berserk Killer launched a wedge at him, he too quitted the field. The slaughter went on until late afternoon. My sword had been blunted long ago and I drew my seax to end the lives of the enemy who were too badly wounded for the healers. They were followers of the White Christ but they were warriors and they deserved the chance to go to Valhalla.

Wearily I made my way back up the hill. I was too tired to be joyous and I passed bodies of our clan ascended the slope. Eiril Jorgesson, Asbjorn Ulfsson, Kolbjorn Olvirson and Olaf the Bear would not return with us to Raven Wing Island. I reached the body of the chief I had slain. I took the cross from his neck. It would make a fine and appropriate present for Mary. He had three rings on his fingers. I took them. One had a skull upon it while the other two bore jewels. His sword was not worth anything and I left it.

I reached Ulf who was standing now. He held our two bows in his hand and he pointed to the two animals we had taken. "Here are your ponies, Hrolf."

I shook my head, "One is yours."

"You gave me a bow for it was something I would love. I give you my pony for I care not for them, save to eat, and you have an affinity with them. Come hero. Let the two of us drown in ale this night!"

We were surrounded, as we headed back to Dyflin, not only by our clan but other warriors too. Thorgeir Sigurdsson put his huge arm around me. "I could see that Ulf Big Nose was a warrior who could fight but you look as though a strong wind would blow you over. You barely took a blow and you made that son of the chief, Connor mac Murchad, look foolish. He and his brother were both known as champions. I think the High King gambled and lost."

"What do you mean?"

"He put them up to it. He thought to weaken that flank. If the heart went from your men and with our allies fled then they could have rolled our line up. It seems it did not go to plan."

I nodded, "*Wyrd*."

"Aye, as you say, *wyrd*."

Warriors we had never seen before came up to Ulf and me just to stand close to us. They looked at my helmet, my armour and my sword as though they had some magical powers.

"Is this the sword touched by the gods?"

"No, but the same smith who made Ragnar's Spirit made Heart of Ice. He is a good smith."

"It must have cost you much gold?"

I shook my head, "It was a gift from the Dragonheart."

Siggi White Hair, Rurik One Ear and Arne Four Toes closed around us. "Let them have some peace. They have won a battle. We will head back to our drekar. Later will be the time for stories and questions."

I led the two ponies. I had placed Ulf's weapons and my shield upon them. "Where do we sleep tonight?"

"I am guessing the warrior hall."

"I would be just as happy to sleep on the drekar. I do not wish to answer questions all night."

Ulf shook his head. I could see that his knee pained him, "We must. It is how others learn to be warriors."

"Ulf is right, besides Jarl Gunnstein must reward the Jarl. Had we not attacked then we might still be fighting."

"Yes Siggi but Hrolf's charge which we followed drove the High King from the field."

"And that is another reason, Rurik One Ear, why we should attend. The Norns sent us here. Had Lars Larsson not lost his temper on the Sabrina then we would not have raided Ynys Môn and been so overloaded that we had to come to Dyflin. Then Jarl Gunnstein would have lost his land. We are toys in the hands of the Weird Sisters. We have to attend, Hrolf, and we have to smile and answer questions. Resign yourself to it."

"I will leave my mail, helmet and shield on the drekar then. It is strange having warriors wishing to touch them as though they were magic."

"Then you are privileged, you know how the Dragonheart feels. I would leave Heart of Ice there too. But it is understandable. They wish some of your luck or skill to rub off on them."

The others decided to do the same. I had a kyrtle I had not worn. Mary had made it for me. I would wear it. Arne Four Toes told Sven and the ship's boys of the battle as I changed from my mail. I would have bathed in the river but it was not clean water. Instead I used the pail of sea water we kept by the steering board and sluiced away the blood from my naked body.

"You have no wounds but you can see where you took blows. Bagsecg will have much work repairing your mail."

Ulf nodded as he began to dress, "But after this raid we will have much coin." He pointed to my ponies. "And Hrolf has increased his herd."

Sven the Helmsman shook his head and said, vehemently, "I am not having them shitting their way back to our island!"

Siggi shook his head, "You will not have to. The Jarl is going to hire a knarr to transport our treasures. He may have to hire two if Jarl Gunnstein rewards us too!"

With the smell of blood gone from my body I dressed again and put on my spare sealskin boots. I let my hair hang loose after I had combed it. I could not be bothered to plait it. I just put my seax in my belt. With luck there would be meat at the feast. The Jarl and his three hearth-weru arrived. Vermund had lost part of his nose and his already ugly features would be disfigured even more by the long scar down one cheek. It did not seem to bother him for we had won and the hearth-weru had protected our leader.

The Jarl was both happy and proud. He embraced first Ulf Big Nose and then me. "You have given us more glory today than some clans achieve in a lifetime. We have many men who wish to take the places of those who fell. We will sail back with a full crew. And tonight Hallgerd's father is throwing us a feast. Ulf, Hrolf and myself will sit on his high table. We are to be honoured!"

The Jarl decided that the clan would travel together. We would not be eating indoors, there were simply to many of us but the main square had been filled with tables. The main meat would be the horses and ponies which had been killed in the battle. I was grateful that I, at least, had saved two. Beer was in abundance. As we entered the square, for we were the last, every warrior banged his dagger or seax on the tables. It was a cacophony of noise. They cheered. Our names were shouted for it was rare for champions to fight. It was humbling for all the warriors gathered had battle rings and the experience of many sea fights and battles yet the name they chanted was Raven Wing. There were three empty seats by Jarl Gunnstein. Jarl Gunnar and Ulf Big Nose took the two on either side of him. I sat next to Ulf. I noticed that only the two princes of his allies were present. Their men had not covered themselves in glory and their punishment was to be kept from this celebration.

I was determined to keep a clear head but I fear I was the only one. Ulf drank as though tomorrow would never come. In truth I did not blame him. He had had to walk to the feast using the broken shaft of a spear and the beer would numb the pain in his knee. The healers had done their best but the blade had scored his

244

bone. Even when it healed it would ache. The others who drank as much as Ulf, had no excuse save that they had fought in a great battle. The food was plentiful if not particularly well cooked. That was to be understood. I ate because I was hungry and the food stopped the beer going directly to my head.

Before he became too drunk Jarl Gunnstein Berserk Killer stood. "When Jarl Gunnar Thorfinnson asked for my daughter Hallgerd to be his wife I knew him to be a good man and a fine Jarl. After today I know that he and his crew are more than that, they are heroes all!"

This was the cause for even more applause.

He leaned over to me, "And I have to tell these two champions that I have another daughter, Hlif, who I would be more than happy to give as a bride to such men as you."

Ulf was already incoherent and so I answered, "That is a fine offer, Jarl but until I have my own drekar I cannot be the husband your daughter deserves."

I saw Siggi nodding. I had said the right thing. "A good answer but I feel it will not be long before Hrolf the Horseman leads his own band of warriors. Jarl Dragonheart told me that you had something about you and today I saw it."

I saw the briefest of frowns flicker across the face of Jarl Gunnar Thorfinnson. Then he smiled broadly and shouted, "And he will make a good leader too!"

"In that case I can only offer you gold!" he waved his hand and Thorgeir walked over. He carried two golden objects in his hands. "These are two of the torcs from the dead Hibernians. Their chiefs wear them and they are ancient. I give them to you with the promise that when you visit my city you will both be exempt from taxes and shall stay in my hall."

I stood, "I thank the Jarl for both of us. It was an honour to fight alongside you and your brave warriors. I was among heroes this day!"

245

Once again it was the right thing to say. Everyone banged the table again. I sat and prayed that the speeches were over.

They were. I was close enough to the two Jarls to hear their conversation. "After the battle I sent my scouts to find out what they could. The enemy is in complete disarray. They have fled to the west. Then our allies said that they left their wounded to be slain by their scouts They are many miles away now! It was a complete victory. The alliance is broken asunder. We captured a couple of Munster warriors. Before they died they told us that the King of Munster is angry at being left on the field. He did not lose many men but he feels let down. In a month or so I will send emissaries. If I can ally with him too then the High King will never dream of trying to attack me again."

"I am pleased that we could help."

"You could have your own land here too, you know? These savages do not know how to fight. We lost less than forty men today and there are almost a hundred and fifty of theirs slain not counting the wounded and those who will never fight again. Had we had better allies or horsemen then we could have ended the threat permanently."

"I may take you up on your offer but we still have much to do on my island. Neustria is weak and we can raid there at will. The land of the Saxons also offers much opportunity for profit. From what I have seen of this island there is little coin to be made here."

Although he leaned in to speak privately I still heard his words for he was drunk and speaking loudly. "You do not take money, you let people trade in your town and protect them. You make your money from the taxes. You tax the ships which moor, you tax those who buy and you tax those who sell. They are willing to pay, believe me. It is a simpler way to make money than risking life and limb. That was fine when I was a young warrior, now I like my comfort."

246

The discussion was ended when the entertainment, in the shape of acrobats, arrived. I had much to think on as I watched the successful warriors drink themselves into a stupor.

Chapter 16

I had to stay until the end. Ulf was to sleep on the drekar but he would not leave the feast while the Jarl was in the hall. So it was that we were amongst the last to leave. Siggi was able to stand and so the two of us carried Ulf back. He was heavy and it took some time. We were the last ones to head back to the drekar. Our berth was at the far end of the quay and we had to negotiate many warriors who had just fallen asleep wherever they fell. They lay in the streets, under tables. They were everywhere. Ulf was a hardened drinker and he was not unconscious. He might not be able to walk but he could talk or ramble, at least. He mumbled to us as we walked, "We showed them half naked wild men? Eh Hrolf? We showed them."

He was not waiting for a reply. I glanced at him and his eyes had closed. Siggi chuckled, "He is right, Hrolf. Perhaps we should stay here. There would be no danger from men like that." He hiccupped. It seemed to take him by surprise. Despite the fact that he sounded as though he was making sense he was still drunk for he giggled. The huts and buildings were close together as this part of the town was close to the river. It was a popular place to live. At the end of one narrow alley way leading to the river a group of warriors was drunkenly fighting. I heard no metal on metal, just the sound of fists striking flesh. It would not do to get involved and besides I was tired.

"Let us slip down here."

We turned down a narrow passageway behind a large storehouse. No one had decide to sleep here and we found the going easier. I knew we were close to our drekar and just had to turn right at the end of the storehouse and walk alongside it to reach our drekar which lay at the end of the warehouse. Had Ulf Big Nose not been drunk I have no doubt that he would have smelled them but he did not. Just before we turned I caught their smell. It was the same smell as the concoction they used to spike their hair. There were Hibernians nearby.

"Siggi! Danger!"

Drunk or not Siggi trusted me and my judgement. His hand went to his seax, "Then let us get back to the drekar and be away!"

As we turned to move towards the river I saw them. There were four of them. They stood twenty paces away at the end of the warehouse. They were waiting. It was an ambush. Ulf chose that moment to let out the loudest belch I have ever heard. They turned and, seeing us, just raced towards us with weapons drawn. We dropped Ulf and, drawing our seaxes stepped over him to defend his defenceless body. Siggi roared, "Raven Wing! Raven Wing!"

I prayed that there was a deck watch who would hear us. We were outnumbered two to one and we had been drinking. I doubted that the four wild men who hurtled towards us had. They were armed with short swords and daggers And I saw that they had had cloaks to disguise them. That gave me hope. The passage was narrow and they would not be able to swing as freely with a cloak about their shoulders. I was faster than Siggi and as we closed I decided to use one of their tricks. I dived and rolled at the leading warrior. He did not see my move until the last moment but, even so he almost caught my head as he swung his sword. I hit him with my outstretched hand and seax. It drove deep within his guts. I kept hold as I landed and I twisted. He gave a scream which sounded like the death throe of a wild animal. Warm blood cascaded over me. My shoulder crashed into the shin of a second man who could not swing for fear of hitting his companion.

I sprang to my feet and reached up to grab the sword hand of this second warrior. I heard a noise from the end of the storehouse. Someone had heard our cries and there was the sound of noise from the drekar. Even if it was just the ship's boys then we might have a chance. The warrior whose sword I held stabbed at me with his dagger. Instinctively, in the dark I fended it off with my seax. The blades rang together. I stamped down on his foot. I knew they did not wear boots. At the same time I pushed his sword hand against the warehouse and twisted my seax. The edge found his leg and I sawed back and forth. I felt his blood begin to pour. He pulled his left arm back and stabbed at me again. I was slower this time and I felt his dagger slide across my back. I felt blood drip.

I must have cut something vital in his leg for he went limp in my arms. I whipped around. One warrior lay trying to hold his guts in but the fourth had raised his hand and was about to decapitate an unconscious Siggi whose body lay draped over Ulf. I pulled my arm back and drove the seax up through his ribs. As his back arced I grabbed his sword hand. I pushed up into his body diagonally. When my fingers touched the jagged edge of his ribs he stopped moving. I had pierced his heart.

Sven the Helmsman and Harold Fast Sailing appeared armed with a half dozen ship's boys. "What happened Hrolf?"

"Treachery! We were ambushed. Siggi is hurt. We must get help."

We carried the two of them back to the drekar. Some of those less drunk than the others were staring at us as though they were dreaming. I saw the Eriksson brothers, "There are four dead and wounded Hibernians. Fetch them aboard we need to find out where they came from."

They hesitated and Sven snapped, "Do it!" They both nodded and left. "Fetch light. Karl Swift Foot stand guard at the end of the gangplank."

Ulf looked no different save that, having been laid down, he had fallen asleep but Siggi had been wounded. There was blood on his head and his white hair was stained red but it was his side where we saw the serious wound. He had been stabbed. We stripped him and saw that he had a deep wound to his side. It bled. If we did nothing he would die. Hold him still!" Sven grabbed the torch which Sigurd, the ship's boy, had brought and he held it to the wound. Siggi, although unconscious jerked and thrashed in our arms. There was the smell of burning hair and flesh. Smoke rose but when he pulled the torch away we could see that the bleeding had stopped. Harold poured water over the wound to cool it. "Cover him in furs. Sigurd, watch him."

As Sven the Helmsman turned with the torch Harold Fast Sailing shouted, "Hrolf, you are wounded too!"

I had forgotten the wound I had suffered. They pulled my kyrtle from me. Oddly the thought which came into my head was not the wound but the cut. Mary would not be happy that her good work had been ruined. "Hold the sheerstrake while I examine it." I grabbed the sheerstrake with both hands and peered into the black water of the river.

I felt his hand, amazingly gentle, as he ran it over the wound. He said nothing but I suddenly felt heat and then had the most vicious pain I had ever felt. I dropped to my knees as he seared my side too. When Harold threw water upon the seared wound it felt like a blessed relief.

They helped me to my feet. Rurik had risen and the sights, sounds and smells had helped to sober him. "You were lucky there, Hrolf. It will just be a fine scar you have to show to your grandchildren. You will live and that is good."

The four dead Hibernians had been brought aboard. Each clan had different symbols and markings. I noticed that these four all had long hair and it was not tied back. They had it spiked and it was in the style of Connor mac Murchad, the man I had killed in single combat.

"These look to be those we fought today but how did they get into the town unseen? The Jarl said his scouts had said our enemies were all fled. And there were sentries on the gates. There is treachery afoot."

"We will have to keep watch this night for I fear the feast has dulled the senses of all those within these walls. Tomorrow we must unravel the knot!"

I donned an old kyrtle and wrapped myself in a cloak. The pain from the cauterized wound would not let me sleep and so I sat with Sven and Harold and we kept watch. Dawn seemed to take an age to arrive. I had time to think. The four had been waiting for Ulf and me. The place they had chosen to wait meant that they could watch as we came back down the quayside. They were looking for us specifically. Had we not deviated because of the fight then they would have had us before we could draw our weapons. It was only the fact that I had smelled them first which had allowed us to avoid death. Had these dead men been oathsworn? Had they come of their own accord or had someone ordered them? I did not know these people nor how they thought. The Franks and the Bretons would not have done this. They would have had vengeance but used different methods. This was a quick and deadly response to a combat initiated by the dead brothers. I did not understand it.

Ulf woke first. He sat up and rubbed his head. "That was a drink and no mistake." He turned and looked at Siggi lying next to him. He laughed, "That is the first time the old goat has had more to drink than me."

I held my hand to help him up. "He was wounded, Ulf. We were ambushed last night by these four." I pointed to the bodies which lay by the mast.

He became alert. "The two of you slew four killers?"

Sven nodded, "Aye and Hrolf suffered a serious wound too."

Ulf clasped my arm, "Does Jarl Gunnar know of this?"

"No. We have yet to speak with him."

He shook his head, "I should have been like you, Hrolf, and drunk less. I thought we were safe here."

We donned our mail for there had to be retribution for this treacherous attack. My back felt tender even with the padded kyrtle between the mail and my new wound. We were about to leave when Gunnstein Gunnarson, who had stayed close by the Jarl, ran up. "There has been murder. The guards at the north gate have been slain."

Sven the Helmsman pointed to the cloak covered bodies, "And we have killed their killers."

"I had best return to the hall. They will wish to know this."

As men came back and heard the story they armed. Siggi was almost a father to us all. He was the eldest of the warriors and the fact that he had come so close to death made them angry. He stirred not long after Gunnstein had left us. His groan made us turn.

"I thought to wake in Valhalla. What happened?"

They looked at me. "You were knocked out and the last Hibernian was going to slay you. I killed him."

"I owe you a life, Hrolf."

"No Siggi for I owe you far more and it was Sven who sealed the wound." I pointed to the cloaks, "These four murdered the guards at the gates. That is how they gained entry."

He nodded, "I feared treachery. This is just incompetence from the guards but they have paid with their lives."

Jarl Gunnstein appeared along with Jarl Gunnar and their hearth-weru. The Jarl of Dyflin uncovered the bodies. He scowled, "They are the kin of Connor mac Murchad. I recognise the clan markings."

We looked at our Jarl. It was for him to question his father in law. He asked, "But the scouts said that the enemy had fled west. How did they come from the north?"

He looked bleakly at Jarl Gunnar, "They did not do their job. I should have sent my scouts. I apologise. The fault is mine. I have lost men and yours have been wounded when you were my guests. I will make amends. We will hunt this clan and destroy them." He nodded to me and Ulf, "When I return I shall bring you their heads."

Ulf Big Nose shook his head, "No Jarl Gunnstein Berserk Killer. We will come with you. The blood of one of ours was shed and we will take revenge."

"But you are both wounded."

"Aye and we are warriors of the Raven Wing Clan. We do our own killing!"

While we prepared to go hunting those who had sent the killers the two Jarls went back to the hall to speak with Mal mac Rochride. He was the prince ally who had sent the scouts out.

Ulf spat over the side, "Prince! Any jumped up warrior who fancies a title calls himself a chief. It means nothing."

I was worried about Ulf and his leg. "I know we cannot keep you from this hunt but you cannot walk."

"Who are you to tell me so?"

"I am the warrior who has scouted with you, Ulf Big Nose, and remembers your words about moving swiftly. The Jarl's wife with child before her can move faster than you." I paused, gauging his reaction, "and you know it." He nodded. "Take the pony. The Norns sent them for a purpose did they not?"

"Aye you are right!" he shook his head, "I preferred it when you were an ignorant young warrior. Your head is becoming too wise and you show much courage facing up to an old man like me!"

"You taught me well."

We were ready by the time Rolf Arneson came to fetch us. "The Jarl questioned our ally. When he sent for his men he discovered that two of them were in the pay of Conchobar mac Donnachada. After they had been tortured and told all the Jarl gave them the blood eagle. I do not think that Mal mac Rochride had ever seen it before. He was a chastened man. We go to their village, Áth Truim. It is twenty miles from here." He looked at Ulf, questioningly.

"I ride one of Hrolf's ponies. I will not hold you up."

He nodded, "The men you killed are of the Cenél Lóegairi clan. It is one of their strongholds."

Ulf looked up at the sky. "We had best leave unless we wish to fight at night."

"They wait for us at the north gate. Many men had left for their homes this morning. It will not be a large band we take. The Jarl does not wish to take his allies and he leaves a garrison to guard the town. We will have to make do with the men we take."

Ulf's long legs almost reached the ground but I could see, when he mounted, that he would find this much easier than walking. What I was not sure of was his ability to fight. No one had suggested that I stay with Siggi and the drekar. Perhaps they saw my face. I would not leave the treacherous attack unpunished . Nor would I allow others to fight and, perhaps, die for me.

The two Jarls led. They too rode ponies and were followed by their hearth-weru. Ulf and I had brought our bows. We knew that the Cenél Lóegairi clan had a palisade but Mal mac Rochride assured us that it was not large enough to stop us. We were sceptical. So far we were less than impressed with our allies. I had had two wounds and both were in my back. The one in my left shoulder had healed well. Would the one on my right side heal either as quickly or as well?

We marched in silence, without songs. We marched with firm resolve to avenge ourselves. We marched all through the morning. We halted briefly at a stream to take on water and for some warriors to empty their stomachs. We had lost warriors in the battle and Siggi had come close to death. There was grim determination amongst the twenty five of us who marched. The rest, the wounded and the drekar crew, would guard the drekar and watch for further treachery. I had managed to sharpen my sword. It had been almost blunt after the battle. My shield needed repairs but that would have to wait. My helmet and mail had not suffered as much as some others but we had no spears. The heads from the shattered spears would have to be taken home and Bagsecg would repair and refit them to new shafts.

The road was flat but it was not Roman and, in places, it was uneven. However we made good time and in the middle of the afternoon we saw the wooden walls less than a mile away. I could see a river but it guarded the stronghold from the north and not from the south. It was obvious we had been seen for we saw people fleeing towards the open gates. We stopped a mile from the walls while we prepared. We drank first and then we prepared for battle. We tightened straps and adjusted helmets. We slid swords in and out of scabbards. We waited for the orders to advance. Compared with the strongholds in the land of the Saxons and the Franks this was little better than a pig pen. There would be little preamble. The plan was simple. We would march up to the gate and batter it and the wall down. Many of Jarl Gunnstein Berserk Killer's men had axes and they were angry that their comrades had been slain at their gate. They also felt that they had let down their guests, us.

There was no discussion and no offer of peace. Then we marched again. Ulf and I did not go in the front rank. We took our bows and halted two hundred paces from the wall. While the double shield wall marched towards the gate and the shallow ditch we released arrow after arrow at the walls. Until we had hit eight men they discounted the effect we would have. After that we had no targets. I handed my bow and my arrows to Ulf. "You can ride to the gates but I must march."

He nodded, "May the Allfather be with you."

I brought my shield around and drew my sword. The movement sent paroxysms of pain coursing through my body. I gritted my teeth. I could not let pain stop me. Already I could hear the axes as they pounded on the gate and the walls. Those within had not had time to prepare and there were few stones and rocks to hurl at the attackers. The few they sent were easily blocked by our shields. Even so a few lucky javelins had got through and I saw some of Jarl Gunnstein Berserk Killer's men being dragged away from the walls. It was the wooden walls which fell first. Had we been more rested we could have climbed them but the twenty five mile march had taken its toll after the battle the previous day. I reached the line just as Rurik's axe smashed through the wall. He hit it again and again to widen the gap and we entered the town.

The wild men who had survived the day before threw themselves at us as we made our way through the hole Rurik had made. We did not enter as a band but in groups and Rurik, Arne and Gunnstein Gunnarson had to fend off a furious attack until others reached them. The Eriksson brothers made up for their poor attitude before the last battle and they launched themselves at those trying to get at Rurik and the others. The ferocity of their attack and their mail and weapons cleared a space and allowed the rest of us through. The Jarl and the hearth-weru followed Jarl Gunnstein through the gateway further to our right. I heard Jarl Gunnstein Berserk Killer shout, "Kill every man and boy! Let none live!"

I followed Rurik and Arne as they ran towards the wooden hall in the centre of the town. It was on top of a small hill and their warriors were retreating towards it. The women and children fled behind a wall of screaming warriors. They shouted at us; I had no doubt they were curses. They called, no doubt, on their One God to save them and still we advanced. One man, obviously determined to die heroically, hurled himself from the ranks of the retreating warriors to attack Vermund and the Jarl. He threw himself high in the air and brought his sword down to try to split the Jarl in two. Vermund and the Jarl both put their shields up at the same time. The Jarl brought his sword across. It bit deeply into the side of the warrior who, even while dying, still cursed and howled at us. His sword slid off the two shields. There was no possibility that these men would die easily. They might be Christians but that was but skin deep. Beneath their skin beat the hearts and spirits of barbarian warriors.

We moved in two lines and I was in the second behind Arne Four Toes. We moved relentlessly forward. Part of that was tiredness and part a desire to ensure that no one escaped. Jarl Gunnstein was showing the local tribes that he ruled here and not the High King. We stopped just thirty paces from them. Most of them did not use shields and could not make a shield wall but there were two men who looked like minor chiefs. They held shields. Their eight oathsworn had small wooden shields. If they used them then they would be kindling!

One of the chiefs steeped forward. He ranted, raved and shouted. Then he stopped. Thorgeir translated. "He says that the Cenél Lóegairi are an ancient people and this land is theirs. You have killed their nobles and they have had revenge and the killers now lie dead. Soon we will lie with them. Their god will give them victory over pagans!"

When our men heard that they began to jeer and howl. Jarl Gunnstein Berserk Killer said, "Hrolf, step forward. Thorgeir tell them that this is one of the warriors who killed their noble and the other is taking his rest."

As I stepped from behind Arne they saw my distinctive shield and helmet. They had seen them on the battlefield the previous day. One young warrior, an oathsworn suddenly ran out from the barbarian line. He punched Thorgeir out of the way with his shield and raised his sword to take my head. He was fast. Luckily my shield was facing my front and my sword was out. His sword clattered into my shield with all the weight of his body behind it. I reeled slightly. Then I stepped on to my right foot as I brought my sword around in a long sweep. There was no subtlety in the stroke. I hit his shield and it splintered. My sword bit through the leather and into his arm. As I had reeled so did he but I was upon him. As he fell I raised my shield and smashed it down on his windpipe. He lay still.

I was angry. I raised my sword and shouted, "Raven Wing Clan!" I ran towards their lines and their chiefs. My brethren and the rest of Jarl Gunnstein's warriors followed. I hit two men, a chief and one of his bodyguards with my shield as I stabbed into the stomach of the chief. I tore the blade out sideways and ducked as the body guard tried to take my head. I brought my sword up into his groin. I felt it grate along bone and then I ripped it out. The two lay in widening pools of blood. I saw two young warriors with swords who jumped high in the air to kill me. One was thrown back by an arrow. I plunged my sword into the second and turned to see Ulf with his bow. He was astride the pony. He was there at the kill. He was able to see the men and boys of the village be slaughtered. None asked for mercy. They fought when they had lost arms, legs or parts of their face but inevitably their twitching bodies stopped moving and they died. Our warriors went around every body and chopped the head from them. We wanted no one to feign death.

"Bind the women and children! Search the men for treasure and then burn their bodies in the hall. This will be a blackened reminder of the folly of challenging Jarl Gunnstein Berserk Killer! Put the heads of the dead on the palisade!"

I went to the body of the chief I had killed. I took his torc. He had no cross but he too had two rings. One had a skull upon it. I took it to be the symbol of the tribe. As I had thought their Christianity covered deeper, pagan beliefs. As the bodies began to burn Thorgeir came to me. "I am sorry Hrolf the Horseman. I should have stopped that barbarian."

"It was *wyrd*. We began this feud with our arrows when we slew their leaders. It is right that it ends here now."

When the fire caught and the flames leapt high into the sky we turned and headed home. We marched through the late afternoon, beyond dusk and arrived back in Dyflin after dark. Extra guards were placed on the gates so that we could sleep easy in our beds. We slept aboard our drekar. We had made a Blót in the Sabrina and that along with the spirit of our drekar would keep us far safer than the Jarl's guards. I was so tired that I fell asleep in an instant and slept so soundly that I was in the same position when I woke the next day.

Jarl Gunnar went to arrange a knarr just after dawn. We had much to take back with us. Jarl Gunnstein insisted on paying for the hire of the knarr. It was not a purely generous act. He would sell the slaves we had captured in Áth Truim. He would send us our share but he would make more profit from the arrangement. Our Welsh slaves and grain were loaded on the knarr, along with our two ponies while the gold, swords and treasures we had taken from their dead were placed on our drekar. The Hibernians did not use mail but they liked gold and silver. We were all much richer.

Three days after the battle we left the Liffey and headed out to sea. It would be a three or four day journey home for we had to travel at the speed of the knarr and we had empty benches.

260

Those warriors who wished to leave Jarl Gunnstein Berserk Killer's service and join our clan would have to serve until Midsummer Day. The Jarl was loath to leave himself short of men but by then we would have a second drekar for we had made enough to be able to seek the services of Bolli of Cyninges-tūn. Jarl Gunnstein Berserk Killer had offered to sell us his new drekar but Jarl Gunnar knew the kind of drekar we wanted. It would accommodate more men and we would be able to defeat more enemies. Our clan was growing.

Epilogue

Our island had never looked as good as we sailed towards my cove. Hrolfstad was the obvious choice to land the knarr. The wooden quay meant that we would not lose either slaves nor livestock. While the able bodied left the drekar with me those who were still suffering from wounds, like Ulf and Siggi, sailed around to Raven Wing Bay.

Mary and Gille were there to greet me as I landed. They had seen the ships. Gille told me later that Mary had gone there twice a day to watch for me every day since I had left. He laughed as he told me that Dream Strider had told him that I would be coming in soon. This was Gille's first time watching for me. It had been Dream Strider which had made him do so. We took the slaves off first and they were herded and led across the island. Each carried something we had taken. The time they had spent in the slave pens had made them realise what their future held and they were resigned to it. They were passive as they headed south. Next we took the grain. Until carts could be fetched it would stay at my farm. Finally it was the livestock which was taken off. I took the ponies off first as the knarr rode lower in the water and it was easier. Gille was delighted and he and Mary led them up to the pen. We would have to enlarge it soon. For now its small size would help my five animals become a family.

After the livestock had been taken the hearth-weru carried the treasure which the Jarl had accrued. We each had our own treasure but, as Jarl, he had more. He had enough to buy a drekar. It would be a bigger one than *'Raven Wing'* and would be built at Cyninges-tūn. As the knarr turned and set sail for Olissipo where she would trade, the Jarl walked alone with me to my home.

"You have brought much honour to the clan. I would offer you the chance to become hearth-weru if I did not know that someday you will leave me." He nodded, "The Weird Sisters have decreed it so, it is *wyrd*. But know you that no one on this whole

262

island is held in more honour than you. Whatever you decide in the future and wherever you travel I will always remember what you did for us."

"I have no plans to leave yet. I am still learning. I must become a horse master and I must learn to lead. I have learned much watching others."

He looked relieved, "Good for I thought with all your gold that you be away before harvest time."

"No Jarl. I will not leave yet."

That evening I gave Mary the cross and Gille one of the skull rings. He liked it. I told them of some of the things we had done. They knew of Ulf's injury and Siggi's so it was inevitable they would know that I had been wounded too but the fact that I walked well and did not appear to be troubled made it easier. A month after our return the Jarl and Siggi left on the drekar to pick up our new men and to order the drekar. He had barely been gone two nights when Gerðr went into labour. I was grateful that Mary and Gille were there for I am not sure I would have known what to do. Gille had helped his father and Mary was a woman. She knew what to do. The young colt was healthy and golden. He shone like gold. It was the horse from my dream! We called him Copper. Mary wanted a name which was not Norse and neither Gille nor I wanted a Christian name. It seemed right. As we watched the gangly colt take its first faltering steps it seemed like a symbol of us and our lives. We were taking our first steps as a family and a clan. Where would they lead us? The gods and the Norns knew the answer. We just lived the best that we could.

The End

Glossary

Afon Hafron- River Severn in Welsh
Alt Clut- Dumbarton Castle on the Clyde
Andecavis- Angers in Anjou
An Oriant- Lorient, Brittany
Áth Truim- Trim, County Meath (Ireland)
Balley Chashtal -Castleton (Isle of Man)
Bebbanburgh- Bamburgh Castle, Northumbria.
Also know as Din Guardi in the ancient tongue
Beck- a stream
Blót – a blood sacrifice made by a jarl
Blue Sea/Middle Sea- The Mediterranean
Bondi- Viking farmers who fight
Bourde- Bordeaux
Bjarnarøy –Great Bernera (Bear island)
Byrnie- a mail or leather shirt reaching down to the
knees
Caerlleon- Welsh for Chester
Caestir - Chester (old English)
Cantewareburh- Canterbury
Casnewydd –Newport, Wales
Cent- Kent
Cephas- Greek for Simon Peter (St. Peter)
Cetham -Chatham Kent
Chape- the tip of a scabbard
Charlemagne- Holy Roman Emperor at the end of
the 8th and beginning of the 9th centuries
Cherestanc- Garstang (Lancashire)
Corn Walum or Om Walum- Cornwall
Cymri- Welsh
Cymru- Wales

Cyninges-tūn – Coniston. It means the estate of the king (Cumbria)

Dùn Èideann –Edinburgh (Gaelic)

Din Guardi- Bamburgh castle

Drekar- a Dragon ship (a Viking warship)

Duboglassio –Douglas, Isle of Man

Dyrøy –Jura (Inner Hebrides)

Dyflin- Old Norse for Dublin

Ein-mánuðr- middle of March to the middle of April

Eoforwic- Saxon for York

Faro Bregancio- Corunna (Spain)

Ferneberga -Farnborough (Hampshire)

Fey- having second sight

Firkin- a barrel containing eight gallons (usually beer)

Fret-a sea mist

Frankia- France and part of Germany

Fyrd-the Saxon levy

Gaill- Irish for foreigners

Galdramenn- wizard

Glaesum –amber

Gleawecastre- Gloucester

Gói- the end of February to the middle of March

Greenway- ancient roads- they used turf rather than stone

Grenewic- Greenwich

Gyllingas - Gillingham Kent

Haesta- Hastings

Hamwic -Southampton

Haughs- small hills in Norse (As in Tarn Hows)

Hearth-weru- Jarl's bodyguard/oathsworn

Heels- when a ship leans to one side under the pressure of the wind

Hel - Queen of Niflheim, the Norse underworld.

Herkumbl- a mark on the front of a helmet denoting the clan of a Viking warrior

Here Wic- Harwich

Hetaereiarch – Byzantine general

Hí- Iona (Gaelic)

Hjáp - Shap- Cumbria (Norse for stone circle)

Hoggs or Hogging- when the pressure of the wind causes the stern or the bow to droop

Hrams-a – Ramsey, Isle of Man

Hrofecester-Rochester Kent

Hywel ap Rhodri Molwynog- King of Gwynedd 814-825

Icaunis- British river god

Issicauna- Gaulish for the lower Seine

Itouna- River Eden Cumbria

Jarl- Norse earl or lord

Joro-goddess of the earth

jǫtunn -Norse god or goddess

kjerringa - Old Woman- the solid block in which the mast rested

Knarr- a merchant ship or a coastal vessel

Kyrtle-woven top

Leathes Water- Thirlmere

Ljoðhús- Lewis

Legacaestir- Anglo Saxon for Chester

Liger- Loire

Lochlannach – Irish for Northerners (Vikings)

Lothuwistoft- Lowestoft

Louis the Pious- King of the Franks and son of Charlemagne

Lundenwic - London

Maeresea- River Mersey

Mammceaster- Manchester

Manau/Mann – The Isle of Man(n) (Saxon)

Marcia Hispanic- Spanish Marches (the land around Barcelona)

Mast fish- two large racks on a ship for the mast

Melita- Malta

Midden - a place where they dumped human waste

Miklagård - Constantinople

Leudes- Imperial officer (a local leader in the Carolingian Empire. They became Counts a century after this.

Njoror- God of the sea

Nithing- A man without honour (Saxon)

Odin - The "All Father" God of war, also associated with wisdom, poetry, and magic (The ruler of the gods).

Olissipo- Lisbon

Orkneyjar-Orkney

Portucale- Porto

Portesmūða -Portsmouth

Condado Portucalense- the County of Portugal

Penrhudd – Penrith Cumbria

Pillars of Hercules- Straits of Gibraltar

Ran- Goddess of the sea

Roof rock- slate

Rinaz –The Rhine

Sabrina- Latin and Celtic for the River Severn. Also the name of a female Celtic deity

Saami- the people who live in what is now Northern Norway/Sweden

St. Cybi- Holyhead

sampiere -samphire (sea asparagus)

Scree- loose rocks in a glacial valley

Seax – short sword

Sheerstrake- the uppermost strake in the hull

Sheet- a rope fastened to the lower corner of a sail

Shroud- a rope from the masthead to the hull amidships

Skeggox – an axe with a shorter beard on one side of the blade

South Folk- Suffolk

Stad- Norse settlement

Stays- ropes running from the mast-head to the bow

Stirap- stirrup

Strake- the wood on the side of a drekar

Suthriganaworc - Southwark (London)

Syllingar- Scilly Isles

Syllingar Insula- Scilly Isles

Tarn- small lake (Norse)

Temese- River Thames (also called the Tamese)

The Norns- The three sisters who weave webs of intrigue for men

Thing-Norse for a parliament or a debate (Tynwald)

Thor's day- Thursday

Threttanessa- a drekar with 13 oars on each side.

Thrall- slave

Tinea- Tyne

Trenail- a round wooden peg used to secure strakes

Tynwald- the Parliament on the Isle of Man

Úlfarrberg- Helvellyn

Úlfarrland- Cumbria

Úlfarr- Wolf Warrior

Úlfarrston- Ulverston

Ullr-Norse God of Hunting

Ulfheonar-an elite Norse warrior who wore a wolf skin over his armour

Vectis- The Isle of Wight

Volva- a witch or healing woman in Norse culture

Waeclinga Straet- Watling Street (A5)

Windlesore-Windsor

Waite- a Viking word for farm

Werham -Wareham (Dorset)

Wintan-ceastre -Winchester

Withy- the mechanism connecting the steering board to the ship

Woden's day- Wednesday

Wyddfa-Snowdon

Wyrd- Fate
Yard- a timber from which the sail is suspended on
a drekar
Ynys Môn-Anglesey

Maps and Illustrations

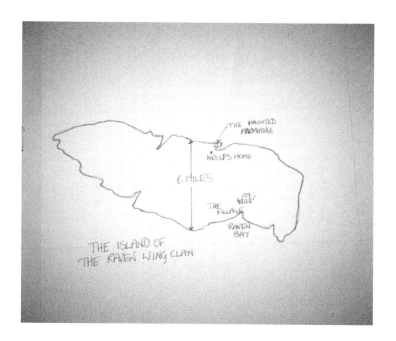

THE HAUNTED FARMHOUSE

HROLF'S HOME

6 MILES

THE VILLAGE

RAVEN BAY

THE ISLAND OF THE RAVEN WING CLAN

Griff Hosker 2016

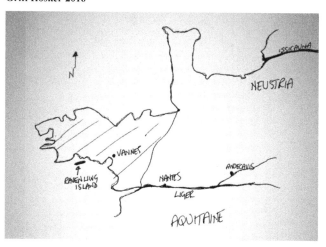

N

ISSICAUNA

NEUSTRIA

VANNET

RAVEN WING ISLAND

ANDECAVIS

NANTES

LIGER

AQUITAINE

Griff Hosker 2016

Map courtesy of Wikipedia

Charlemagne's Empire

Courtesy of Wikipedia –Public Domain

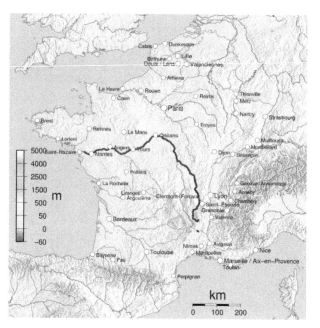

The Loire

272

Historical note

My research encompasses not only books and the Internet but also TV. Time Team was a great source of information. I wish they would bring it back! I saw the wooden compass which my sailors use on the Dan Snow programme about the Vikings. Apparently it was used in modern time to sail from Denmark to Edinburgh and was only a couple of points out. Similarly the construction of the temporary hall was copied from the settlement of Leif Eriksson in Newfoundland.

Stirrups began to be introduced in Europe during the 7th and 8th Centuries. By Charlemagne's time they were widely used but only by nobles. It is said this was the true beginning of feudalism. It was the Vikings who introduced them to England. It was only in the time of Canute the Great that they became widespread. The use of stirrups enabled a rider to strike someone on the ground from the back of a horse and facilitated the use of spears and later, lances.

The Vikings may seem cruel to us now. They enslaved women and children. Many of the women became their wives. The DNA of the people of Iceland shows that it was made up of a mixture of Norse and Danish males and Celtic females. These were the people who settled Iceland, Greenland and Vinland. They did the same in England and, as we shall see, Normandy. Their influence was widespread. Genghis Khan and his Mongols did the same in the 13th century. It is said that a high proportion of European males have Mongol blood in them. The Romans did it with the Sabine tribe. They were different times and it would be wrong to judge them with our politically correct twenty first century eyes. This sort of behaviour still goes on in the world but with less justification.

The Vikings began to raid the Loire and the Seine from the middle of the 9th century. They were able to raid as far as Tours. Tours, Saumur and the monastery at Marmoutier were all raided and destroyed. As a result of the raids and the destruction castles were built there during the latter part of the 9th century. There are many islands in the Loire and many tributaries. The Maine, which runs through Angers, is also a wide waterway. The lands seemed made for Viking raiders. They did not settle in Aquitaine but they did in Austrasia.

At this time there were no Viking Kings. There were clans. Each clan had a hersir or Jarl. Clans were loyal to each other. A hersir was more of a landlocked Viking or a farmer while a Jarl usually had ship(s) at his command. A hersir would command bondi. They were the Norse equivalent of the fyrd although they were much better warriors. They would all have a helmet shield and a sword. Most would also have a spear. Hearth-weru were the oathsworn or bodyguards for a jarl or, much later on, a king. Kings like Canute and Harald Hadrada were rare and they only emerged at the beginning of tenth century.

Hermund the Bent is an actual Viking name but I do not know why he was called Bent. It seemed appropriate for my villain. Harald Black Teeth is made up but the practice of filing marks in teeth to allow them to blacken and to make the warrior more frightening was common in Viking times.

The wolf and the raven were both held in high esteem by the Vikings. Odin is often depicted with a wolf and a raven at his side.

The battle at Rochester Bridge is based on the famous incident at Stamford Bridge in 1066 when three Vikings held off the whole of King Harold's army until warriors went below the wooden bridge and killed the Vikings from beneath by stabbing their spears through the wood of the bridge. Rochester Bridge was made by the Romans!

I apologise for the complications of the names and the plotting of the Irish kings. I did not have to make them up. The events leading up to the battle outside did happen and the High King was murdered himself a couple of years later. High King was similar to being a Mafia boss. There was always someone trying to take over. There was, as far as I know, no battle between the Irish and the Vikings in 825 but as neither civilisation had good written records it is hard to find hard evidence. The Irish warriors did not wear armour. Until the arrival of the Vikings they had no need for their enemies fought as they did. Their courage was unquestioned and they had managed to conquer what is now Scotland but the Vikings proved a stronger enemy. By the end of the ninth century the key strongholds in Ireland were all controlled by the Vikings. History would repeat itself when Henry II arrived with his Normans three centuries later.

Books used in the research

British Museum - Vikings- Life and Legends

Arthur and the Saxon Wars- David Nicolle (Osprey)

Saxon, Norman and Viking Terence Wise (Osprey)

The Vikings- Ian Heath (Osprey)

Byzantine Armies 668-1118 - Ian Heath (Osprey)

Romano-Byzantine Armies 4th-9th Century - David Nicholle (Osprey)

The Walls of Constantinople AD 324-1453 - Stephen Turnbull (Osprey)

Viking Longship - Keith Durham (Osprey)

Anglo-Danish Project- The Vikings in England

The Varangian Guard- 988-1453 Raffael D'Amato

Saxon Viking and Norman- Terence Wise

The Walls of Constantinople AD 324-1453-Stephen Turnbull

Byzantine Armies- 886-1118- Ian Heath

The Age of Charlemagne-David Nicolle

The Normans- David Nicolle

Norman Knight AD 950-1204- Christopher Gravett

The Norman Conquest of the North- William A Kappelle

The Knight in History- Francis Gies

The Norman Achievement- Richard F Cassady

Knights- Constance Brittain Bouchard

Griff Hosker
July 2016

Other books

by

Griff Hosker

If you enjoyed reading this book, then why not read another one by the author?

Ancient History

The Sword of Cartimandua Series (Germania and Britannia 50A.D. – 128 A.D.)

Ulpius Felix- Roman Warrior (prequel)

Book 1 The Sword of Cartimandua

Book 2 The Horse Warriors

Book 3 Invasion Caledonia

Book 4 Roman Retreat

Book 5 Revolt of the Red Witch

Book 6 Druid's Gold

Book 7 Trajan's Hunters

Book 8 The Last Frontier

Book 9 Hero of Rome

Book 10 Roman Hawk

Book 11 Roman Treachery

Book 12 Roman Wall

Book 13 Roman Courage

The Aelfraed Series (Britain and Byzantium 1050 A.D. - 1085 A.D.

Book 1 Housecarl

Book 2 Outlaw

Book 3 Varangian

The Wolf Warrior series (Britain in the late 6th Century)

Book 1 Saxon Dawn

Book 2 Saxon Revenge

Book 3 Saxon England

Book 4 Saxon Blood

Book 5 Saxon Slayer

Book 6 Saxon Slaughter

Book 7 Saxon Bane

Book 8 Saxon Fall: Rise of the Warlord

Book 9 Saxon Throne

The Dragon Heart Series

Book 1 Viking Slave

Book 2 Viking Warrior

Book 3 Viking Jarl

Book 4 Viking Kingdom

Book 5 Viking Wolf

Book 6 Viking War

Book 7 Viking Sword

Book 8 Viking Wrath

Book 9 Viking Raid

Book 10 Viking Legend

Book 11 Viking Vengeance

Book 12 Viking Dragon

Book 13 Viking Treasure

Book 14 Viking Enemy

Book 15 Viking Witch

Bool 16 Viking Blood

Book 17 Viking Weregeld

Book 18 Viking Storm

Book 19 Viking Warband

The Norman Genesis Series

Rolf

Horseman

The Battle for a Home

Revenge of the Franks

The Land of the Northmen

Ragnvald Hrolfsson

Brothers in Blood

Lord of Rouen

The Anarchy Series England 1120-1180
English Knight
Knight of the Empress
Northern Knight
Baron of the North
Earl
King Henry's Champion
The King is Dead
Warlord of the North
Enemy at the Gate
Warlord's War
Kingmaker
Henry II
Crusader
The Welsh Marches
Irish War
Poisonous Plots

Border Knight 1182-1300
Sword for Hire
Return of the Knight

Modern History
The Napoleonic Horseman Series
Book 1 Chasseur a Cheval

Book 2 Napoleon's Guard

Book 3 British Light Dragoon

Book 4 Soldier Spy

Book 5 1808: The Road to Corunna

Waterloo

The Lucky Jack American Civil War series

Rebel Raiders

Confederate Rangers

The Road to Gettysburg

The British Ace Series

1914

1915 Fokker Scourge

1916 Angels over the Somme

1917 Eagles Fall

1918 We will remember them

From Arctic Snow to Desert Sand

Wings over Persia

Combined Operations series 1940-1945

Commando

Raider

Behind Enemy Lines

Dieppe

Toehold in Europe

Sword Beach

Breakout

The Battle for Antwerp

King Tiger

Beyond the Rhine

Other Books

Carnage at Cannes (a thriller)

Great Granny's Ghost (Aimed at 9-14-year-old young people)

Adventure at 63-Backpacking to Istanbul

For more information on all of the books then please visit the author's web site at http://www.griffhosker.com where there is a link to contact him.

Made in the USA
Monee, IL
13 December 2020